What people are saying about

HAPPY NEW YEAR, DARLING!

"Bennett is a storyteller! Weaving messy scenarios and tying characters motivations together is her forte...can't put it down, waiting for the sequel!"

Mina Diamos, *Metro L.A.*

"This housewife's solutions to her problems are unique and bold...this book is a fun read!"

Barbara Stokes, *Ridge Writers on Books*

"Her writing pops with reinvented clichés like 'going out on a twig' and '24 hour nagathon' describing her less than successful attempts at parenting the delinquent Devin. All in all, a chick book for chicks who prefer their comedy edgy."

Penny Bernal, author *Cool Classics*

"Not only does Veronica capture the desperation so many women are feeling in their marriages, but she adds the twist of a con job and an illicit affair to tease us into loving this book. "

Kat Hutchison, *buybooksontheweb review*

"I couldn't put the book down; I loved the back-story of the mom and teenager struggle. It was compelling on so many levels."

Megan Willingham, host
Authors, Books n' More, AdviceRadio.com

"Veronica, you have a great story so full of intrigue! Now I have to ask, how much of it's true?"

Frank Truatt, *Morning Show WTBQ-AM*

"Some good laughs, some hard life lessons and a memorable upchucking scene in the linen closet, and I was ready for the denouement. Congratulations Veronica on your first novel, personal courage and fulfillment."

Dean Rod, *Songwriter*

Happy New Year, Darling!

By

Veronica Bennett

ISBN 0-7414-2584-X

Published by:

INFI∞ITY
PUBLISHING.COM

1094 New DeHaven Street, Suite 100
West Conshohocken, PA 19428-2713
Info@buybooksontheweb.com
www.buybooksontheweb.com
Toll-free (877) BUY BOOK
Local Phone (610) 941-9999
Fax (610) 941-9959

∞

Printed in the United States of America

Printed on Recycled Paper

Published March 2006

This book is dedicated to you, the reader. Thank you for holding my debut novel in your hands.

VB

"Fiction is the truth within a lie."

Stephen King

Thanks to Ken Joyce, Tamara Madison, C.J. Grove, and Andrea Abbate.

·

Special Thanks to Alina Eydel whose art appears on the cover and within. www.AlinaFineArt.com

Special gratitude to the lyricists of my favorite songs and their publishers, for song lyrics quoted. Permission pending.

Chapter 1

STEPPING OVER AND OUT

*Life is not measured by the number of breaths we take,
but by the moments that take our breath away.*

Anonymous

Now I'm no Jackie Collins, but I do know more than I should about having an affair with a celebrity. Oh, and that pesky wife of his? *Puhleeeze.* Don't get me wrong, I'm no homewrecker. In fact, our affair has made my lover a model husband—when he does get back home. Hey honestly, he's more fulfilled, so I've done that couple a world of good. Hold your applause.

It all started about a year ago. Completely unexpected, however. It was a Saturday morning much like any other Saturday.

"Come on, it is eleven o'clock. Get up, Devin. All of you, in fact," I added wearily as I stepped over the sleeping bodies littering my seventeen-year-old son's floor.

As I swept the curtains open, the late morning sun revealed a textbook display of teen vice. A Domino's pizza box with cigarette butts jammed in the crust like a grove of trees, balanced on top of a pile of discarded clothes. Beer bottles were vertical ashtrays, floating more cigarette butts in the flat, amber brew. A video had long since ended, leaving only the bright blue screen and loud hiss of an experiment gone bad. The stale smell of pot and perspiration from five adolescent boys hung in the air, overpowering my perfume. Teetering between the lumps, I pulled back the curtains to secure them and made my way toward the door.

"Get out! I mean it. What the fuck?" Devin snarled from the corner of the bed, flipping his head up like a serpent. "What are you doing? Get out bitch! There's no reason to get up, I just went to bed….get that light outta here!"

"There are too many people here. One, two, three, four…all of you go!" I left the room quickly, checking my watch, noting the seminar would begin in 45 minutes. It was so unnerving to open his door in the mornings and see random, lanky strangers sleeping it off on the floor. One wondered about this new breed of traveler and what accommodations they passed up, preferring Devin's hospitality, with its dirty floor, no pillows and four others, all in a 12 x 14 foot bedroom. I used to ask names, but it was hard enough connecting a name to a face and impossible connecting a mumble with a lump.

Sliding into my Honda Accord, I took some deep breaths and began the familiar head debate. Why do I upset myself before a meeting by going into his room, the crash pad for stoner-slackers? The retort reminds me that I am a good (if ineffectual) parent and I have to see who's still breathing every morning. It would make a bad impression on the coroner if five teens began to decompose in my house because I'd let them sleep in too many days. The weekends are always the same. Where were their parents? How did I become the Slacker-Wrangler? Evicting kids every Saturday and Sunday was as natural as bringing in the paper. Lately there were more strays than usual.

I sped through my suburban neighborhood, and thirty minutes later I entered ASCAP'S Sunset Boulevard parking lot. Checking my wallet, I felt sentimental about the last $20 hiding in the zipper compartment. Solemnly, I handed the parking attendant the currency, nodding a brief goodbye to President Jackson, as I read the sign, $7/ First Hour. As I got out of the car and walked into the foray, I warned no one in particular, *this better be good.*

ASCAP, the American Society of Composers and Authors and Publishers, had seminars periodically to educate its members of its services. Today a panel of prominent composers and attorneys would discuss songwriting and marketing. Since my husband, Raymond, is a composer/musical genius, my list of errands included making him famous. I was reminded often, much the same way other wives are reminded to pick up the dry cleaning early. Yeah, sort of like that. Today, I needed to learn how to market and sell the several thousand CDs of original guitar music stored in our garage. I do mean *today*. The music was lovely, but so is a coaster to place your drink on, and if these puppies didn't start selling quickly, I'd have to justify their use anyway I could, to bring in some money.

With the speed and determination of a woman on a mission I brushed past Mickey Owens, who was also headed for the elevator.

"Oh excuse me, I guess I was in a hurry, oh, wait... hey? Mickey!" Extending my hand, I said, "Veronica Bennett." I smiled at the singer/composer I'd booked for a casino gig four years ago.

"Are you speaking today?" I asked as we both stepped into the elevator.

"Veronica! How great to see you. It's been a while. You look great! How are things at the casino?" Mickey asked.

"Well, I don't work as Entertainment Director anymore. They closed the show room for remodeling and never re-opened it. I've been working at my home office, booking entertainment, for, uh, various places." I vaguely explained, trying to sound confident and breezy, not like someone who worked as a slob in pajamas, chomping on toast in bed while waiting on-hold with the William Morris Agency. The last time I booked Mickey, I had two assistants, a plush entertainment office and a fat expense account.

The elevator doors opened. "Good to see you," Mickey said over his shoulder as he exited into the meeting room.

As he walked away, I remembered a happier time when I was on a payroll, schmoozing with national acts whose "people" kissed up to me for bookings. Now, I was just another face in the sea of hopeful songwriters listening for tips on how to "make it in the music business." Actually, I was worse off than the other faces, since the room was filled with hopeful songwriters whose artistic heads were filled with musical pictures, white pages dotted with black notes of "tomorrow's new sound." I, on the other hand, was here as a mercenary. I needed a miracle: to turn CDs into bread. Although I didn't live out of my car, I had a mortgage payment that surfaced like the fin of a shark on the first of every month. In the three years since I'd been laid off, my savings had dwindled down to a pile of loose change on the dresser.

My husband's words echoed in my head as I entered the meeting room, "Veronica, I am only going to tell you one more time. Now get out there and sell those CDs. You aren't bringing in any real dough with the bookings. There it is! Thousands of dollars worth of music product for you to unload. Don't tell me about the phone bill or anything else while those boxes are still sitting there."

I slumped into a seat in the back row next to several Bohemian types engrossed in animated conversation. Glancing at the floor, I quietly kicked off my shoes and noticed a bright mustard-colored stain on my black suede pumps. A closer look revealed it literally was mustard. Apparently while wading through my son's room this morning I'd squished the condiment package and was now wearing the tasty spread.

****

As I walked toward the car, my high heels clicked and echoed a steady rhythm in the cement underground parking lot. As the drone of heel-toe, heel-toe resounded through the aisles of cars, I heard the patter of new feet, as a breathless Mickey Owens caught up with me.

"Hi, what did you think of the seminar? Did you get

anything out of it?" Mickey asked, as we fell into step marching alongside the corridors of cars.

"You were very funny, Mickey, the best speaker, 'cause you weren't there to educate, just to amuse, and it was great," I smiled at the friendly face beside me.

He had sandy colored hair with an Irish-ruddy complexion. His sideways grin gave Mickey an expression hinting that he knew a secret you wanted to be in on or at least some irony may be taking place. This quirk was as charming as it was accidental. Mickey Owens was always on the brink of amusement, rather than constantly "being on" like Robin Williams or so many of the national acts I'd worked with. His quick wit spiced with self-deprecating humor put people at ease, no doubt contributing to his immense popularity as an artist and celebrity personality. At fifty-five, he looked like Jeff Bridges, ever the mischievous adult. The lines on his face looked like creases from a long bus ride.

"I don't take this stuff too seriously. Coming from the heart, well, that's what song writing is all about, right? In the seminar someone always asks, 'which comes first, the lyrics or the music?' The answer of course, is—"

"The phone call!" We said in unison and laughed.

"Seriously, did you learn anything?" Mickey turned to me, as he approached his black Porsche, keys in hand.

It occurred to me to ask, "Where can I sell a set of 980 cocktail coasters—I mean CDs?" But I censored my automatic response and shrugged. We stood looking at each other a moment and I said, "Today's music doesn't seem to honor the serious composers. Have you heard Linkin Park? That group is on a heavy, heavy AM/FM rotation and the chorus to the song is '*Shud up, I'm talkin'* to you!' growled by some scary guy. I have to hear it every time my kid rides in my car with me."

Mickey looked at his watch, and I took the cue.

"Hey, great to see you, continued success, sorry I got carried away," I said hastily.

"How about a cup of coffee? Do you have time for a

5

piece of, I don't know, pie?" He asked with a grin.

"Uh, yes, pie is good," I agreed lamely.

"Victor's Deli, on Bronson at Franklin, do you know it?"

"Sure I'll see you in a few, Okay? Thanks."

Conversation flowed easily, the atmosphere more like a reunion, rather than the second time you've seen someone in four years. We were finishing each other's sentences and sound-biting our own stories to cover new topics quickly, as there was so much to say. Laughter broke out at our table, and then a serious comment would lead to a philosophical peek into the wisdom of my table companion. Show biz anecdotes with unpredictable story endings slid seamlessly into jokes, gossip and current events. It felt like channel surfing with Mickey on every TV show. One minute a street-smart, wise-crack'n, little delinquent sat before me, then the conversation clicker would land on a program where Mickey was the elder statesman for the young aspiring songwriter; he was eloquent on every channel.

Describing himself as the "Luckiest Man in the World," Mickey validated the claim with humility, as my mind wandered back to my house, and how different our worlds were. I recalled the morning wake-up call to Devin and my effort to gingerly step around the stoned teens, barely hidden bongs and grease-stained food bags. With disgust, I considered the mustard packet that my high heel pierced, its yellow ooze now joining the other stains on the beige carpet.

As Mickey chirped along, I marveled at how great this day turned out to be, meeting a person who billed himself as "The Luckiest Man on Earth." It was hard to know if the years had been kind to him. His career must have started and stopped a few times in the last twenty years, but his aura of positive energy was contagious, and I basked in its warmth like a cat on a windowsill.

"Did you decide which pie you want ma'am?" Our waiter was back for the third time, since his former interruptions of our anecdote-a-thon were futile.

"I can't decide between blueberry or pumpkin."

"Get both," Mickey chirped.

When I asked the waiter to bring me change for the parking meter, Mickey said, "Why didn't you ask me for quarters?" It never occurred to me to ask him for anything. The one time I booked him I dealt with "his people" until after the show. We sat quietly for a moment and I remembered something funny, and recalled that he hugged all of his fans that came backstage the night of the show.

"Oh yes, I am a hugger," he confirmed with a shrug.

"I am a patter," I said, with Swedish pride as I demonstrated the upper-arm pat of approval on him. Then, suddenly warming to him, I said softly, "You wrote one of my favorite songs in the world, *'Look at You.'* I sang it when I played piano professionally."

"Where did you play?" he asked, modestly sidestepping his own achievement.

"High-end hotel lounges mostly," I looked away. Reminiscing for a moment, I was playing the grand piano, at the Top of Five on the 42nd floor of the Bonaventure Hotel. The L.A. skyline was my twinkling curtain, and I was a diva. Now it seemed so long ago. With a jolt I fell back into the present, like nearly falling out of bed during a dream.

When I looked back, his eyes were still on me. We sat in silence for a moment, and I said, "I used to sing your songs. I sang *'old souls find new life in hearts that are listening like ours'*." The lyrics hung in the air, and suddenly I felt my face get hot and my eyes sting. I was embarrassed at having said something so intimate across the table, with nothing between us but blueberry pie and coffee cups. Inhaling deeply, I willed my tears back to the corners of my eyes. Bowing my head, I opened my eyes larger making room for the salty sadness to retreat. Drops splashed on the Formica tabletop.

"I'm sorry. I'm…I'm not unstable, it is just, well, it's an honor to… know you. I really respect your work." Without looking up, I felt his hand take mine across the table.

Sensitive to the weeping pie-eater, our waiter made another U turn away from our table.

"Oh baby, you are so open, it's okay. Baby, baby…it's okay, really, it's okay…" Then, lightly petting the skin on the palm of my hand, he said in a solemn voice, "it's an honor to know you too."

I had to choose now. Should I bolt to the bathroom, wash my face, blow my nose, re-apply lipstick and resurrect my importance? I wanted to run and hide, anything to escape this moment. More renegade tears plunked on the table as I kept my face down. If I walked to the ladies' room, I would still have to come out, and reclaim a dignified posture suggesting the crying didn't happen. That somehow seemed worse.

"Do you feel this?" Mickey put his hand a half-inch from my palm and an invisible force pressed an energy current into my skin.

"How did you do that? Is that a trick?" I gasped, happy for the distraction.

"I don't know how I do it. Feel this. Can you feel this?" Again, circling with a slow movement, more pressurized air on my palm, yet his hand never touched mine.

"Sometimes it helps to pretend there is an ice cube in your hand, and you squeeze it to melt it. It's a technique to center you…" he explained, now on the Health Channel.

"I never met anyone as open as you are," he added tenderly, "don't be embarrassed."

Thoughts swirled around, me reminding me I was in the company of a successful composer and recording artist and I was making a fool of myself by crying for no reason. I was tough. What was happening?

I had become a warrior-citizen in the angry house called home. This was no overnight transformation. After years of urging my husband and son to attend anger management classes, or try meditation, or yoga, or Prozac or prayer, or de-caf, or at least eat less red beef, I gave up. The bar was lowered to, "Please don't throw anything bigger than a lamp." They grudgingly abided by that rule. Now, I leaned into the walls as Raymond and Devin stormed by, flinching at the occasional object thrown past me. But I was done being scared of them; I wouldn't break down. Let them try and grind me to dust, the battlefield was my territory too-- even as the uninvited slept there. Their violent mood swings were crashing waves and like a cork I floated on top of the angry sea we called "home."

That Saturday, in a deli, with an hour of kindness and a magic hand, I cried for the first time in months.

&&&&&&&&

.

Chapter 2

BOOKIN' BOOGIE

Anxiety is only the wait between the here and then.

Fritz Pearls

"Yes, I'll get right back to you, Dr. Allen, with a price for the string quartet. Oh yes, and the harpist? Okay, I'll check her availability, too." Quickly signing off with my client, I hung-up the wireless phone and walked out of my closet. I hoped Dr. Allen didn't catch the true ambience of my office. The out-of -tune electric guitar whined through the house, penetrating the walls of my upstairs bed-room/office. The drummer whacked a cymbal, jarring my last nerve.

"Turn it down, down there!" I hollered, running down the stairs. My words vanished, overruled by the squeal of high-pitched feedback.

Devin's punk/rap songs were performed by sullen teens with lofty ambitions and no musical training or talent. With an abundance of guitars, amps, mics and recording equipment, our home had become a breeding ground for Snoop Dog wannabes. The closed-in patio became a "hands on" music studio for children to make lots of noise, like that special part of the kids museum, only there was no closing time.

Devin's homies were all suburban stoners, aged 16-20, and he was Mister Hospitality. Devin was home-schooled, and his pals were unemployed or high school dropouts, so everybody was available 24/7 to make music.

Thin, hollowed-eyed teens wearing the regulation uniform baggy pants sagging below their boxers, drifted in and out of my home all day and night. The zombie parade avoided eye contact, which was fine with me, since I gave up trying to know them long ago.

I shouted, "Devin, may I speak with you? Turn that down!" Since the random notes at volume eleven drowned out my words, I unplugged the cord connecting his Strata caster guitar to the huge Marshal amp.

"What the fuck?" He spun around and saw me for the first time.

"You guys have to keep the volume down! I can't talk on the phone upstairs with the sound this loud!" As I surveyed the room, glaring at the six or seven slackers, there was no response.

I continued, "Anyway, Devin, you have an audition at 3:30, and you need to get ready, so have these guys leave."

Turning to the drummer, now part of the peanut gallery on the couch, I said, "Really, you guys have to go now." Expressionless, they sat patiently staring out the window or lighting cigarettes. The drummer made brief eye contact, regarding me casually like a piece of lint on a shirt.

"Devin! Get them moving!"

With my son's cue, the group slowly began migrating toward the door. Leaving was merely a temporary inconvenience, since the Slack-fest generally wandered back in, once I was working upstairs. Periodically, I would ask them or tell them (depending on the crowd size) to leave again. Un-offended, the kids would slowly shuffle out the door and smoke on the sidewalk in front of the house. The zombies would huddle in a smoky, denim circle until a car would roll up and the teen-wave would wash out to sea until the next day.

The Slackers never spoke to me. Although they were individuals, it was hard to tell, since they seemed to be sharing a brain, much like the Borg on "Star Trek," only stupid. The spreading slacker organism had insidiously taken over my house. From my kid's room, they oozed onto the enclosed patio, and after reaching a certain number, eventually spilled onto the sidewalk. Their Borg-like survival skills somehow equipped them with antennae for when Raymond was home. Then they became invisible, holing up in Devin's room for hours, maybe days. Often just a thin trail of smoke escaping from under the bedroom door betrayed their presence. The last thing I wanted was to go in there.

Today Devin assured the Slackers they could return in a few hours, and after they left, he took a shower.

Devin's therapist suggested acting lessons to funnel his negative energy, and it proved to be a good suggestion. Improvising with the creative drama coach made the greatest improvement in Devin's behavior. Classes were fun, and he liked it. Apparently, my little con-artist-in-training brought convincing characters to classroom sketches. The class was $45 a session and lasted three hours, which, for my money, was better than the shrink who charged $125 for 50 minutes. Devin got an agent and was beginning to get auditions from Agency West.

I called to him as he left the house, "Good luck with the audition, Devin. You look really cute!" I was hoping he'd be the "sirloin" at the cattle-call audition.

He answered cheerfully as he walked out into the glare of the afternoon sun. "I love you Mom, thanks." He wouldn't let me give him directions, and we had already argued about what to wear, so now it was up to him.

As he drove away, I wistfully thought of him as a runway model. Great bones, thin, gorgeous and not built for work, unless the job is smoking cigarettes while brooding. Judging from Calvin Klein ads, there is a handful of those jobs.

Women are drawn to his aloof manner, and I've seen him work his magic at every opportunity. Sheena Williams, head of Agency West squealed, "Wow, we could use your energy around here! You are what we're looking for. Most of our calls are for Caucasian teen males that can play young."

God blessed my son with a gorgeous earth-suit for this lifetime. But, if the Universe is fair, and I'm not sure it is, then it also cursed him with sloth. His body houses a lazy entity who won't work or do anything that doesn't connect him with immediate gratification. His contribution to society is Windex-blue eyes, strong jaw, thick hair, engaging smile, slim physique and an ability to con. Like a used car salesman on the last day of the month, he hammers away, begging, throwing tantrums and lying to convince you to do his will. With the vigor of youth, he has time on his side. But I'm a strong contender, too, and we go to the mat everyday.

Perhaps today's audition will pan out, and provide at least a temporary future for Devin. Certainly good-looking sloths have found fortune in the entertainment field. If there truly is a job for everyone, consider the study that found marijuana users had a lower sperm count than the rest of the population. The guys in the study were paid to smoke pot and pleasure themselves. Too bad it wasn't on-going research, with benefits. They could have relocated the lab to Devin's room.

Trudging back up the stairs to my office, my eyes were brimming with tears because I love him so much, and I'm exhausted by our daily battle of the wills: me trying to blast the Protestant work ethic into my son. For whatever faults Raymond and I have as parents, we have always worked hard and can't stand sloth. Devin may have seen our struggle to make a living and didn't want to put in the effort it takes. Even if it's just getting a pencil and writing anything down. He just plays guitar, talks on the phone and dabbles in drugs.

True, most musicians struggle, but their art makes them happy and that is the payoff. Devin saw his guitarist father always angry and, I guess, decided he didn't want to work. Or perhaps it was me who spoiled him rotten. There hasn't been a change in five years; how long do I have to pay these dues?

As I picked up the soda cans and crumpled Taco Bell bags strewn on the floor, I heard the phone ring in the distance. "If I only had a real office!" I complained to no one in particular as I scrambled up the stairs, three at a time, to catch the phone by the third ring.

"Entertainment," I sang into the phone. "No. I don't book strippers, or any smut, of any kind!" I said righteously, clunking down the phone receiver with a thud.

"If I don't get some bigger acts and better clients I'll be booking chia pets next." My dog's ears went up and the prospect of someone actually listening to me was encouraging. Taking the dog's face in my hands, I looked at her.

"Something's gotta give," I whispered, "Buffy, hey, your nose looks like an electrical outlet."

&&&&&&&

Chapter 3

THE HUNGRY HEART

Kisses are a better fate than wisdom.

ee cummings

To me, the place of passion and "through-the-fire" kind of love is located at the bottom of the heart, that pointy V. Some people's hearts are all round at the bottom: they don't have the edge. Their heart might look like a nice fat pair of lips. My heart has a distinct empty V at the bottom—which needs filling. I'm happy for the contented folks, with the lips-shaped hearts, as much edge as a Frisbee. However, some of us (reader, you may be one) have a Hungry Heart. Like the Bruce Springsteen song, everybody's got it, and that V at the bottom seeks passion.

Blessed or cursed, your soul-mate-seeking love antenna invisibly extends from your aura. This thin sensory organ is even more active on clear windy nights. Symptoms may include crying without explanation, or buying sexy lingerie for yourself. The point is, cupid's arrows are growing in number and the quiver on your back is so heavy you're apt to fall.

So, the Hungry Heart pulls out an arrow, and shoots it off into the unknown on a long, lonely night. A few weeks later, he is there. That is my story. Can you blame me? Go ahead, it doesn't change anything: my arrow hit Mickey. I saved our first email exchange.

TO: Mickey

FROM: Veronica

Date 2/14

    Dear Mickey, I decided to share with you my diary entry. Dear Diary, Today I had coffee with someone I booked a while back and I was very proud of myself for being brave and pursuing the friendship. Everything was normal except for the fact that I cried giant drops, scaring our waiter into an early retirement. As I tried to explain I was not unstable, my table companion was quite consoling. Then he zapped my hand with energy, causing especially dense air to push between our hands and then melted an invisible ice cube in my hand. Other than that, it was a pretty normal day."

    I know you are busy (just look at your desk) but I do have one burning question. How often does it occur that your hand can push air and energy to another hand?" Is it every day? With everyone? Tell me, magic man.

Fondly,
Veronica

TO: Veronica

FROM: Mickey

DATE: 2/15

    Hi, I leave for Ohio tomorrow. Nothing that happened at the Deli has ever happened before...not like that...I've played with my aura and pushed the air around...but never into the hand of another open heart that couldn't hide her vulnerability or caring...It was really beautiful and when we left I wanted you to get in the car with me and stay with that energy...I've said too much...So, my openhearted flower of Studio City, no need for cynical cover with me...I love your spirit and that's just the beginning...

Kisses, Mickey

Have you ever been the object of intense interest and emotional scrutiny? Where every nuance of your body language is significant to the sensitive and observant eye of your partner? No? Well, me neither, 'cause I'm married. However, blueberry pie and several cups of Java with an associate led to more sugar and stimulation than I ever imagined. Talk about antennae? Mickey has antennae the entire human race will be equipped with—in about five thousand years. This man can dial in intimacy with a look. Combine that with a chatty girl who doesn't know she shot a Hungry Heart Arrow, and well, that is the stuff love songs are made of. Now I'm singin' it all day. Familiar theme, catchy tune, good to dance to: Dick Friggin Clark would even agree!

Oh, and the emails—hmmm. Who knew just being me would inspire this kind of attention? Now I'm the proud recipient of first class, lyrical love letters.

Being Me had been good up until a few years ago, before I lost my job as Entertainment Director at the casino. Then things went south, like to the middle of the Earth. A foreclosure notice from Washington Mutual is eminent. There's a chance I've received it, but then-I don't open the mail. Currently Raymond and I are teetering between homeowner and squatter. Now I see why the realtor made such a big deal about us qualifying for a loan; at the time I thought she was such a nit-picker. Technically, we *didn't* qualify until I healed the sickly documents using the magical powers of White Out and a copy machine.

I do, however, have a few things going for me. I can still fit into my college cheerleader uniform; I have green eyes and shoulder-length, auburn hair, and I'm thirty-three… kinda. Come on! We've all heard that "forty is the new thirty" and I've embraced the notion as a personal motto/medical fact stopping short of printing the slogan on my stationery and checks. If there were two words to describe me, I would have to say "glib" and "nurturing." If there were four, I would have to add "foolhardy" and "deceitful". Anyway, this suburban warrior had had it up to here with her husband and son. The ground was tilled for what was to come.

Back to the emails. I inspired the letters and I'm lickin' them up like frosting in a bowl. Or, more accurately, wolfing them down like a dropped T Bone in a dog kennel. There is minimal guilt, since it seems ordained by a higher power. Magic pushed energy between our hands, spirits collided in an empty deli. Too curious to be cautious, I needed to ride it out, while Mickey's catchy tune played in my heart.

As if dating wasn't tough enough (my being married and all), seeing a celebrity on the down-low came with a lot of restrictions. Starting off with a dazzling fireworks display, a couple months later, we were down to the bottle-rockets. I'm all dressed up with nowhere to go.

Mickey had appeared in the *National Enquirer* a couple times since I'd known him, so his paranoia about our being seen in public was justified. As he was visibly uncomfortable sitting with me in public, I took to carrying a steno pad opened to a page, as if jotting notes for an interview. We always met in coffee shops or delis and always before 3:00 p.m. Looking back, it was considerate of me to pretend to be working with him; however, using the notes to write this story was probably less than angelic.

****

To say my relationship with Mickey is hanging by a thread understates it; it's hanging by a spider's last web. A recent argument proves the point. In a moment of bravado I challenged Mickey to find another woman who would go along with these idiotic restrictions. With a haughty swagger, I stated, "You won't find someone else who'd go along with this! Never going out—imprisoned by the four walls of a hotel room...all our private conversations are paced to fall in between sandwich deliveries by waiters...blah, blah, blah..."

Mickey calmly looked up from the spy novel he was reading in our hotel room and said, "I don't need someone. I shouldn't have had someone and wouldn't look for it anyway."

Oh yeah. This self-described Luckiest Man needs an affair like Michael Jackson needs Tito. Right. I forgot.

When he spoke at the ASCAP meeting a few months ago, I remember he humbly stated why he felt so blessed. With commercial and critical success, he enjoyed financial comfort, had two healthy children from a prior marriage, was actively philanthropic, and enjoyed good health. (I noticed at the time he didn't add happily married.) These comments weren't bragging sentiments, just expressions of gratefulness. Similar to the feeling I had yesterday when I had enough money to pick up my dry cleaning. Something I didn't brag about, but yet was grateful for at the same time.

If the rich get richer, perhaps the lucky get luckier. The Hungry Heart Arrow penetrated this man, catching us both unaware, and now I'm devoted to him. What I am to him remains to be seen. You, the reader, will have a better perspective on that, since I'm standing too close to the flame. After reading my story and private emails, you may conclude I'm just a rich dessert that can be enjoyed or gently pushed away from the table with a smile. This man's plate is full, and yet?

Right now my home is on the brink of foreclosure: a burden I carry alone since my husband is volatile. My faltering booking agency has three phones ringing, which isn't as good as it sounds. Usually I'm dodging bill collectors' calls, while stepping over passed-out teens. At last count in the garage there were 3,874 CDs I needed to sell.

Once I was proud and successful, but circumstances have painted me into a tight corner and the paint isn't drying any time soon. For now, Mickey is my own Fantasy Island. With all of the chaos around me, I'm able to tune out the roar and listen to his whisper. My lover's touch, and the recordings of his love songs, fuel this one-way ticket to passion's netherworld, where I (along with the rest of the world) personalize the romantic lyrics. Gazing across a hotel pillow or a Formica tabletop, Mickey's expressive eyes remain fixed in my mind.

If you'll excuse the cliché, meanwhile back at the ranch, comes to mind. As far as my delinquent son and inattentive husband are concerned, the only thing that sets me apart from a maid is a uniform. I exist to serve them. The soundtrack of my life is a blasting rant of punk obscenities screamed by our son's band. Or, if one would choose to go to the soundproof garage/studio, Raymond is running guitar scales, or writing jazz. Have I mentioned they are both very important artists? I like being a mom and wife, but I get no gratitude or respect from them. It's tough working and taking care of the house as well as being booking agent and bouncer/narcotic squad for the neighborhood.

Raymond? For the past seventeen years, anniversaries included, our only "quality time" is spent watching a video, while he frenetically plucks Dorian scales to a metronome's incessant click. I guess we're having fun, but I get the feeling I'm missing so much of the story, since I'm unable to hear the dialogue.

I honestly can't tell if I deserve to have an affair, or I'm rationalizing immorality. It's a rhetorical question since I'm already in too deep.

While scrubbing floors, pulling weeds, and folding boxers, my mind is spun out, breathing in passions fleeting memories and exhaling the futility with a sigh.

&&&&&&&

Chapter 4

THE FEMININE MYSTIQUE

"I don't lie! I just have a gift for fiction!"

Dialogue from movie,
State and Main

Rushing out of my house in a sweatsuit, ponytail and no makeup, I was signaled by my neighbor Janna, from across the street. Hiking up my rhinestone bustier, underneath the gray stained sweatshirt, sent a cringe of guilt.

"Veronica? Do you have a minute? I saved some dog bones for Buffy, and I want to give them to her, if you have time." Janna flashed her radiant godly smile for an instant and turned away from pushing her youngest child on the swing. The happy toddler smiled as she bobbed from the ropes and board hanging from the tree. Janna went to her porch and grabbed a plastic bag on bones. Judging by their simple lifestyle, I suspected the matriarch of this Mormon family of seven didn't have meat too often. The few times I'd stopped by at the dinner hour, it looked like scones and jam, or fruit and rice. Her children are as thin and white as slices of Weber's Bread. Surprisingly, their borderline malnutrition didn't affect their brains; they made better grades than my son.

"Gee thanks Janna. Is that a new apron you're wear-ing?"

"Oh yes, thank you. I made it at the Relief Society Meeting last week," she answered with a modest giggle, lowering her big brown eyes.

Having been a Mormon myself until I turned 18, I always recognized Janna as the mirror image of my divine self: we were so much alike, living on the same street, shopping at the same stores, chatting about our husbands. Our kids went to the same schools, only I just drank a pot of coffee, was wearing a scandalous teddy under my sweatshirt and was minutes away from hooking up with my lover at the Sheraton.

Contemplating her tranquility, and pure feminine, albeit earth mother beauty, I wondered how I could get some of that. Even wearing my Victoria Secret vamp-o-rama outfit, she out-woman's me. A pure feminine aura surrounds her, and I always wanted Janna to be, well, my mom. Push me on that swing, with that look of love. Sing to me, and laugh good-naturedly when I spill something. You could almost smell a home baked cookie in her apron pocket.

Janna looked like Juliette Binoche, with the ever-present sweet smile Juliette flashed to the camera, in the movie *Chocolat*. Her positive and serene energy had a calming effect and left me feeling blessed while in her heavenly aura; like having a Dali Lama in the burbs. However, no time for serenity now, Mickey is pacing inside the Sheraton Suite, and I'm late.

"Off to work-out at the gym?" she inquired sweetly.

"Uh, well, kinda," I stammered, hoping she didn't notice the coffee on my breath, or the perfume on my neck, or me eyeing her apron pocket for a cookie.

"I don't know how you do it?" Janna mused.

"Huh?" I said lamely.

"I have to hand it to you! It's hard work to lie on the floor doing sit ups," she smiled, nodding her head with a newfound appreciation.

"Yes," I said simply, bracing myself for a random lightning bolt. With my hand to my heart, I felt the lumpy rhinestone necklace dangling on my cleavage through the stained sweatshirt.

"Bye, thank you for Buffy!" With that I ran across the street, chucked the doggie bones over the fence and jumped in the car. Hey, I'm not about to get that gross gristle on my freshly manicured hands. That dog can chew his way through the baggie. This is Studio City, the dog should be grateful he doesn't have to penetrate fur and skin to gnaw that bone.

Since Mickey never takes me anywhere for fear of being seen, and I have the need to get dressed up, I decided to treat him to a "Teddy Fashion Show." If all goes well (and how bad could it be?), maybe I'll write an article about it. My spin, of course, is a tad different than the typical *Cosmo*-slut advice. If that sounds unkind, it is. They are way too promiscuous. I think you should only be a slut with someone you really almost think you could some day be in love with, if you aren't mistaken.

Dear Cosmo Readers, Once you have decided to jump ship for a few hours, follow these instructions: Tell the lump on the couch watching sports, you're going to work out. Then bolt out of the house wearing a stained, stretched-out sweat suit and your hair in a rubberband. If you wear glasses, put them on too, or buy a pair to complete the costume. (Hopefully, a heavenly neighbor won't detain your lusty mission.) As you race down the freeway, you need to apply heaps of eyeliner, lip-gloss, and Tuscany Perfume. Then, hair spray the stupid ponytail while it is still up, so your hair will be extra full when you take the rubber band out. While at the stoplight, grab those hot, high-heel pumps and replace the groddy tennis shoes. You planned ahead to wear a teddy, so pull over on a side street, ditch the sweats and put on that cute full-length coat you have jammed into your gym bag.

Keep in mind the underground parking lot of hotels may be dark, so apply make up while driving on the freeway, the light is better. Drivers who honk at you are just starting to notice your glamorous transformation, so don't be concerned if the angry honks drown out the blaring radio. (The road rage you cause may be due to driving 40 miles an hour while you draw on eyeliner with a steady hand.) Don't look over, do what I do. Just bounce along with the radio, knowing you are lookin' good.

As I turned into the underground parking lot of the Sheraton, the radio was playing *Midnight Train To Georgia*, by Gladys Knight & The Pips. I joined the Pips in the chorus, *"I'd rather live in his world, than be without him in mine--- mine---mine."*

Stepping out of the car I had transformed into a sweet smelling, surprise-under-the-coat vixen. My voice echoed in the cement structure as I headed for the elevator, singing, *"His world—my world—his world—my world..."*

****

Returning home I was a blithe spirit, re-living the tryst. Since Mickey's wife was out of town we were able to meet at night. This prompted my festive teddy ensemble complete with garter belt and thigh high stockings. My boom box played the sultry music of Diane Krall as I slinked around the hotel suite. (If slunk is a word, I did that too.) Equipped with a raspberry-scented candle, and Sees's Chocolate bridge mix, I personalized our hotel room; the temporary nest that would hold our love until checkout time.

Taking moral inventory, I reflected on the hot love-making scenes, as I sped down the deserted freeway. We always make love two or three times a night, as if storing up orgasms for a rainy day. If we get caught, there will be more than rain; there would be a monsoon with Biblical flooding.

It occurs to me Mickey's wife may support their family. How else could she hold such a death grip on him, or at least, such a sense of entitlement? I suspect they found each other during the lean years, in between successes. She picked him out, and perhaps brought him and his two children into her big house and continues to foot the bill. Now, as an indentured servant, he can't purchase his freedom even if he wanted to, there must be trunks of emotional baggage. So what? I'm not available either.

Returning from the rendezvous was becoming problematic. Rounding the corner of Moorpark Avenue, I gasped to see Raymond's car in the driveway. It was 11 p.m. and he wasn't supposed to be back until about midnight.

Jolted into the present, with fear mounting, I need to get back in the house without arousing suspicion. Pulling over to the curb a few houses away, I recall the Goodwill bag in the trunk of the car. There may be an all-purpose dress inside, I hope, shaking the bag out into the dark trunk of the car. Hmm, here's something that could have been worn to a meeting.

Changing in the front seat, I eye the glove compartment and in a flash of genius, I dig out some labels that were stashed in the back. With a pen, I quickly wrote my name in big letters, under the *Hello My Name Is* section, and smacked it on the wrinkled dress. With dum, dum, dum-dum, dum, dum sound of the *Mission Impossible Theme* going on in my head, I sped up to my house. I turned off the car, and ran around to open the trunk For late "re-entries" to the house, I always had a Vons Market bag handily filled with non-perishables, dog food, coffee, paper towels, etc. Grabbing two bags, I entered the house.

"I thought that meeting would never end," I announced wearily, rushing into the kitchen, with my head down.

"The Neighborhood Watch Group goes on and on..." I yelled over my shoulder as I slammed cupboards open and shut putting away items, and started up a bag of microwave popcorn.

"Where've you been?" Raymond growled.

"Is this too buttery? It's so hard to know which one to get, 'light butter,' 'movie style.' I was thinking of inventing popcorn incense, it smells so good it just—"

"Where were you, Veronica? I couldn't go to work tonight because my car's battery was dead –then when auto club came, they said it was the alternator—no, I don't want any popcorn, quit putting that in my face!" he huffed with frustration.

"Oh, my gosh! That's terrible, what did you—"

"I called a cab, one couldn't get here 'til too late, the reception was only a couple hours, and so I had to call the client and cancel!" His voice went up an octave, "I needed your car!"

"Oh, Raymond, how awful, were they mad?"

"No, it was Betsy Klein, a regular client, so she was cool, but I could've used YOUR car—but I didn't know how to find you!" Looking from side to side, almost thrashing with frustration, he bellowed, "I guess I better give you back the cell phone!"

With that, my guilt and sympathy instantly fused into an electric bolt of aggression. "Gee, I always wondered what it would be like to have a cell phone in case of emergencies—like last year when MY car broke down on the side of the 405—at two a.m. coming home from work."

With the rapid pace of a trained prizefighter, I went in for the punch. "Well, that wasn't considered an emergency, was it Raymond?" Feeling sassy from the alcohol still in my system, I took the offensive and challenged my husband with dripping sarcasm, "I mean, you needing to drive my car, well, now THERE'S an emergency." Turning on my heels, I climbed the stairs, slammed the bathroom door, locked it, took off my clothes and got into a steaming hot shower.

As I washed Mickey's scent off my body and sobered up from the drinks, I shuddered with relief. The tension seemed to melt off me, swirling around the drain. The hot water temporarily spared me from questions, buying me time to sketch out an alibi for the night. It never mattered.

Through the bathroom door, Raymond shouted, "I got a call from Jill, at the Ritz-Carlton, and they need me to play at a wedding or some deal on New Year's Eve. It was just guitar for the ceremony. I told them my price, and they said okay, and then I told them my price for the reception with the band, it's in the same room, and they said okay to that too."

I ignored the voice on the other side of the door, and gargled straight Listerine, replacing the distant taste of Tequila masked with buttery popcorn.

Raymond knocked on the door. "Did you hear all that? I doubled the price being New Year's and then added on more, and they didn't bat an eye." I nodded silently inside the bathroom and he continued, seeking a response.

"I guess some big shot is getting married and renting out a whole floor—it will be a money makin' night," he chuckled nervously. Raymond had segued from the controversial topic of who's getting the only cell phone, to a more important subject: himself.

In a big robe, I emerged from the shower with wet hair dripping and make-up stains under my eyes. The desired effect was to be as unappealing as possible. As Raymond sat in the chair facing the bed, he polished his Inez classical guitar tenderly. Holding up the instrument proudly, he remarked, "Doesn't that look beautiful? I used to use Turtle Wax, but this polish works better." Then, in a reverent tone, he almost whispered, "The sad part is, most people don't even notice how beautiful it is."

"Yes, it is sad," I said.

Holding the guitar at arms length he narrowed his eyes with appreciation, then with the tenderness one would extend to a sickly child, he set the instrument down.

I got in bed and turned out the lamp.

"Hey, what are you doing? I'm in the dark!" Raymond exclaimed.

"Sorry," I said.

Trying to fall asleep was impossible. His indignation about the rightful owner of the cell phone was still bubbling inside me. I laid awake recalling the incident that shaped my behavior and my own marriage of convenience; his convenience. When exactly did it grind down to dust? A couple years ago, it's been that long.

As Entertainment Director of a casino, I had to stay for the second show on weekends and after taking care of all the stage manager duties, I would get home between two and three in the morning. This particular night my car sputtered to a stop on the freeway at 3 a.m. As my old Taurus died, so did the power steering and electrical; so it was impossible to flash the lights.

Adrenaline pumped through my body as my head got busy with dread. In the silence of the deserted freeway, the only sound was my breathing, like a scuba diver at the bottom of the sea on borrowed air. As the windows fogged up I waited. My job entailed too much responsibility to drink at work, and my head was alert and fully aware of the dangerous situation I was in. To get out and walk in my short dress was unthinkable; let alone, the impracticality of heels on gravel.

Finding a sandy beach towel in the back seat, I quickly wrapped it around my shoulders and shivered like a wet terrier, cursing myself for leaving my jacket in my office. Then I waited, and waited. Do I accept a ride to the call box? Or, all the way to a gas station?

At 3:11 a.m. I decide to only accept a ride from a female. After a moment of resolve it occurred to me there weren't other females on the freeway at this hour. So, my "ride criterion" also included a sweet old grandpa type. But, are they out cruising around the 405 freeway after nine p.m.? At 3:15 I'm so cold, I decide to jump into the warm car of anything that pulls up, since I am dying of boredom anyway. Most likely it will be a stoned teenager and I can handle that. However, being an expert on stoned teenagers, they aren't out to help anybody. So what is the profile of anyone who stops to rescue a Ford Taurus on the shoulder of the 405 heading into the Valley? As if the universe read my mind, two cars race by at a break-neck speed. Oh, that's the population out at 3 a.m., drunks. Most likely a burley, tattooed, toothless parolee on PCP will stop by, on his way home from a gang initiation. Offering to take me to a call box, he'll get spontaneous and speed to a deserted shack in a remote desert town like Lancaster, and skin me alive. Afterwards, he'll preserve my drenched-in-blood-ensemble by hanging it in the shed to dry, like a crisp bouquet of dead flowers. I've seen those profiles on Court TV.

Giving in to the drama, a tear formed when I next visualized my friends and family at my funeral. Raymond would be extremely agitated that he had to make the arrangements; making arrangements was my job.

Raymond's dad gave me a cell phone a few months earlier, expressing concern about my driving home from work late at night. (This was before everyone from pre-teens to rodeo clowns had cell phones.) After two weeks Raymond confiscated the cell phone, assuring me he needed it more than I ever would. Even if I could call him, Raymond unplugs the phones when he comes in at night, so his sleep is undisturbed. This habit is not malicious, but it is indifferent to any help his wife or son may need, before 10 a.m.

As random cars raced past me, I went back to imagining my funeral. There was a sick satisfaction knowing my husband would face tough questions from his father about the whereabouts of my cell phone. I saw myself as Raymond sees me, like an employee; an employee who is only relevant while in your service. Like the gardener; we don't consider what his life is like once he leaves the parameter of our yard. That must be what it's like for Raymond. An hour before his gig I am valuable. "Fill up the car, pull the contract and put it in the front seat, find a tie to go with this, make copies of this chart, write checks for the band, put a bottle of water in my car, slide your naked torso under mine for six minutes, find my keys…" At the end of the night, he returns home glowing from praise and flushed by expensive wine. He unplugs the phone and sleeps like a baby.

My watch says 4:05 a.m. As I sit on my hands for warmth, a car rolls to a stop behind me, and I hear the sound of two doors slamming shut. The windows are so fogged up I don't have a clue who's approaching. Not happy to hear two good Samaritans crunching up to the door, I wait, holding my breath. With no visibility out the window, and no power to lower it, I open the door and prepare to be fierce or grateful.

"Car trouble, ma'am?" a tall policeman inquires, and with a measure of concern, adds, "This is a nice view of the valley at night, but not a good spot for a little lady to be stranded." His partner chuckled uneasily and said, "I'm not sure I'd want to be walking along this freeway here, Gomez."

"Do you want us to call your husband, to pick you up?"

Sheepishly I explained my husband unplugs the phone so he can sleep, so it wouldn't help. On the ride to Denny's, where I would call a tow, I reviewed this scenario through the policeman's eyes. Later, at the doughnut shop, the two of them would later discuss my merits as a wife. "She looked pretty cute, so her old man must have put up with a ration of shit with her—to not care like that," Gomez would say biting into a maple bar.

"Yeah, you never know how may times he probably bailed her ass outta jail, just got sick of getting the calls, most likely," agrees his partner.

Luckily the tow-guy was nice enough to drive me home after pulling my car to an auto repair. Climbing into bed at 5 a.m., Raymond didn't know the difference. In the morning I was miffed, then hurt, then sullen about the repossession of the cell phone. My father-in-law had more concern for my welfare than my husband. What about the woman he loves or at least the mother of his child driving home in the middle of the night for six years?

Raymond is a nice guy, but emotionally shallow. I often told him "his thimble runneth over" when it comes to love. Lying in bed, with my back to my husband, I went over the familiar metaphor. What happens when you don't take care of something you have? You lose it. Like the bike that gets you around, that you use everyday yet you don't bother to lock up, or put away. After a while you don't even use the kickstand, you carelessly drop it on the lawn and don't give a glance to the thing that helped you get around every day. Well, somebody up and rode your bike away.

Our wedding night I went to bed with a husband I loved and one who loved me. Seventeen years later I'm with the same man, who is as emotionally invested as a college chum who drank too much at a frat party, and woke up in bed with a girl from his chemistry class. Bike in the yard? Last Sigma Chi to leave a toga party? Forgive the mixed metaphors, but that's marriage with Raymond.

Through the years and tears I had warned my husband, "if ever I leave you, it's because you don't love me enough." He would bat the air with his hand, and say, "Women? Can't live with 'em, and can't do the bookings without 'em. Hey, just kidding around. Don't look at me like that!"

&&&&&&&

Chapter 5

SCAMORAMA

The illusion which exalts is dearer than 10,000 truths.

A. Pushkin

If I could re-trace a thousand steps leading to the disaster that took place on New Year's Eve, the first step was Mickey and I staying at the Ritz-Carlton Hotel. My folly began with a get-rich-quick scheme, inspired by a table tent-tent advertising the hotel's extravagant New Year's Eve Party, taking place in a few months.

While brooding, as I waited for Mickey's return, I studied the ad carefully. Apparently, for a mere $40,000, a guest could bring in the New Year with this snazzy package: Seven course dinner, dancing the night away, luxurious suite, Champagne Brunch on New Year's Day, and unlimited food and beverages. The fee included round trip airfare to any of their luxury hotel resorts, anywhere in the world. Aside from the airfare, hmmm…that's a pretty steep cover charge for a weekend. Oh, and all you can eat? There isn't a woman over size 8 in the hotel; it's not like an open bar at a frat party. These people are moderate in their habits (with the exception of over paying).

Putting the ad in my purse, I started wondering: Who is that person that could pay forty grand for a 24-hour party for two? And, what could the Ritz possibly include to justify that kind of money? They should throw in sex for that. Or, something even more dangerous and exciting. Love! How would it feel to have unlimited cash and no one to share the most anticipated, romantic night of the year? Sure, the hotel provides the setting, but how could a lonely, rich person find love? Sex is easier; you can rent a body. But, how about renting a romantic fantasy? What is it worth to feel adored, cherished and loved? There goes another year down the drain. The last day on the calendar and hope has exhausted all possibilities that you were loveable. Every interaction is motivated by finance or polite obligation set in motion years ago.

Crossing the room to the mini-bar I liberated a Snickers and a bottle of Perrier. Then, plopping into an overstuffed chair in front of the window, my thoughts drifted past the ocean's horizon. I book entertainment for a living, and I'm on familiar terrain when it comes to fantasy and deception. I book entertainment, hmmm. Perhaps I could book a fantasy; all I really need is one customer. Like a detective, I must zero in on the profile of a lonely, wealthy, love-starved man in need of sincere attention and love.

A man who is estranged from his family; maybe his bitchy wife gets the kids on that holiday. A successful businessman, who also wants to be a successful *family man*. He's used to having things his way; to spend that night alone would scream defeat, in an otherwise orderly world. Or, at the very least, he wants the hope or suggestion of love by a beautiful and attentive woman. He secretly fantasizes of spending just one weekend with "the one that got away."

Fantasy is the key. It may be his college sweetheart, or his business partner's wife, but he has an ideal woman in mind. This classy and beautiful Angel who stares at him adoringly while he drones on about nothing, is even better in a swank setting. It completes the picture he has of himself. Joyously, he toasts in the New Year. With the classic beauty at his side, they celebrate their success with him as loving eyes lock across the flutes of champagne. Never mind that the workaholic will dive back into business on the following workday, forgetting the "woman at his side." All the better.

Perhaps a well behaved, model child joins the happy couple in the dining room, then disappears with the nanny, following dinner. This leaves an evening of dining and dancing culminating in a romantic, sensual interlude. This man deserves the best; he needs the complete illusion of happiness, even if the clock is ticking. It's expensive, but what does he care? My phantom client makes money while he sleeps. He probably lost forty grand in a casino one night, and has *only bad* memories the next day. This fee will buy him some lasting memories—if it's done right. This opportunity is unique. Heck, this type of man likes adventure! I book entertainment, I book events and I can book a fantasy. After all, this is just a small, small party. Should I find an actress slutty enough to have sex with a stranger? It will be hard enough to match a description of his Dream Girl. Or, do I find a hooker and send her to charm school? I'll have to figure that out.

"Hi, are you there? This is me missing you," Mickey's voice sang out from the adjoining room of the suite. With the heavy clunk of the door shutting, I was jarred from my daydreams and I jumped up as he entered the suite.

"Baby, I'm sorry rehearsal took so long. They were having trouble with the sound check and then—hey, is that new? You look adorable!"

"Well, yes, actually, it is new. I 'found' some money in my purse at breakfast last week, and well, you bought me the outfit." I said, turning around slowly so he could get the full effect of my pantsuit and dainty lace camisole.

"You are so beautiful, how did I get so lucky?" he asked my neck in a sweet embrace.

"You have always been lucky, we know that, Mickey," I smiled.

Making good use of the embrace, Mickey swung me around and we started dancing as he sang the words to the Cy Coleman song, *"The best is yet to come, now won't it be f-in-e-? You think you've seen the Sun? You ain't seen it shine..."* Now as corny as this may sound, it works. We had danced enough times in various hotel trysts to have some good choreography. In these luxurious settings, I imagined I was on the movie set of a musical, with Mickey singing the score. Our exquisitely decorated suite had the added benefit of late afternoon sun, making amber stripes across our dance floor.

"Out of the tree of life, I picked me a plum..." sang my leading man, as he confidently dipped me low, supporting my back with strong arms.

We napped, ordered room service and then he was off to perform at the charity event, held in the ballroom of our hotel. Mindful of my potential boredom, he suggested a Pay TV new feature movie or a visit to the indoor swimming pool, for the next three hours. Assuring him I would be fine with a long bath and a good book, we kissed good-bye at the door.

Although Mickey's departures were a disappointment, there were times when I welcomed the spaces in our togetherness. It seemed I needed time alone to sort out all the special moments and words spoken. Like flowers just picked, I stored these in *memory vases*. Reviewing each compliment, filing away hints of our (implied) future, didn't he say the best IS yet to come? Filing away innuendoes about his growing dissatisfaction with his marital status, filing away hot love scenes, how I rose to the occasion – didn't I? Well, that memory vase was always blooming.

With a sigh of gratitude for my life at this moment, I went to the desk and took the leather bound stationery folder from the drawer. Glowing with the afternoon's delight probably gave me the confidence to dream up the biggest payday for any party I ever booked. Going out on a limb, okay a twig, I wrote the ad.

Happy New Year, Darling!

Plan now for a fantasy dream come true. Bring in the New Year at a lavish resort, but don't stop there! Spoiled in luxury, you will be joined by your estranged lover. *You know,* that special one and only who *should be with you on this, the most romantic night of the year.* We can provide that certain woman, who until now was unavailable to you. Is a family part of your holiday magic?

We will recreate the loving family you deserve. Call Veronica for a discreet consultation appointment.

First, I'll write a loose script, based on the information given to me by the client, then hire an actress who matches the physical descriptions and is strong at improvisation. I can delicately explain to the gentleman/client that the actress playing the part of his fantasy date will be called away from the dining room at the last minute, due to an emergency. Then, he'll get a call to his room from his "mistress," who happens to be in the hotel. She asks permission to come up for one last romp. Most men are cocky enough to want a woman on the side as well as the trophy wife. So, since it's your dime buster, you get two beautiful women, ten minutes apart. That's the only way to solve the problem of a talented actress having to put out. It's the classic Freudian Madonna/Whore complex with glitter spelling out Happy New Year on a cardboard tiara.

Now, as bizarre as this may seem, I'm not crazy. My friend Dianne is a Beverly Hills Matchmaker, and when a gentleman flies in for the weekend, and stays at the Beverly Plaza Hotel, for example, she arranges a breakfast date, lunch date, pool date, cocktail hour date, dinner date and dancing date—all for Saturday. (Photos were sent ahead for prior approval.) Each girl is on her own, in her given time slot. Incredibly, Dianne arranges about fifteen introductions in the space of a single weekend. Her matchmaking service is not about prostitution—just successful men being introduced to beautiful women. She charges her gentlemen clients a lot. So, I intend on doing the same. Say, $30,000.

Hey look at me now! I've got two feet firmly planted in the clouds. Hmmm, booking a New Year's Eve fantasy party and my personal love life? Which is the bigger illusion?

&&&&&&&

36

Chapter Six

IT TAKES MONEY TO MAKE MONEY

If you got the dough, I got the show.

Veronica Bennett

Raising then risking the money needed to place an ad was a nerve-racking experience. It cost a whopping $1,050 for a month in the classified section of Los Angeles Magazine. Could it attract a Hungry Heart with a silver lining?

After a lukewarm response to the treasures at my garage sale, I had to lower the decency bar another couple rungs to raise the money. More about that later, first the garage sale.

Naturally, there were lots of Raymond's CDs to sell (his original guitar music), but my neighbors seemed more interested in slightly stained Tupperware than broadening their musical horizons. The big-ticket items were: a rabbit fur jacket, Devin's microscope, and a Play Station, with about fifty games. The Play Station had gathered dust in the garage, after I confiscated it in a pot and beer raid. It was supposed to be returned after one month of good behavior. That month never came, since Devin shrugged off the punishment with a chuckle. Apparently, entertainment trends had changed for him. Like trading in Legos for Hot Wheels, Devin "was chill" about never seeing the once-beloved video games, once substance abuse was an option.

There was a large book section at the garage sale too, featuring *Chicken Soup For The Teen Age Soul* (volumes one through three), *The Drama of the Gifted Child,* and *Teen*

Etiquette Guide to the New Millennium, to name a few. A haggard lady bought the *Back in Control Handbook for Parents*. As I took her dollar I said, "You will probably like your kid a whole lot better after reading my notes in the margins." She gave me a worried look, horizontally stretching her jaw, revealing her bottom teeth, and scurried away.

There were several broken guitars that had been shoved aside for newer models, and I cashed-in on those. Raymond wouldn't notice they were gone, I reasoned.

By the end of the day, there still wasn't enough money. So, I'm not proud to tell you what I did next. Okay, I prepared for the labor-intensive, Veronica's Portable Pet Shop. It had bailed me out before, and by-golly, it worked again. The following Saturday, Devin and I answered all the "free puppy/free kitty" ads in the classified section of the newspaper. By driving all over the valley, posing as "to a good home" candidates, we ooohed and ahhhed a couple puppies and kitties from each litter. Now you're wondering if we made stew. No, no, just because veal tastes good, I don't assume anything.

My neighbor, Lindy, let us store the animals in her garage (since Raymond would have a fit if he knew). Then, early Sunday morning we bathed and ribboned our bounty and transported them in plastic laundry bins to the grassy parking entrance of a busy mall. I cut Devin in for helping and he came through with four cute baby ducks he swiped from the pond at the park. Our zoo was decorated with a couple helium balloons to attract customers. We gave away Baggies of dog and cat food with each purchase, and hawked 13 dogs and 15 kittens, and four ducks before security ran us off. By then we were out of stock, so it didn't matter. At $15 a pet, we brought in $480.

The day the ad came out was pretty exciting to me. It looked good, but it was hard to be objective; time would tell. Lindy dropped by for Happy Hour, as was our informal custom on Friday afternoons. Entering the house with a walking-knock, she went to the liquor cupboard, poured a shot of Cuervo Gold tequila, drained it, sank her teeth into a wedge of lime and set the glass down with a loud clunk. She then poured club soda in a tumbler full of ice, and flopped into a chair with a loud sigh.

"What do you think of this, Lindy?" I handed her the magazine folded back to the page of the "Fantasy Date" ad. Reading the ad slowly, she started to laugh.

"This looks like a typical Veronica scheme. So this is all you bought with the garage sale and portable pet store! Is it? Where do you get these ideas?" she asked as she refilled the tiny shot glass. "Out of necessity I guess," I muttered, suspecting I had shown it to the wrong person. "I have some good ideas," I said defensively. "Some of them, okay none of them, have caught on—that's all." I whined.

"Oh, don't start feeling all sorry for yourself 'cause you invented the bottle of water," she taunted.

"Hey, *I did* invent the portable water—ten years ago! Come on, it was pre-cursor to the modern bottle of Evian," I reminded her.

"Just that it was a mayonnaise jar, but come on," Lindy said. "The design lacked something since the glass jar chipped at the bridge of your nose, every time you took a drink," she cackled as she recounted a tale that had been told too many times.

"The point is, it was a portable drink of water, an alternative to soda. They came up with the uncola, and I came up with the un-can," I said reaching for the understanding of the Jose Cuervo bottle.

"The un-can? The UN-popular, heavy, breakable, fat ol' jar..."

"Enough," I said, folding up the magazine and putting it in the top desk drawer. Somehow, the tequila spliced memories of past entrepreneurial schemes into a montage of I Love Lucy-esque mishaps. Shaking my head, I finally joined her in laughter.

"Seriously, Veronica, this ad looks good, but you are forgetting one thing. Guys that are rich can always get a date.

And what? You're gonna charge them a bunch? How much to set them up with a—fantasy?"

"Well, I was thinking, $30,000. Which includes the whole weekend of dining, dancing, suite, champagne brunch the next day—" I was interrupted by Lindy choking, she managed to sputter out, "Go girl! If you can pull this off, but that is pretty steep!"

We didn't say anything for a few minutes. Sitting on the floor with her legs in a lotus position, she began stretching into yoga poses. I admired Lindy's world, where everything was obvious to her.

Lindy was born with keen instincts, street smarts and a certain common sense that was uncommon to me. Not a college graduate, she may have been the smartest woman I knew, and she was making a living selling roofing supplies. With a shiny, brown blanket of hair to her waist, she was a brown-eyed beauty with a 40-carat mischievous smile. Roofers are a no bullshit pocket of society, and my best friend could have out-crassed Roseanne, with her remarks. So incongruous with her appearance; she was Heidi with a hangover.

"Lindy, there are sentimental rich guys, too, who love to be in love. My scheme makes it attainable—if only for—well, a weekend." I said.

As Lindy stretched into the cobra pose she squeaked, "I've seen those guys on freak panel shows, the men who marry ten wives—is that the romantic guy you're trying to nab?"

"Oh yeah—I know what you mean. No, this ad is reaching a high class, lonely romantic, not the guy who leaves a trail of wives in several southern states," I explained, joining her on the floor. "Those guys are cads, it's true, but honestly, you gotta hand it to the emotionally available, risky guy who falls in love so thoroughly he gets married every time."

"No, YOU gotta hand it to them, I think they're jerks," she corrected me.

After holding the poses, we both curled ourselves back up and headed for the kitchen.

"Did you turn off your phone? Or, are you not getting much business," Lindy changed the subject.

"I turned off the phone for happy hour, and Devin and Raymond are gone, which makes it an even happier hour," I said, refilling our glasses.

Earlier that day I ushered Devin and his crew out the door with these parting words, "The music studio is closed Friday afternoons, go find jobs." Raymond was at a gig, and now it's Happy Hour, where my best friend and I had important things to do, complain, stretch, and drink cocktails. With one foot on my inside thigh, I reached straight arms over my head and clasped my hands. Lindy did the same.

As the sun set and the room found shadows, I started to loosen up too. "Love-hungry people are from all walks of life. It's a human quality and romantically-risky men are my favorite flavor," I said philosophically. "There's a man out there who will put his money where his heart is—or was, to experience 'the one that got away' years ago."

"You might get a swinger from The Marina City Club. You know, one of those professional playboys with gold chains," Lindy said as she shook her shoulders imitating the wild and crazy guys portrayed on vintage Saturday Night Live episodes. "Fan--tahhh-see whoa—man, with big American breasts!"

"No, no, you got it all wrong, Lindy. I hate those cel-lophane, cell-o-phone, fake tan, gold--chain-wearing, American Express card flipping, lounge lizards. Those guys just want to buy you a gin and tonic. My potential client..." Feeling the need to take a dramatic pause, I noticed for the first time this client could be real, "is a different animal. He is sensitive, an idealistic dreamer, who has—oh, lines of poetry committed to memory," I explained, gazing off to the furthest corner of my living room. "Ughhh, is that a spider on the wall?"

Breaking the yoga-induced serenity, Lindy pulled off her shoe, ran to the corner and jumping high, slammed the shoe on the dark spot of the wall. "Money for borrowed love?" she said, catching her breath, "isn't that called prostitution?"

"No. Oh, thanks for taking out the spider. No, money for sex is prostitution. I'm interested in re-creating a 'love memory,'" drawing little quotations in the air, with my fingers, I hoped would clarify the distinction. "A time in history when he had *that*."

"Well, I'd say you're about a hologram away from *that* happening," she said sarcastically.

"Hologram? That's a big word for a roofer," I retorted snidely.

"Star Trek," she said, nonplussed. "You're just trying to get this guy on the Holodeck, without having the technology. I get it."

"This is a journey into the unknown, without holograms, I'm afraid," I said starting to doubt the whole thing.

Lindy refilled our club soda glasses and, raising hers as she handed me mine, we clinked the glasses. "Hey, go for it, Veronica. Have you still got a gazillion CDs in your garage?"

I nodded.

"Is that rehab place still bugging you to pay for the unrehabable?"

I nodded again. "Yeah, yeah, my life sucks. I'm behind in two mortgage payments, the phone bills are racking up and I haven't booked Brittany Spears lately. Pssst, it's not happening. My last two bookings, besides Raymond, were a Mariachi band and a chain saw-juggler. I feel like a suburban Broadway Danny Rose, in that Woody Allen movie. Only *he* had an office." I sniffed. "How far down the talent food chain do I have to slip before I change professions?"

"Yeah, it's too bad you can't go back to singing, but then, like you said, with no one home at night this place will turn into a full-time youth hostel."

"Emphasis on the hostile," I said.

Entering the kitchen, I grabbed a bag of chips and started to eat my way to the bottom. "I'll drown myself in salt," I grumbled.

"Seriously, Veronica, there is this um, um…water skiing squirrel on video. I've seen it. He's not that good though…" Lindy slurred. "With, ya know, what you know about pets and your contacts, maybe you could find a better one."

"Thanks for showing me the underbelly of the bottom of the talent barrel." Speaking in a voice reserved for first grade teachers, I said, "Lindy, there are no jobs for rodent/aquatic entertainment. Give me that bottle of tequila, you're cut-off!

"Help! I love this business, but maybe I can't keep the booking thing going." My whine had gone up a notch to full yelp. "Somebody better see that ad! Should I renew it in four weeks? I don't have the money to take it out again! I have to let them know in twenty days if I'm going to renew—"

"Hey, don't ask me! I just came in for a drink," Lindy stated. "What about Raymond? He's always working, where's his money."

We slowly grazed through the kitchen cupboards, combining foods that have no business in the same sentence, let alone the same stomach.

"Raymond's last two albums were produced on our three Discovery credit cards," I said.

"You have four albums now? Ffff, that's bad." Lindy scolded no one in particular.

"We're still paying off the margaritas Raymond bought me when we were dating," I said.

"I guess you 'discovered' one thing," Lindy said, making the quotation marks in the air around the word "discovered." "A margarita at 22% times seventeen years adds up, to…" she trailed off.

"Ffff, like you'd know, you're so buzzed," I said, laughing at my friend.

"I may be buzzed, but I'm not trying to hook up a dude for thirty grand."

"When I need roofing supplies, I'll call you. Right now, I'm booking a romantic fantasy. I know about romance and fantasy. I know about booking, so just step back and watch me rock," I challenged her, with a tequila-induced bravado. Had we not been drinking, this much truth would have remained under the surface.

"Sorry, Veronica, I 'spose you can do anything you set out to do," Lindy hugged me as we drifted toward the sentimental aspects of tequila.

With a renewed vigor, we cried out, "book it!"

"Oh, oh, try this," I cut a piece of sharp cheddar cheese and sandwiched it between two slices of apple. "This is the best orange and green breadless sandwich you'll ever taste. Here, this is dinner. Come on, it tastes like a caramel apple, really, try it!" I popped it into her mouth.

With the fruit and cheese sandwich in her mouth, Lindy gave me the one ounce of support I had needed all day. "Yeah, I guess you have good ideas. That was good. Make me another one. Get me some water—where's the mayonnaise jar of water you invented?"

&&&&&&&

Chapter 7

RUNNING

*Out beyond ideas of right doing and wrong doing,
there is a field. I'll meet you there.*

Rumi

"Well Noodles, you can never say *that* again!" I growled softly into the phone.

"No, wait listen! When you said Monday—I was thinking you meant *next* Monday, not *this Monday*-Monday!"

"Noodles, that's exactly why the calendar uses numbers—"

"Ya but, I didn't miss it. In eleven years I've never missed a show!"

"You weren't on stage last night, which means—you can never say that again!"

"Eleven years, *I've never* missed—"

"You can never *say that* again! I'm telling you that sentence is retired! I have to take the heat from the club owner and I'm sitting here trying to—I gotta go, I'm getting another call," I clicked the lever and with gritted teeth, I sang into the receiver, "Entertainment."

"Veronica? Hey, babe don't hang up, I got your message and really, I wasn't *that* dirty,"

"Al? Well, the club owner said—"

"Veronica? Come on, you know my act! They were laughing! So the middle-act doesn't show up, so I have to stretch, and well, I had to pull everything out."

"Did you say tits? Did you do the joke about the dog's tits?"

45

"Well, yeah, that isn't *raunchy!* It's a social statement about how animals don't take sex for granted, like you never hear a dog saying, 'wow, that bitch I had last night? She had ten tits.' They were laughing I tell ya!"

"Al, it may be a social statement, I agree, but some people are offended by that word. Men can't laugh when they're sitting beside their wives. These hotel shows have to be conservative. You're jeopardizing the whole comedy series when some lady complains, and some lady did."

"Hey, you should feel lucky I was there! Most guys couldn't have done an hour and ten. Noodles didn't show up! So, I'm getting his money too, right?"

I looked at my watch, I was supposed to leave fifteen minutes ago. Mickey was picking me up on a corner of all things, so the timing was important.

"Al, I'm sorry Noodles didn't show, and you were great to fill in the extra time. Let me figure it out and I'll adjust the check, gotta go."

Mickey was supposed to pick me up on the corner of Highland and the 101 freeway. I was waiting by the Hollywood Bowl, shying away from the occasional honk and whoop of passing cars. I was five minutes late and it seemed he was at least six minutes late. Each green light released a new pack of cars, and I hated scanning the speeding shapes for his black Porsche.

"Wow, you look great!" he said through the window, as his car slowed to the curb. Gratefully sliding into the leather seat, I wondered if my perfume was still valid.

"Ready to run, gorgeous?"

"I definitely need exercise, this will be fun. So, where is this place? Some secluded trail?" I asked, as I leaned over to kiss his cheek and then re-tie my tennis shoe.

The phone rang and Mickey pushed a button, and launched into a short conversation with a friend that ended with, "I love you, man," and hung up. The phone was barely in its cradle, when the phone rang again. With an apologetic look and a shrug, he whispered, "This won't take long."

This time the call was his son, and signing off from the brief encounter, he spoke the words, "I love you, so much."

Turning to me he, placed his hand on my knee and smiled. "So, today we get all hot and sweaty with our clothes on, huh?"

As we rode along toward Topanga Canyon, I fell silent. For some reason I didn't want to talk; my good mood was fading. Mickey asked me what was up.

"I guess it's just a Hollywood thing, I don't know," I stammered.

"What? You'll have to fill in a few more dots, what is 'a Hollywood thing'?" he asked.

"Mickey, since we are always alone—together, and we haven't interacted with others, I notice and think it's weird that almost every time you speak on the phone, you tell the person you love them or *love them sooo much*."

"What does that have to do with us being alone? You aren't making sense," he said calmly. "Hollywood?"

"I guess if I knew who these loveable people are that you love, it would make sense. But as it stands, every time we're in the car and I hear you talk to people—you love them by the end of the conversation."

"Veronica, that was my son, are you serious?" Turning up Laurel Canyon and then right into a narrow road with a gravel parking lot, we parked on the side of the hill. He turned off the car and looked at me as he took my hand.

Gathering steam, I said, "I've heard you speak to your agent, your manager, your housekeeper, your kids—sure, but your publicist? It seems those words fly out of your mouth with every telephone breath you take."

"Wasn't that the original lyric that didn't make it in the Sting song?" He started singing, *Every Breath You Take*, and got out of the car. Stretching first, then grabbing two water bottles, we headed up the tree-lined trail into the hills that separated Hollywood from the Valley.

"You're laughing, Mickey, but I've heard you declare love to three people, and it isn't even noon. I gush when you say those words—I thought it was more special. Well, let me

47

say, I think the words, 'I love you' are more exclusive; well, to me they are."

"That's apples and oranges! With you I am *in love*.

"I love *you, Earth Angel*," he said, kissing my finger tips.

"That's the problem. An apple and orange are too much alike, both round fruits. I think the difference should be, oh, apples and gorillas."

"Those are both living things," he said, gamely, seeming to enjoy the new hiking game. In the spirit of being playful, he said broadly, "The way I love you, is the difference between a 747 Jet, and—liver pate`. But, you are right, there needs to be a better word."

"I've heard Hebrew has nine words for different kinds of love." I said.

"Since we don't know any of them, we'll have to make up one. How's 'iggy-wop'?"

"Huh?" I asked, "Is that the new word?"

"Yes, I iggie-wop you and no one else." He pulled my arm gently leading me off the trail toward a Eucalyptus tree. As we kissed, his hand slid up my back, and he gently pressed his knee between my legs. Leaning against the gray bark of the tall tree I was supported from all sides.

"I love you so much, how could you doubt it, baby?" Mickey cooed in my ear.

"How much?" I said. "Show me with your hands, at the same time, I'll show you. Ready?"

He nodded.

"One, two three!" Mickey stretched out his hands about three feet apart; at the same instant, my hands stretched about three and a half feet.

"Oh, gosh," I said with mock disappointment.

"No, my measurement is more," he explained quickly. "In iggy-wop, we measure from the ground up—so it's clearly, I love you more. This is more—than that."

"Why was your other hand out there to the side then?" I asked giggling.

"Because, my right hand, if you notice carefully, is pointing behind you at that great, big buzzing bee!"

"Help!" I said, running away. As he grabbed me, we swung around in an embrace.

"This is me loving you..." he said, passionately breathing into my neck and kissing my collarbone.

"No horse play," I murmured.

"Maybe just a little. Pony play is okay, isn't it?"

"What now?" I asked his shoulder.

"Let's go eat," he said stepping back. "Enough outdoors. Anyway, it always makes me hungry."

"Where? Is there someplace to eat around here?" I said softly.

"How about—room service? Would that be too... too... you choose the word, Veronica."

"How unathletic of you," I said.

"How optimistic of me," he grinned.

"How unhike-like of you," I said.

"It's hard to like the hike, when I would rather smell your hair than all of the outdoors. When we're together, I don't want to be watching my feet step on leaves, finding the trail. I want to be looking at your face, your deep, sad eyes. Veronica, I wonder sometimes, is everything okay at home?"

I didn't move or answer.

"I don't want an in-depth account, Angel, but at times your eyes express a sadness beyond—beyond what is going on with us."

Hugging him close to me, I looked over his shoulder at the wind gently bending the smaller branches of the massive tree. Making the most of our time together, I chose to leave out the dark parts of my home life. Mickey assumed I had typical teenage son problems, like acne and lost skateboards. As long as my family wasn't on an episode of COPS, when he tuned in, I could just leave the domestic dramas in the closet.

"I'm fine," I smiled and we resumed walking up the trail in silence. The dilemma of choosing a restraining order, or home security system to keep Devin and the migrant teens from squatting at our house, constantly weighed on my mind.

Appearing in Family Court was necessary to get a restraining order on a minor, and it cost $250.

The only other alternative to get him out of the house was Club Fed—jail. The thought of turning my only son in for selling drugs paralyzed me. Since we couldn't afford a security system to seal his bedroom windows, everything stayed in its unfixable state. For years, every day became riper for some disaster, inevitably hurling us over a cliff of disgrace and financial ruin. It's like a Jack in the Box, on the last note of the tune. The tin door is ready to spring open with a drug bust, overdose, car accident with tangled, dead teens or possibly a brawl where Raymond breaks his uninsured hand or finger. No wonder Raymond unplugs the phone at night.

Today Mickey sensed my preoccupation when I got inside the car. When I complained about his terms of endearment, the thin curtain of smiles was dropped. Following the adulterer's unwritten code, our time together was devoid of the practical tedium of day-to-day living. In "Mickey Time" we discussed art, music and kept a running critique of pop culture. Besides looking my best, I made a concerted effort to be amusing and at the very least, informative. (I left the bleating sobs of how I missed him for my pillow, or late night walks with the dog.) To introduce the Jerry Springer element of my life would upset the delicate balance of our bliss. After all, I did have my pride.

"Let's order room service, I'm hungry too. Iggy – wop? Did I say that right?" I said, slipping my arm around his waist.

"Veronica, if there was a word for, 'just past always' …I'd use it when I promise love to you. But, for today—it's iggy-wop." He locked his arm around mine as we headed toward the car and the Sheraton.

&&&&&&&

Chapter 8

NOT EVERYBODY LOVES RAYMOND

You know what my husband does that really pisses me off?
He comes home.

Andrea Abbatte

"Veronica! Get out here!" screamed my husband from the front yard. It was scary sound, not a health emergency, but an angry summons. I apologized to the client on the phone, whose event I was booking. Viola versus third violin for the classical ensemble would have to wait.

"This asshole says we haven't paid the electricity bill, and he's turning it off! Now, tell me! WHAT'S GOING ON!"

"Look, Mister, you can't swear at me! I'll file a police report for verbal abuse," said the portly city worker whose shirt was monogrammed "Lloyd." With measured restraint, he turned to me, "I can't help you, lady."

"I give up!" Raymond shouted as he kicked a dent in the wheel well of my Honda, which was parked behind the city truck.

"I don't know how I got behind..." I stammered. "Can we pay you now? Let me get my checkbook—ah, Lloyd," I said weakly to the city worker whose career choice put him into these dramas daily. As I spoke, he eyed Raymond, and the freshly dented car, with contempt.

Since Raymond valued his hands, his fits of anger were often expressed by kicking objects. The dent in my Honda Accord was only the first upset of a day promising disaster.

"Look lady, I've been out here before. You didn't pay the bill, I got orders to cut off your electricity and you deal with it in the main office. Here's the number." Handing me a cardboard disconnect notice, he drove off with a screech.

Raymond yelled "fuck" and threw a Snapple bottle across the yard, where the glass hit the house with a crash. Small kids gathered on the sidewalk, relishing the interruption of an otherwise dull morning in the suburbs. A big white truck was mildly interesting for the kids, but a grown-up kicking a parked car and throwing a bottle at a house was fascinating. The profanity shouted at volume ten sent my neighbor Janna scurrying outside, prepared to reprimand an insolent teen. Seeing the esteemed classical guitarist in mid-tantrum proved somewhat embarrassing for all of us, so like a mother hen she ushered her brood toward her door.

When the city truck screeched away, I was left on the sidewalk hiding behind the large Edison Company Disconnect Notice, staring at the grass. I raised my eyes just enough to see Janna glance over her shoulder at the squeal of the truck. Her little sons were alive with excitement. You couldn't get better than this on a quiet morning. Cursing, truck peeling out and a wild kick to a car were a testosterone circus for the budding boys. Taking a particular delight in somebody's mom getting yelled at was the highlight of the morning's macho-fest. Standing on the grass, I was as paralyzed as a lawn jockey, and twice as subservient. I wanted to follow Janna's kids into the house to watch Sesame Street and eat a cookie from her apron, but Raymond broke the spell when he bellowed.

"What's it gonna take to get you to take care of these things? Huh? Huh? You tell me? Now, get in the house!" he growled behind clenched teeth, suddenly aware we had cleared the happy street of birds, children and retirees watering their lawns.

"Hey, Dad, way to go!" Devin yelled from his bed-room window. "If Dad was just a little more white trash, he'd be hittin' Mom!" Devin's comment was met with more hoots and laughter from inside his room. Apparently, the slumber party was just waking up.

Once inside the door, the questions came hard and fast. I didn't mind the questions so much, it was the answers that were tough.

"When's the last time you went through the mail?" Raymond snapped.

"A few weeks ago, I guess—maybe three?" I replied.

"What's wrong with you? I make enough money!" Not waiting for an answer, he sighed so strongly I think the lamps swayed.

"I can't figure out how much is in the account, so I was waiting for the statement to come—and then pay the bills."

"The statement comes—what? Once a month? So, you just let the mail stack up and stack up?" Then pausing, his face clouded over with a new pain.

"We better not be paying any late fees!" Cackling like a madman, he got sarcastic. "Oh, this is just *g r e a t!* Are you telling me now, we have to pay *late fees*?" With eyebrows raised, his eyes got even wider, intensifying the inquisition. After a beat, I took a deep breath and met him nose-to-nose.

"Thanks for denting my car with your flying foot! Now, that'll stay broken, like everything else around here!" I said fiercely. "I *should* face that stack of mail. I *should* be able to add and subtract, but the days go by, booking talent, doing contracts, teaching Devin the definition of osmosis for home school, cleaning, sending invoices to our accounts, making copies of charts for the musicians, alphabetizing your music book, putting the charts back in order after each gig, laundry, shall I go on? Since the bills don't have a voice they just sit over there in silence." I sat down exhausted from the fight. "Well, sometimes the magazines have a teeny, little voice and I grab them, but you know—"

"Is that supposed to be funny? I give up!" he roared, shaking his head wildly, looking around the room for support. There was no Greek chorus for this tragedy, even the dog had bolted through the pet door.

"I'm really sorry, it just takes so long to go through the stack and juggle who gets paid." I pleaded with my husband.

"What about that garage sale? What happened with that fiasco?" His arms flew in to the air only to flap back down at his side like a wooden toy whose string was pulled from the bottom.

"I'm glad you brought that up," I said, buying time. "I used that money to place an ad for our entertainment services in Los Angeles Magazine, you know, holiday entertainment. Since I knew the cost of the ads, I figured I would buy an ad the size of –what ever we made at the garage sale. It was, you know, separate. Anyway, I'm really sorry about the electricity being turned off, I'll go down to the Edison Company and give them the $35 cash. You can go back to practicing, okay?"

"Oh yeah, right! Unplugged," he grumbled, heading back to the garage/studio, slamming the screen door for punctuation. Have I mentioned the foot holes in the screen?

Defending my place in the universe was futile, since we had no power. The Edison Company assured me it would be turned on within 24 hours. However, the verbally abused Edison man, Lloyd, chose not to file his paperwork on Friday, so the 24 hours started after the weekend; such is the revenge of the city worker.

It was a dark and melty weekend. The next two days Raymond was a rocket of anger; Devin and I clung close to the candle lit walls as he raged past us.

****

Raymond had a right to be mad. He made a respectable living playing guitar, but it was costly keeping him outfitted in expensive clothes suitable for yachts, gallery openings and snooty fundraisers. He had several tuxedos as well as expensive suits, Tommy Bahamas Casual Wear, a new car and so on. All contributing to the image of Southern California's Premier Classical Guitarist.

As the darling of society's cultural elite, he played all the "Lifestyle of the Rich and Famous" type parties. His regular gigs smacked him right into a setting of Architectural

Digest every night. These homes were equipped with private car museums, heliports, high tech home theatres and small zoos. Mingling with the patrons of the arts led to more bookings in posh resorts, and occasionally some island hopping of his own. Raymond was comfy with the ultra rich, where cocktail banter included stories of hot-air ballooning in Africa, and private jet maintenance.

Pulling out the ironing board, hangers and wrinkled shirts, I decided to make myself useful with the remaining daylight. Grabbing a thick orange extension cord from the garage, I ran it out the living room window, over the backyard fence and plugged it in to my neighbor's garage. Pressing heat into the cuffs and collars of the tuxedo shirts, I tried to uncover the root of my husband's angst.

Maybe our home life is just north of Tobacco Road, but his job is perkadelic. How many excuses do I make for the angry, white, male who is handsome, talented, and, like Dorian Gray, keeps getting better looking? Supervising all areas of his grooming, feeding him well and handling all his bookings (as well as my own booking business), do I get credit? No, people are constantly shoving me aside for a view of the guitarist who looks like actor Jeremy Irons. Considering his great bone structure, perfect skin, innate athletic ability, musical talent, great wife and healthy-delinquent son, shouldn't that stand for something? What do I have? An angry husband with great bone structure.

We are living in the same house, with much the same circumstances. Except he's doing his life's joy playing classical music on sunset yacht cruises, eating lobster with clients. I'm booking talent all day, stepping over stoned teenagers, and eating Kraft Macaroni and Cheese over the sink. My own son doesn't want home cooking, preferring fast food with his friends. Since I'm happy, I resent his right to brood. When Raymond and I met I was a singer and I gave it up for the family and to help him with his career. Why can't the shallow praise of strangers sustain him as it did me? Ambition and envy are his demons.

At the end of the night when Raymond pecks the cheek of the hostess, bidding her good-bye, does the client ever wonder what's on the other side of the musician's door? Could they imagine Raymond The Musical Genius coming home to the pounding thud of Dr. Dre's rap music blasting? As he steps over a skateboard cursing, the dog escapes through the hole he'd kicked in the screen door, a few months back. Irritably, he's faced with the nightly struggle of opening the door with one hand, while holding the guitar case in the other, as the dog makes a run for it. Chasing Buffy back inside, he then "critiques" Devin's music with caustic scorn as Devin scrambles to turn off the music and evacuate his homies. Raymond climbs the stairs and finds me hiding from the teen-scene below. There in my splendor, eating ice cream in bed while watching a video from the 99-Cent Video Store. Wearing braids, and glasses, and most likely a few blops of ice cream on my PJ's, I'm no prize. It's a far cry from the glamorous world he just left.

For him coming home is like a rich, basketball player returning to a Bushman's hut in Africa. Admittedly, Raymond deserves better. He's rich man trapped in a poor man's body; he'll tell you. But, it could also be said, I deserved to be the bike that gets put away and not taken for granted. As I sprayed starch on the front panel of the tux shirt I told the ironing board, "Don't even use a kick stand—nope, just drop the bike on the lawn, it will be there in the morning, or will it, Raymond?"

Like swimming under water, my husband has been holding his breath, waiting for fame. When he gets a record deal, then life will begin, and he'll come up for air.

His car pulled into the driveway as I hung up the last of the shirts. Slightly swaying from premium cognac, Raymond entered the house and went straight to the kitchen to see what was melting in the fridge.

"We have to do something about this. I just saw a roach," he announced wearily, motioning his head toward the kitchen.

"When we get the check for tonight, I'll get extermina-tors to come out here. How about these candles, maybe poverty is romantic?" I submitted for consideration, as I looked up from matching socks by candlelight.

"I'll tell you what's romantic, and it isn't this," he said menacingly. "The house I just came from? You couldn't believe it." He slammed the dark refrigerator door closed, realizing he couldn't identify the food. He clucked in disgust, "You could eat off their marble floor." Raymond's eyes narrowed slightly as he tried to draw up the vision of perfection he left only an hour before.

"You could eat off our floor, too," I said matter-of-factly. "And, at least on our floor, you could get full. I walked through the kitchen barefoot the other day? And the bottom of my foot looked like a pizza, with all the little scraps of food stuck on it." I chuckled at my joke, alone. Raymond started upstairs shaking his head, when we heard a mild commotion outside. Devin and a friend stumbled in the front door, already laughing at some joke in progress.

"Hey Dad, good one! I like the uh, atmosphere of the house, all candles and shit, like that movie—what's that old movie?" he turned to the mental midget beside him to prompt his memory. "Dawg, what was that old movie with candles?"

"*The Gas Lights*? Where the husband drives his wife insane? Yes, that was a great old movie!" I was impressed we shared a cultural experience and he knew the classic.

"New Jack City, yeah, that was it," Devin said. "That movie was tight, with the crack house all lit up with candles and shit—" he said turning to his friend.

"You can talk to your mother about the candles. I gave up a long time ago," Raymond scoffed, as he swatted the air, batting an imaginary insect, or perhaps a curse.

"Speaking of décor, what was that glob of yellow and white mess on the sidewalk in front of the house?" I asked my son.

"Huh? Oh yeah—right, that. Well, Jeff bet me five bucks, I couldn't fry an egg on the sidewalk, you know how everybody is always, like, saying it's so hot outside—"

"Don't tell me," Raymond said from the stairs, no doubt regretting he'd almost escaped to bed without knowing this.

"Well, so, like it was hot today, but this ass-clown didn't tell me I needed to use like oil?" Devin said, as he playfully karate-kicked Jeff. "So, no, I'm not paying you, fool,"

"Why didn't you call Buffy over to eat it?" I said.

"No, dude it was like nasty for reals," Devin explained, as he swayed toward the dark kitchen.

As my son and his buddy drifted away with more laughter than the occasion called for, I folded up the ironing board. Feeling stupid that the power was shut-off for a measly couple hundred bucks, I reviewed the details.

After the credit cards were maxed from Devin's rehab, there was never any cushion, so to speak. So, if the checkbook was low, or I hadn't balanced it, I didn't bother opening the mail. For daily expenditures, I raided Raymond's pockets, he sold random CDs and always had tip money. He never noticed the money missing, since he never hung up his clothes anyway, so his pants became a cloth ATM.

Food wasn't expensive. Because we never ate together, I stopped cooking big dinners. Devin only wanted fast food with his friends at odd hours, and Raymond dined at events. My diet was basically, *girl food*. Dinner might be a couple handfuls of crackers, a hard-boiled egg, a banana or a bowl of cereal.

The lesson from this debacle was to always pull out the utility bills. "Start with those, Veronica," I scolded myself. The ominous pillar of bills would have to be dealt with tomorrow, in the bright sunlight. As I blew out the last candle, I climbed the dark stairway toward bed.

&&&&&&&

Chapter 9

THE FISH ON THE LINE

We will not solve the problems of the world from the same level of thinking we were at when we created them.

Albert Einstein

Racing up the stairs to catch the phone on the third ring, I breathlessly answered, "Entertainment." I can't describe the sensation I got when I heard the formal voice on the line say, "I am inquiring about the New Year's Eve Party described in *Los Angeles Magazine*-classified."

We arranged to have coffee at the Roosevelt Hotel in Hollywood. It has a lovely open lobby/restaurant with a history of old Hollywood's glamour, tacitly implying romance.

Simon Bestock is sixty-five, looks like Ichabod Crane's thinner brother, walks hunched over, and has a history of acne on his gaunt face. This man's idea of a workout is using the eraser briskly on a crossword puzzle. His frame is so fragile; his clothes look like the hanger is still in them.

After tedious attempts at small talk, I took a deep breath and solemnly launched into a speech I'd memorized on the ride over.

"As a professional matchmaker and event planner for ten years, I have found, Mr. Bestock that—"

"Please call me Simon, my dear," said a formal voice attempting to be friendly.

"Thank you, er, Simon. Anyway, a well-planned eve-ning, an exquisitely planned evening, is my forte. From the centerpiece on the table to the artist's performance, a client's evening is flawless when I am in charge." I indicated air quotation marks, when I referred to the artist's performance.

Clearing my throat, I continued, "I can, uh, will orchestrate a perfect evening for you—a party of one. The artist in this case is the ideal woman," I paused and sat up straight, as if the very mention evoked reverence, "you'll spend the weekend with." With no expression on his face to go by, and no questions from him, I just kept talking. "The actress, playing your perfect partner, enjoys your company and, with the background you provide, she will be well versed on the special things you like to talk about, as well as an uncanny physical likeness to—"

"Opera? My deceased wife Gwendolyn was an opera singer, an amateur in community productions. Is that possible Ms Bennett?" He asked quietly, almost in a whisper. Leaning forward, his posture suggested eagerness.

With visions of the *Phantom of the Op*era and all the disaster it implied, I responded confidently, "No problem."

This was an unexpected turn, but this man was my only response to the ad; to rerun the ad would mean paying again on Thursday. Do I dare run the ad another month and hope for the best? Can I shake him down for a deposit today? Clearly the man was interested; as he rambled on, my mind raced as I tried to gauge the situation. At home Raymond was breathing down my neck with prying questions like, "How much are you bringing in this month?"

Testing the water, I said, "With all that is involved, it would be comforting to leave this meeting today knowing the evening is in the planning stages, sir, Simon, sir."

"A soprano's tremolo in an aria is so crucial to the performance, consider Beverly Sills…" he said.

Recalling the threatening voice of a bill collector on the phone this morning, the only sill I was considering was the window sill-getting ready to jump. Steadying my voice, I looked Simon in the eye, "A deposit today would seal the date."

"Do you enjoy the libretto?" he asked.

"Le bread-o? Would that be the French word for bread?" I offered tentatively.

"Libretto? Oh my, it is the spoken text of the opera, of course you're joking. You're a witty one, Ms Bennett!" he said, with a hearty laugh. Joining him in the laughter, it was a welcome comic-relief point for both of us.

He then reached into his wallet, which was a very good sign. However, he produced a photo of Gwendolyn. The thin, wispy brunette even looked haunted while living. He held her photo with two hands, as I leaned in and we both examined the conservative-looking face of a woman about thirty-five. I mumbled something about her beauty as he rambled on. Picturing myself gripping a walker for support while I booked bands from the pay phone of my rest home, at age 87, I was suddenly jarred from my daydream. My fish-on-the-line was staring at me, apparently he'd come to the end of his sentence. Having no idea of what he said, I took a shot.

"To find an opera-singing actress to fit this description is exactly the challenge I love, Mr. Bestock. For your convenience, I took the liberty of bringing an agreement, which outlines the terms, deposit schedule, and confirms the price of thirty thousand dollars, all in."

As he labored over the simple contract, I wondered about delivering an intellectual-type improvisational actress, fitting the description of the photo on the table.

"One question, Ms Bennett."

"Oh, please call me Veronica," I smiled broadly.

"Are we to assume that a sexual union will take place on this occasion?"

"Certainly," I said gravely, and handed him the pen.

Hoping at least one woman in that elite category lived in my time zone, would put-out and also be available on New Year's Eve was tomorrow's challenge. Today, watching his hand write the check, I caught myself licking my lips. Quickly I inserted my tongue back into my mouth, and the check and the photo in my purse, and bade him good-bye. Pfff, how hard could this be? I wondered while waiting in the Valet parking line. As Simon Bestep rolled out of the hotel driveway in his Lincoln Town Car, I took out the check to admire it one more time. A five thousand dollar check made out to our Entertainment Company.

Driving home slowly, I contemplated my successful action. I had to savor this moment, before the details of accomplishing the task buried the joy. Relishing my gift for granting fantasies, I wondered how I might rescue other love-starved citizens in the world. Heck, forget the love-starved abroad, how about in my own zip code. Truth be told, Mickey's marriage probably could be improved with my guidance, leaving Veronica the Love Doctor with a moral dilemma. If I were truly on a mission to make Mickey happy, in a marriage that used to work, I should suggest Prozac. It changed a friend who had been rigid and controlling, so the same treatment might benefit Mickey's wife.

Helen Owens had Mickey Owens on a short leash. If he were a dog, he'd be tethered to a tree, on a one-inch steel chain wearing a choke collar and muzzle, staring through an electric fence. Although he's a happy puppy, with cool toys in the doghouse, his wife's constant vigil has to be suffocating. She calls him three times an hour with such emergency bulletins as, "I just lost two pounds." (In case he doesn't recognize her when they next meet?) "Where are the scissors? How do you spell Rockefeller?" Mrs. Mickey's voice really carries and she talks fast, like an auctioneer. "Bring home this, and get me that" is shrieked into Mickey's cell phone and passes through his other ear, making me privy to her petty concerns and complaints from any point in our hotel room. Those spousal check-ins are how I came to know her; the shrill voice escaping the seal of phone receiver and Mickey's ear is so annoying, I want to call down to the front desk, and complain –like reporting a noisy ice machine.

Day spas, shopping on Rodeo Drive, lunch, private dance lessons, therapy, Pilates, dog-walkers, gurus, hair, nail and hoof appointments fill her day. With no marketable skills, no charity work and no artistic projects, what is there to admire? Raise you hand if you think she'd be the first person voted off Survivor Island. It seems he denies her nothing. Yet why do I get the feeling he wants to kill her, right after he does the dishes?

So, I have no qualms, okay, maybe two qualms, about borrowing her lap dog a few hours a month. Mrs. Mickey is an example of what happens when you tighten your fist on a handful of sand. Regardless of her surveillance efforts he still comes out to play with me. He deserves the fairy that occasionally creeps into the yard late at night, and clips the chain when everyone is sleeping. Mickey is like the abused yard dog tied to the tree, with a master barking commands.

Back to my dilemma, if I were a true humanitarian, I'd airlift in a basket of tranquilizers and drop them on his porch; judging by her voice, she definitely needs a mood elevator. If her personality improved, and she calmed down, could their marriage be saved? Dare I suggest Prozac? Since he deserves to be happy, I should do that for Mickey.

What about the client and the $30,000 fantasy date? Should I tell him his expectations are unreasonable? *Am I just swindling him?* No, Simon Bestock is willing to risk the money, so let the show begin. Mickey is willing to risk the wrath of his controlling wife for stolen moments running in the wind, so let the show continue.

Pulling up to the ATM I quickly endorsed the deposit check and fed it to the metal slit which consumed my bounty with a low hum. Withdrawing $20 for gas, I breathed a sigh of relief. Finally able to pay the $1,500 balance owed to Obsidian Trails, my son's last rehab facility, was a major victory. There may be leftover money for the credit card minimums too. The mortgage could wait.

Approaching my street, I considered the risk. What am I risking? Perhaps my business license and litigation if Bestock changes his mind and wants his deposit back. Now I'm liable for the deposit at the very least and $30,000 if it falls apart at the end, after his money's been spent. More significantly, I'm risking my belief in love's magic;

manufactured in Besteps's case, and earned in my own. By taking chances to see Mickey, I'm invested. I believe and trust he's my perfect love. If Raymond discovered the betrayal, I'd lose my freedom to come and go; and that's all I've got. After a horrific scene, he'd watch me like a hawk. From then on, life would be tainted with suspicious hostility—instead of indifference. I would be lonely and grounded. These romantic dream-schemes have got to work.

&&&&&&&

Chapter 10

THE LINE FORMS TO THE LEFT

To risk nothing is to die more. That is how you die.

Steve Brooks

Dear Diary,

I'm trying to decide if my world has gotten larger or smaller. I have the attention of a worldly, successful, wise man, whose famous friends go by just first names. Yet, I have to justify being seen with him, even in a coffee shop. We can't go out, so my world is small. His name is known, I'm cautiously introduced, my name is to be spoken in invisible ink, vanishing before it settles into memory. Is it love? A large expansive encompassing love that awakens every atom in my body, and makes me breathless and fizz inside-like tiny bubbles speeding up a slender glass? Or is it a tiny love...waiting for emails, chained to a monitor like a dark spinster. It leaves me breathless and intoxicated in a sick, dreamy netherland. Grasping at straws, gasping at air, I'm breathless.

****

Standing in the sold-out line in front of the Rainbow Club, I had time to re-think the outfit I was wearing. The dark pink tank top and colorful fitted skirt was new, and an hour ago seemed pretty fabulous, but, sadly it was "Black & Over-sized Night" at the songwriters showcase for ASCAP and I didn't get the memo on how to dress. Actually, I didn't get invited, either.

Mickey mentioned he was the special guest of the evening and knowing his wife was out of town, I figured it would be safe to show up. What I didn't figure was the line of wanna-be-writers hugging each other, chatting and supporting each other and emoting far too much for my comfort. I'm standing hugless and chatless without anyone to talk to for half an hour. Not to mention, feeling like a float in the rose parade among these drab, intense Bohemians.

Yes, I hate life, thanks for asking. Maybe I should leave now and go salsa dancing. Now there's a population who appreciates color. A ten-minute drive could replace the literate crowd with dancers. I'd swirl in a hot rhythmic trance, executing a graceful cross-body lead, with a double turn and hammerlock into a dip, putting the bohemians to shame. Glancing at my watch every two minutes, I decide spying on my celebrity lover was a new watermark in humility. Since everyone in line is so enthralled in conversation, I'm conspicuously unimportant. Pulling a note pad out of my purse, I decide to jot down something important. Memo to self: Never wait in line for a glimpse of someone I am currently fucking. Officiously I shove the memo in my purse, and stare off to the west, furrowing my brows, as if watching for a ship at sea.

What am I doing here? What if Mickey is courting a songwriting protégé inside? The line is 80 per cent women. Any of them would love to collaborate with a Grammy winning, cutie pie like Mickey. Surveying the competition I decide they are an intense intelligent and over-fed population. Mickey once said, any color he ever got was from the light in the refrigerator, and one might imagine the same of these pasty lyricists, I'm deciding. Waiting in line has brought out the worst in me. I'm as bitter as a coffee bean.

The doorman forgave my deviation from the black and blousy pant uniform and with a broad smile ushers me inside. Finally, breezing past a handful of aspiring songwriters craning their necks, I stand tall.

As my eyes adjusted to the dim light, I squeeze into a pocket of standing space at the bar and order an apple martini. With something to quench my nerves, and a much-coveted speck of real estate at the bar, I settle in. As luck would have it, I'm positioned about 30 feet behind Mickey. Since everyone is facing the stage, he has no idea I'm here. There are no women at his table, so I try and focus on the music. Taking a few long sips I congratulate myself on enduring the friendless line and start to forget my "pity party." This could be fun.

The first act ended and as the stage was changing over, the room was a buzz of conversation. With the spontaneity of a space-shuttle launch, I swoop down on Mickey's table and cheerfully feigned surprise at (one more) chance meeting. After a graceful recovery, Mickey introduced me to Jake, his music director. Complimenting my outfit, the flattery was flying and I quipped about not getting the memo on wearing all black.

"I like this girl!" Jake said laughing, and ordered me a drink from the waitress.

Being my first introduction to a friend of Mickey's it was important to make a good impression. My background as a piano bar singer honed my already strong social skills, unbeknownst to Mickey who only knew me one-on-one.

"Do you want to sit here with us?" Mickey politely offered.

"Fitting another chair at this table is as likely as squeezing in just one more elephant," I said, "but I thank you guys for the drink. Wow, it came quickly. . I'm at the bar just behind you."

"We're doing a spot at the end, why don't you stick around and listen to the new stuff?" Mickey urged me. "Let me look at you, it is so dark in here, move this way so I can see you in the light."

Moving into better viewing light, it dawns on me we've never been out at night. Dressing up and flirting feels natural in these settings, and after gulping my second apple martini, I kind of *was* on a date. The coffee cups from our deli meetings were now transformed into sleek martini glasses, glistening in the moody lights. Blossoming by the second drink, I felt heady and became Cinderella at the ball, among the town's people hearing music and looking beautiful. Seeing my often mundane life through a fairy tale frame, starring me as the heroine, was one of my abilities, like a great back swing in tennis.

"You look wonderful tonight. Stand this way so I can see your face. The light is behind you," Mickey directed from his chair. "Veronica was a singer, Jake. See how lovely she is."

"There is no shortage of singers here," I commented, looking around. "Do you know how many chick –singers it takes to sing *Crazy?*

"Okay, how many?" Jake said.

"All of them," I said. The Patsy Cline Standard was a typical request and every musician knew it.

"I like this girl!" Jake repeated, laughing as he rocked back in his chair.

"I love her." Mickey said smiling up at me as our eyes locked. With the announcement to take our seats, the spell was broken.

"Well, it was great seeing you again, I'll be going," I said brightly.

"Won't you stay and hear my set?" Mickey said, discreetly holding my hand at my side.

"Sure, I'll stay, I would love to hear your new material." A round of air kisses at the table and I floated back to my spot in the back of the room.

The next Alanis Morrisette type spouted her angst in song and it proved to be contagious. The euphoria of seeing Mickey in a date night setting was too fleeting and was now replaced by melancholia. When a fellow squatter at the bar introduced himself offering his business card, I welcomed the attention.

"I'm a partner in a record company owned by Tom Hanks and I'm authorized to sign new talent," Mark Weisman announced with satisfaction. Those words are gold to everyone in this room. We chatted a little and exchanged cards. It was hard to determine if he was bragging or flirting. Perhaps he was drawn to the only color in this dark room, or maybe it was our proximity at the bar, but I had the attention of this good-looking guy. By accepting the record company executive's business card, there may be a possibility to further Raymond's career, it would make my life easier if someone would help me get distribution for Raymond's CDs. Once he hears I'm trying to promote my husband's career, well, we will see.

Declining Mark's offer for another drink, I felt edge-of-smug, that although Mickey is the celebrity and everyone wants a piece of him, I can still attract the opposite sex.

As the music was loosening up the audience, various couples around the room snuggled and I yearned to be half of a couple. Since Raymond worked nights, years would pass without our going out; after all, he was out every night. To lean back against the chair and feel an arm around me would be heavenly. Actually, just sitting in a chair sounds good, since I've been standing since 8:00 p.m., due to the overcrowded room.

Suddenly I felt lonely in the crowd, as the volume of the music raised; it was too much trouble to talk to Mister Big Shot next to me. I went to the restroom, and upon return, I perched on a different ledge at the bar. Watching Mickey finish his first song, I wondered how long I could stay in hiding? Is this a phase, not being seen together after 2:00 p.m.? Or, is this a life style, like a courtesan who meets her gentleman friend privately for years.

"Here is a song for someone special in the house to-night," Mickey says into the mic. My skin begins to prickle and I stand motionless, as if by moving it would disrupt the invisible thread that connects him to me. Although everyone in the room hears the song, I know he sings it to me and I absorb each note personally. It was a heartfelt interpretation of an obscure song from one of his Grammy winning soundtracks. The very song that brought on tears at Victor's Deli about eight months ago. Now it's our song, Mickey's private gift to Veronica, intimately performed in a room that fell silent for the first time all evening. Looking down I saw my tears fall like rain drops on my pink flowered skirt.

Mickey's set closed the show, and he disappeared behind a hedge of fans, photographers, and card palming glombers. I wasn't going to hang around and be the last person to glomb on to him, so I left.

On the drive home my cell phone rang, and my lover and I recapped the evening, punctuated with hot, sweet talk. Mickey described the sensation of watching me from the stage and the compliment-meter was weighing in heavy. Responding with an assortment of sighs, giggles and lusty squeals we drove the empty streets toward our separate homes, enjoying our own erotic version of late-night-pillow talk.

"I am proud of us," I announced just before we said our final good night.

"Why is that, Angel?"

"Tonight I remembered how infatuations are helped along with the lubricant of liquor, music and romantic settings. We have caffeine and stolen daytime minutes. Taking walks, and kissing in cars - stretching out of our seat belts. So much of our words of love are expressed by typing and reading and sighing alone, instead of spoken."

"I know," he said softly.

"Yet, here we are. Laughing, loving each other, staying together in the most inconvenient of circumstances. Yet, due to our fondness, *our immense fondness* for each other, we keep finding our way back to each other. It isn't easy getting together, but once that part is done, it works..."

"You're my Christmas," he whispered into the phone.

"Oh...I find you... totally talented and I admire you, but mostly you amuse me. Mickey I adore you and I do love you when all is said and done."

"I love you so much. Thank you for being my secret."

Sighing, like teenagers, we hung on to the silence, neither one of us wanting to hang up first. Then, I clicked my borrowed cell phone shut. Tonight I borrowed Raymond's phone. Since it's my job to charge it and put it into his car, if he doesn't have to use it, he often doesn't notice it isn't there. Whoops, I forgot.

Intoxicated by the panorama of emotions I'd indulged in all evening, I was exhausted. Tuning down my street, I saw Raymond wasn't home yet, so I carried my euphoria into the dark house.

I was asleep a few minutes when Raymond came in pretty tipsy. He was singing as he got into bed and laughing at something.

"Hey, babe! You shoulda been there tonight!" He said in a loud voice. "You shoulda seen Joey after the gig, this lady starts hittin' on him, you know the client's friend and…"

"I'm sleeping Raymond. Tell me tomorrow, okay?"

"But, you are so cute in the dark, baby,"

"Look Raymond, I'm half asleep, I haven't had a shower, I have a sinus headache and I can't find my allergy pills, I got up really early, I'm on my period. Listen, we could have sex now, but *it wouldn't be good.* Listen, we could, 'A' have sex now *when I don't want to at all.* Or, 'B', have really good sex tomorrow, when—"

"I'll take A," he said quickly.

"Don't you even *want to hear* what 'B' is?"

"*No*, I'll take 'A!'"

"Come on Raymond!" We both laughed a little. "B means *I want to*, I'll be awake and take a bath and wear—"

"I'm takin' 'A'" he stated firmly. Then, rolled me over and pounced.

&&&&&&&

Chapter 11

FOUR & TWENTY LATE SHOW

Illusion is the first of all pleasures.

Voltaire

After giving some thought as to who could play "Gwendolyn" my client's deceased wife, I decided to call Daniella. She was a Hawaiian Tropics model, the actress—not my client's deceased wife. (At least I can't imagine the reserved opera singer I saw in the photo, all oiled up with a belly ring.) Besides being an oily tease for beach promotions, Daniella had the distinction of being a damn good stage actress as well. I recently caught one of her plays at the Fountain Theatre. This week she was working for Anthony The Hypnotist, as his assistant. We agreed to meet after Anthony's show to discuss my "improvisational actress gig for this New Year's Eve." The Four and Twenty Coffee Shop on Laurel was a good halfway spot, and open all night.

"Veronica! Over here!" Daneilla waved from a corner table in the back. I was a little surprised to see four or five people seated with her. A round of introductions ensued, and naturally, I was identified as a booking agent.

"What a pleasure to meet you, Ms Bennett," Anthony said, lighting up.

"Just call me Veronica," I said.

"We were just leaving," he said.

"Veronica, Anthony and the crew needed to go over the schedule for the next couple months, so they came over too, we are just about done," Daniella explained, referring to the various people sharing the table.

"We are all through, and you two ladies can have the table," Anthony said, not moving.

"Isn't Anthony darling?" Daniella proclaimed, not waiting for an answer, she swooned.

"Oh, relax, I'm in no hurry, finish your coffee." I said, pulling up a chair next to Daniella. "Anyway it's nice to meet you Anthony. So this is your closing night this week? I'll definitely see the show next time you're in town. I haven't seen this girl in about a year, so I just heard about the show yesterday—couldn't get here any earlier..." my voice trailed off.

"Ah ha," he said.

"I'm a fan of hypnotism, I've booked these kind of shows before. Do you know Flip Orley?" Anthony shook his head.

I continued, "I thought of becoming a stage hypnotist at one time. I couldn't find someone to teach me. I called Pat Collins The Hip Hypnotist and...."

"Nobody can do my show," he interrupted. "My show is not like anything you've ever seen! Guys try to rip me off, but they can't do it."

"Really Veronica, he is soooo funny!" Daniella said appreciatively gazing across the table with her hands clasped under her chin.

"You've gotta have charisma," I said, agreeably.

Recalling my brief fascination with becoming a stage hypnotist, I was slightly disappointed that this gorgeous man didn't encourage me now to reconsider becoming a hypnotist. So wrapped up in himself, I noticed. With me hypnotizing *and singing* any show would have soared to a new level. "Veronica The Mysterious Chanteuse" would emerge through the back curtain. Wading past conked-out customers, slumped in folding chairs, I would wow the crowd (those that were awake) with a smoky rendition of, *"Good Night, My Love."* But alas, the hypnotist was all aboard a lengthy vain-train of his own rattling on, upstaging even my egotistical fantasies.

"I've been selling out shows for the last five years, eh? You haven't heard of me, since I'm from Canada, but in Calgary...."

It was hard to know if it was a great show tonight, or Daniella's flattery encouraged this brag-a-thon. Or maybe he always floats in a bubble of self-appreciation. It was easy to see why. Anthony was in his late 20's, with tri-colored blond hair spiked like the inside of an artichoke. His teeth shimmered white, his eyes twinkled blue and who knows, there may have been a brain beneath those artichoke-like spikes. His perfectly chiseled features assured a soft life, with a smile that could coax a flea off a dog.

Suddenly Anthony turned to the girl sitting next to him and announced, "I bet I can feel your breasts, and you won't even know it. I bet you –oh, five dollars." Apparently, the girl next to him was a fan who came back stage after the show, requesting to be hypnotized to quit smoking. This being his last night in town, and she being an attractive young redhead, Anthony invited her to come along for coffee, and they could meet privately afterwards. I met "Red" during the introductions at the table.

"I won't feel anything?" She asked cautiously.

"I'll bet you five dollars, right now, you won't feel a thing-but I will touch your breasts. Close your eyes real tight," Anthony instructed quickly.

Once her eyes were closed, he put both hands right on top of her ample breasts and massaged them, saying, "Oh, nice..."

Red opened her eyes wide, recoiled from his touch and shouted, "What are you doing? Your hands are right on top of my –my blouse! Of course I felt that!"

"Oh sorry, I still haven't perfected the trick. Here's the five bucks," he said handing her a bill.

The guys at the table snorted with laughter. I winced, and Daniella shook her head with an expression of amusement, as if watching a kitten play with a ball of yarn.

Red proved to be a good sport and recovering quickly, she joined in with good natured, sheepish laughter, batting the air in front of her, while Anthony moved in close with a fake apology.

Not willing to give the crowd assembled at our table a chance to discuss anything else, Anthony now turned to me and said, "Daniella is a very good assistant, and also a good subject. Watch this." He walked around to our side of the table and standing behind Daniella he put his hand on her neck and leaned in close.

"You are relaxing, with each count you are going deeper and deeper, with each breath you take, you are falling…." He spoke softly close to her ear as her head drooped forward.

"When you awake, whenever Ray, the soundman, holds your hand you will experience the most intense orgasm of your life. You will try and contain yourself, but you get so hot you can barely stay in your chair."

With that, Ray the soundman, started giggling and running his hand down the length of his face, as if to erase any guilt that may be forthcoming.

Anthony spoke a few more words, returned to his seat and clapped his hands loudly. With studied nonchalance, he began mixing sugar into his coffee unaware of Daniella "waking up." Light chatter resumed, and as the waitress dropped off my bowl of chili, I heard Ray the soundman, say to Daniella, "And let me see that ring on your hand. It looks uh-cool." Placing her hand in Ray's hand, I saw the actress take in a slow, deep breath, close her eyes, cross her legs and squirm in the chair. At this time of night the coffee shop was fairly empty except for a few random newspaper readers. Glancing around I wondered if this impromptu X-rated show would get us all kicked out. With a heaving chest and eerie little moans, Daniella stretched her free hand out in front of her, as an aerial artist would reach for an invisible rope. Ray's eyes got big, as he held onto Daniela's other hand. That was quite a breakfast special at the Four and Twenty Coffee Shop.

Suddenly, we all were in the uncomfortable position of witnessing a woman's long, drawn out orgasm at our formica table, and me without the buzz of a couple drinks, like my table companions. This was quite a floorshow accompanying a bowl of chili and a glass of milk. What was the protocol here? Should I be happy for her pleasure? Should I recoil at Anthony's sheer audacity? Do you high-five slap the hand of the pock-faced, twenty-year-old soundman who just got lucky with a girl who, under normal circumstances, wouldn't give him the time of day.

Ray let go of Daniella's hand, and she regained her composure almost instantly. Meanwhile, there was the polite passing of condiments, and awkward banter about new songs.

As I stared into my pile of red lumps, all appetite was lost as I tried to sort this out. Obviously, since I am a talent booker, Anthony's stunt fell under the category of "auditions." After all, in hypnotism there were no auditions per say. I mean comedy hypnotists couldn't round up fifty people, drop by your office, and just start the hilarity. For one thing, who has the folding chairs? But this was pretty vile. Daniella was an actress who picked up a gig for a week working with this evil pretty boy, and now he's turned her into a throbbing, porn star wannabe for any bus boy lucky enough to work the night shift.

"Is she still under, Anthony?" I asked softly.

"Yes," he said proudly.

"Get her back to normal," I said firmly. "Now."

"Hey, sorry, you said you weren't in a hurry…she likes it. One hour of hypnotism is the equal of eight hours of sleep, you know, eh?"

"So far it looks like one week of working with you is the equal of eight minutes of being your pet monkey," I said.

"Oh, well, all rise for Judge Mental," he shot back indignantly. What? Implying I don't understand high art? During this time, Daniella had gone back to inspecting her nails. It didn't occur to me, she might have been faking it with the intention of securing future bookings.

Anthony shot out of his seat and rounded the table, once again standing behind Daniella. In a muffled conference that involved her head drooping and a firm hand on her neck, he clapped signaling the spell was broken. Well, we can hope the spell was broken, not to be tested at church services the next morning.

Ray excused himself to the restroom, to no one's surprise. As we sat in the thick fog of tension, Red excused herself and headed off in the same direction. Daniella, our little erotic friend, just stretched her neck, sighed and finished her ice water. The moments waiting for them to return were unbearable, prompting Anthony to stand up abruptly and throw down some bills to cover the check. He motioned to the other two guys at the table, and with a brief wave over his shoulder, the small entourage headed for the door.

When Red and Ray returned from the restrooms, they were ushered outside by one of Anthony's lackeys.

"How do you feel Daniella? Did you know you were just hypnotized by Anthony? Were you aware... of... well, what was going on?" I asked her.

"Oh, I never know for sure what he's going to do. Don't you love his hair?" she cooed.

"Oh God, Daniella. He's an evil pig. You don't have to be his trained monkey after the show, he had no right to...anyway...you said you were available for New Year's Eve?"

"Well judging from the gig you are offering me, you have no room to talk! Some guy thinks I will be his dead wife, and *he is NOT* hypnotized? Are you sure you don't need to include Anthony in this budget? How am I supposed to pull that off?" Her voice started rising, "Anthony is my friend, I think he's funny. He isn't a pig. Okay, he's a piglet. I know he is bad, but...."

"You know, I gotta go Daniella. I wish you the best." We both stood up at the same time and in a spirit of one upmanship she almost knocked over her chair in the dash for the exit.

Standing in the dust of the stampede, I sighed and shook my head. A meek waitress rushed over to say something to me and for a second, I was glad to see a normal person. In that moment, I wanted to explain everything to, most likely, the only sane person in the room. With indignation, I was gearing up to tell her what a terrible trick had been played on the actress. The waitress and I would establish a life-long bond of sisterhood and friendship.

"Sorry, the bill is $8.32 short, hon," she said.

"Oh, yeah -sure. I've got it right here. I think I do." I said looking through my purse and cursing my rotten luck to be the last one to leave the table. After years of timely exits to the restroom- I should know better. In between the wad of unpaid bills hidden from Raymond and my Fall Collection of Makeup from the 99 Cent store, I discover two crumpled fives in my purse. "Keep the change," I mumble as I skulk towards the door.

"Have a good night, hon," she said wearily, walking away. As I slung my heavy bag over my shoulder, weighted down with library books on opera, entertainment contract and the photos of Gwendolyn, I envied her less complicated life. She was pouring coffee at the waitress station when I left.

&&&&&&&

Chapter 12

COULDA, WOULDA, SHOULDA

Happiness makes up in height what it lacks in length.

Robert Frost

"Happy hour! Who's home? Do I drink alone?" Lindy's voice rang up the stairs. As long time neighbors, we had a walking-knock agreement for our frequent drop-ins.

"Lindy, check this out," I said, pulling my friend into my bedroom/office and locking the door. Producing a folded piece of paper from the toe of a battered, old tennis shoe, I shook out the creases.

"These are my top favorite love letters. I pasted certain emails onto one page, for whenever I'm running out of patience with, everything…"

"You pull out the running shoe."

"Something like that."

"Am I ever gonna meet this guy? Did you tell him I wrote him a fan letter when I was a teen-ager?" Lindy had a habit of skipping subjects quickly, leaving no time for a response.

"Yes, I told him. It's so weird that he has a fan club! I went onto his web site and there are letters from fans, get this, from different countries even."

"I know, I checked out his web site," she interrupted me. "Let's go downstairs for some liquid refreshment, and then I want to see *your* fan letters from Mickey."

"I don't know if I could show anyone –" I hesitated. "Go downstairs and get something for both of us, and I'll read over the page and decide."

Using the rug to flatten out the paper creases, I sat on the floor and re-read the words that soothed me through the last few months of Devin's verbal abuse and Raymond's barked commands. Mickey's words, catapulted my day to day existence from ignoration to admiration.

"You're the hybrid mixing of puzzle and taste...an unsolved chocolate...a sweetness that can't be labeled or identified even...because you keep changing. I like that image...trying to taste you...find the Veronica ingredients...the sugar and cinnamon...my mystery...I've got it really bad tonight

> *I'll love you forever*
> *Tomorrow is too far away*
> *'night Angel, Mickey*

I loved your last letter...your humor is the perfect ballast to your sentiment. It's perfect, like you. I'm changed by your words. They're like a prism, as I observe and remember how our world of Mickey and Veronica spun into its current alignment. At some point you enlarge my ego and at some times I feel small...yet always human beyond a lifetime. We're still quivering with our hello's and sometimes you get a look in your eyes and I'm reading our 'good-byes'...I've never felt such awe and sadness and gratitude at the same time. You belong to the stars and my special prize has been to find your light and know your touch.

> *More please...always more...*
> *tears of kindness and joy...*
> *you're an earth Angel*
> *my first...my last*
> *kisses, Mickey*

My brilliant Angel, It's so fucking sad...wondering where our lives are going to go... Wondering why I've made these stupid choices I've made...wondering when I'll slam the door on this life and choose...

> *light and love...and real happiness...*
> > *you give me all of those things...*
> *and you have a laugh that could restart a heart...*
> > *I want to grow up for you...*
> *Save us both...*
> > *Be your hero...*
> *Grrrrr is the word.*

> > > *I love you so*

> > > > > *Mickey*

(The next excerpt was my response to him. I had glued it on the paper.)

Mickey, I soar when I read your words and they leave me breathless, but I have to notice that you are not longing for Meg Ryan or Cleopatra. It is only me. Your romantic goals are attainable, within reach. It may take more courage than Sweet-Mickey has. That's OK. We all get what we deserve.

> > > > > *Veronica*

The sound of ice cubes clanging against glass preceded Lindy up the stairs. Carefully folding the creased paper to reveal only one excerpt, I handed it to my friend. The others were too personal and being aware of Lindy's short attention span, I chose my favorite email; I'd memorized the last line.

Veronica,

You and I are capable of endless passion...and compassion...making for the best part of my life...and in some ways it appears life itself. You're also the most important woman I've ever met. The most meaningful relationship I've ever had. And that's today. With a river of memories constantly splashing joy on the banks of my dried up life here...You're a life doctor and the best secret I've ever had... xxoo Mickey

"Mmm," Lindy said with eyes opened wide, then attempting a John Wayne impression, "Wow, them there are some mighty powerful words, Missy. Tell me once again, why he stays married?"

Snatching the paper from her hands, I regretted that she chose this moment to drop by, the moment I was caught fondling my lover's words in a romantic revelry. "He's a wuss," I answered.

"So, you want him to leave her so...what? He can be your wuss?"

"I want him to leave her so he can be himself, and not have to live up to her showbiz expectations."

"What does that mean?"

"Recently they went to a premier for a movie—he wrote the title song for *Winning for Losers*. Did you see it Lindy?" she shook her head no, and I continued.

"Once they were on the red carpet, she kept saying, 'no one is interviewing you, I'm so embarrassed! They better seat us with Tom Hanks' and so on."

"That's pretty gross," Lindy said.

"She tells him, 'all my friends ask me, what happened to Mickey's career? I'm so ashamed. What happened? You haven't had any hits in five years! You used to be on top' and on and on. Lindy, she has no idea how messed up the music business is. Trends in music change, and the fact that his career has taken him in the direction of films is the right thing for a composer. So she doesn't hear his songs on the radio, and the red carpet interviewers aren't so quick to come over, who cares? It isn't who he is, it's what he does."

"Sounds like, she was in love with who he *was then*. Now the pressure to crank out the hits for his wife's ego makes it worse," Lindsey said.

"It's just so mean. It just makes him feel unloved. Frankly, he is…unloved by the greedy Mrs. Owens.

"Veronica, I don't know how to say this… I don't want you to get hurt…"

"Go ahead and say the obvious," I said

"Staying with someone who puts him down and having a great girl like you on the side, *is who he is*! That's all he is. He isn't a hero. He's a guy who knows how to talk the talk, but will never walk the walk, and we both know it. Now, if that is okay with you, it is okay with me, and it seems to be okay with him so–"

"Shut up, Lindy," I said evenly, reaching for the drink she had set on my desk.

"Veronica, face it, he likes the abuse or he wouldn't stay with her. You claim he's not materialistic, so it's not the fear of being separated from his money."

"Actually, there is quite a bit at stake. She would get the house and he'd probably end up with just the cat and the Mr. Coffee maker. He isn't materialistic, but we all realize, there would be a huge shift in life style if he had to live on half." There was a murmur of agreement and a silence. Tucking the letter of undying love back into the tip of the worn out Rebock, I said,

"So, you assume he doesn't really love me? Is that your point?"

"They have some deal that works for them. Maybe they have hot sex after she puts him down. Remember hearing about the Alfred Bloomingdale scandal, a few years ago? Did you read about that guy?"

"Yeah, I read about it in the Rolling Stone. Powerful wealthy man –" I faintly recalled.

"He paid his mistress to insult him! Then he died suddenly--as suddenly as someone in their eighties could die--and she sued his estate for the cost of the 'dominating sex therapy' sessions she gave him."

"Lindy, that is too tawdry to even discuss. I'm insulted you brought that up," I said, turning away from my best friend. She crossed the room and gave me a hug. I turned to her.

"I understand the dynamics of feeling unworthy of what you've achieved and some psychological need to be diminished. Maybe, being degraded …balances it out for certain people. I suspect with his wife demeaning him because they don't have a bigger house, keeps him in a state of insecurity. Undermining his self-worth erodes his confidence, so now he can't make a decision without running it by 'headquarters' and any decision that doesn't directly result in more stuff for Helen is vetoed."

"It sounds like you have a pretty good grasp of the obvious and not so obvious. Whatever, Veronica. Just keep in mind, guys in big houses don't leave their wives. Just don't get hurt."

Speaking slowly, plucking words out of the air for the first time, I struggled to explain. "You know what it's like to pass by a store window everyday and notice something beautiful, exotic and frightfully expensive?"

"Sure," Lindy said, taking the last gulp from her glass.

"Has it ever happened that after months of admiring the special exotic thing, you finally buy it and discover it is beautiful and exotic but it doesn't go with anything you have at home?"

Feeling the liquor, Lindy wasn't tracking my metaphor. "Don't you think Mickey and his wife have hot make-up sex after their fights?"

"No, I don't," I said, raising my voice a little, and as a sigh escaped my lips, I turned toward the window and said to the horizon, "I'm an ornate silver tea set, and he lives on a sail boat. He can't take me home, and there's nowhere to put me."

&&&&&&&

Chapter 13

SIMON SAYS

The owl and the pussycat went to sea, in a beautiful pea-green boat. They took some honey and plenty of money, wrapped up in a five-pound note.

Edward Lear,
The Owl And The Pussy Cat

Simon Bestep, the gentleman who optimistically entrusted his New Year's Eve plans to my floundering entertainment agency, was a man whose charm was slow in coming. When he spoke my eyes would glaze over until a word or phrase would jolt me out of the abyss. With embarrassment, I'd realize, I'm half of a meeting. These brief mind lagoons are the result of his blah, blahing-on. Boring topics are more tedious by his monotonous voice.

This particular afternoon, we met to discuss more details of the fantasy date. I was struggling with how to present the fact that he can't have sex with "Gwendolyn."

We spoke briefly about how things were going at his financial planning company. Since these meetings are a getaway from the madness at home, once in chair with a glass of wine in front of me, I unravel like a sweater on a nail.

"Have you read any good books lately?" I asked Simon Bestock.

"Yes, thank you for asking. A fascinating account of the French regime in 1770, as it teetered on the verge of collapsing, as you no doubt know, considering the excesses of the court, it was interesting to uncover the tastes of the high society in the grips of Anglomania…"

Is it something lacking in me? Do I have the attention span of a ferret, raised on MTV? I can't stop my mind from wandering. Wandering around Mickey's life, as I struggle to imagine it. What do Mickey and his famous friends do on a night like this?

Do the wives drink Sangria in a separate area kvetching about the valet parking service at their last party?

"After my Pilates class, we stopped by the Peninsula Hotel for High Tea, and you will never guess who I ran into," a well-manicured Hot House Orchid Type woman reports to her sisters in spoildom. Fading from that fictitious table, I jolt back to the present as my client Simon's mouth was forming words and his eyes were on me.

"And so, Ms Bennett, you can see why the woman portraying my beloved Gwendolyn must have a son." Wow, what a leap from the trudge toward Neoclassicism which was my last recollection of the conversation. No matter, the point was made. Let's see what just happened. A bit tricky to find an opera singing actress whose photo looks like Carol Kane only more haunted. Add to that, she needs to be good at improvisation, available on New Year's Eve and work cheap.

"A son, of what age did you say--? Sir, Simon?" I stammered.

"My stepson attended Webb School for Boys in Claremont, California. It is also my alma mater." He took a deep breath and continued, "Although Chad wasn't my biological son, we would have dinner together on the holidays. That is when he was home from the fine institution, and as such, it would make my evening more complete to have the presence, uh reminder of, Chad—of, better days." Simon looked down as he spoke.

"Oh, did he…? Is he—?" I asked.

"When my wife died, Chad's father's family assumed all parental responsibilities. I haven't seen him in three years. He would be, ah, seventeen now. A nice young man in his Webb Blazer is a picture I long to see."

A second glass of wine was a welcome sight, and as the stiff waiter retreated from our table, I likened it to a nurse distributing a medication to dull the pain of the latest assignment. I try to sip and not guzzle the pinot, and sink back into the comfort of the chair.

I picture Mickey at home being the host and husband of the year. My ghost apparently has access to his house since I'm looking down on what I imagine to be a typical evening at home.

"Whatever you would like dear," I suspect is the catch phrase. I don't know if that is more obnoxious than the catch phrase at my house. "Where are my fuckin' keys?" Or, the ever popular, "When I get back this place better be pulled together!"

Standing in front of the home entertainment center at Mickey's house, he whispers, "Which music selection would you enjoy hearing, dear, before our dance lesson, and dinner?"

Fifteen miles away, on the other side of the universe, an angry voice echoes from the back of my fridge "Doesn't anybody throw away the dead food in here? This celery looks like ribbon!"

Honestly, it's not that I'm a bad housekeeper, just that I'm so understaffed. With Raymond as the King, and Devin as the Prince with surly subjects, I've been ordained to spend all of my days in Slobovia- picking up after them. Never mind I run a booking business. From dropping a wet towel on a bed to a sandwich crust left on a table not the plate, the *crust itself*, is left on a table, these two guys are hopeless. Or, at least get distracted, at the point where a normal person would put "it" or throw "it" away.

Simon's voice jolted me into the present. "You received my second deposit check I assume? And the ten page personal history of my courtship and marriage with Gwendolyn?" Simon asked nervously as he glanced around the lobby of the Beverly Hilton Hotel.

"Oh yes, thank you. The third deposit is due November 1st, I believe." I smiled, and went on.

"I know this is a delicate subject, but we need to be clear about the intimate aspects of your fantasy date. First off, you will meet your lovely *Gwendolyn,* impersonator is such a *strong* word, shall we say, clone? Yes, in the dining room of the lovely Ritz-Carlton restaurant, she will join you. She will appear at your table wearing an outfit like the one in the photo you provided. We have gone to great lengths to brief the actress...er...lovely lady, on topics you enjoy discussing."

Simon smiled for the first time. How sweet is that? In the future people can make holograms of their hottest dates and pull them out like a Blockbuster video long after they're gone. Today is October 12th, and I need to begin casting. The calendar says it's Columbus Day. Like an explorer, I'm out to discover the delicate fabric of this man's romantic fantasies.

"Getting back to New Year's Eve, after a delicious seven course dinner, this will be quite an experience, as it is prepared by one of the city's most renowned chefs. You will enjoy stimulating conversation, dancing, and champagne flowing; however, Gwendolyn is unfortunately called away for an emergency. She will leave the room quickly. At this point your mistress calls your room and tells you she wants to reunite with you on this special night. She informs you she is in the lobby, and is available for a...tryst, shall we say? Since you are alone at this point, and she is eager to join you in your penthouse, well?" With no cue as to his response on the switcheroo, I had to continue.

"It is *your* option to see her and make love one last time. If that is your desire, it is her desire." I paused for a moment and took a sip of wine. Simon said nothing.

"In the morning Gwendolyn will join you for the champagne brunch and the morning will blend into a lazy afternoon. You two will have fun, new memories to share and relive, and brunch will be a glorious way to usher in the new year. The elegant setting, conversation flowing, mutual appreciation..." There was no cue as to how Simon felt, so I babbled on. "Gwendolyn is more generous with compliments than you may remember."

I smiled and leaned forward and in a hushed tone I continued, "She will read the report we provide her, and honestly it will seem like old times. Chad will be joining you for dinner."

We sat quietly and at one point, actually sighed simultaneously, as if watching a poignant scene in a film. Then, catching each other's eyes we nodded slightly in agreement.

"It sounds divine," he said. We raised our wine glasses with a reverence befitting the last signature of an international treaty.

I love this job.

&&&&&&&

Chapter 14

NEW YORK, NEW YORK

A life without love, without the presence of the be-loved, is nothing but a mere magic-lantern show. We draw out slide after slide, swiftly tiring of each, and pushing it back to make haste for the next.

Goethe

Entertainment," I chirped into the phone, in a professional, albeit pajama'd voice.

"Can you talk?" Mickey asked.

"I seem to be doing okay so far," I responded

"You know what I mean," his voice smiled into the phone.

"Hey Mickey, where are you?"

"Nashville. If you lose your privacy, call me back about noon. I need to talk to you about something," then pausing, "It's good."

"What time is it there in Nashville?"

Without missing a beat, he quipped, "Two hours ahead and about twenty years behind." We laughed, and he continued, "Can you meet me Friday in New York?"

Looking over my cluttered desk I inhaled deeply. "I suppose the holiday booking is pretty crazy right now, since it's October, hmmm-yes!"

My time-honored method of leaving town was a nanny gig. Occasionally I worked as a traveling baby-sitter for New Age author Adriana Baker. Her seven-year-old daughter needed supervision during Adriana's book promotions that took place in random cities. Adriana, her daughter, Courtney, and I all went on short junkets. Their "full time nanny" was not always available to accompany the delightful little Courtney, so these out of town jobs came in last minute.

Have I mentioned they are fictional? These people real or imagined weren't likely to intersect with Raymond's world. He'd rather carve his eyeballs out of his head with a grapefruit spoon, than read a book. Therefore, I had a getaway.

After Saran Wrapping four days worth of meals for the fridge, folding all the laundry, watering the plants to the point of flooding, I caught the flight.

A limo driver holding a card with my name met me at JFK airport and rushed me to The Plaza Hotel. It felt like Dorothy arriving at the Emerald City.

Not having been to The Big Apple in years, I savored every New York minute. With my hectic lifestyle, I quickly adapted to the frenetic pace of the city. In the first hour of walking in Manhattan, I saw two cab drivers hop out of their cabs and yell at each other nose to nose; well that felt like a hug from home.

Most people wore black and I saw very few water bottles. There were congenial immigrants gesturing wildly, businessmen in serious negotiations, girlfriends exchanging intimacies, as well as foreign language babble; all passing by me like a cultural conveyor belt.

With days free and being a first rate eavesdropper, I'd walk the city all day. Going a few blocks trailing a couple Wall Street financial wizards, on the brink of hearing a hot stock market tip, I'd jump stride to hear two women discuss their therapy, en route to a trendy restaurant. A right turn on the corner found me privy to the details of an exclusive auction being held by an Israeli art dealer. These meetings ended abruptly at a street corner with a hug good bye. I usually bumped into people's backs-since I didn't know their departure point, and was following too closely. These personal collisions were awkward, and resulted in me grabbing for a clumsy group hug, to the horror of the New Yorkers.

Given a generous allowance for my days alone in the city, I ate well. Apparently, I was invisible to the other diners, who sat inches from me in restaurants, completely unaware of our close proximity. It felt like I was walking into a movie after it started, and I had to catch up on the characters and plot line.

Three ladies dining at The Plaza were overheard saying, "Well, I'm sorry, I just can't see spending $2,000 for a purse." Getting no support from her table companions after a moment of silence, she backtracked.

"Well, I mean for an everyday purse."

My gag response kicked in and I played it off as a coughing fit. Two thousand? On a purse? Are *they* taunting me too? Recalling the day before Devin and I ransacked the couch for change so he'd have spending money while I was away. Given his booming "bud" business, he probably didn't need it, but we mothers do try to provide.

When a four-year-old was being obnoxious in a posh restaurant and screeched when his father tried to reign him in, the man glanced around furtively and with a deep voice announced to our side of the room, "Brandon doesn't have a particularly narrow sense of boundaries."

In front of the Plaza Hotel I watched cutting-edge hiphop dancers spin on their backs to the delight of the street crowd. As the audience grew, an Irish cop stopped the show. Two officers stood talking to each other in a thick Irish brogue, and I leaned in to hear this comment,

"Whale ya knaw Patrick, the Irish don't worry about the future, they choose to get on with the past."

When Mickey was free from meetings, the days were even more fun. He bought me a purse from a toothy Jamaican street vendor. Knock-off purses were sold for $30 just steps outside Bergdorf Goodman Department Store. There were also great sunglasses, watches and scarves in the $20 range. I was so delighted with the knock-off, Mickey surprised me the next day with the real designer purse from the Dooney & Burke store, the price tag read $325.

We held hands inside my coat pocket and walked in the tall shadows of skyscrapers. Chatting and nibbling hot ginger-sugar candy, we strolled past trendy scenesters dining alfresco on Madison Avenue.

"Mickey, you eat so much calamari I suspect you're putting squid on the endangered species list," I said as we exited the Nosidam Café. "Yes, from now on your new name is Squidly. And, Squidly, how wonderful the food is here! How will I be able to remember this wonderful place? Nosidam? What a strange word!"

"It is Madison spelled backwards." Mickey said, "and you don't need to remember where it is, I will always take you here."

"I don't know what to say, but, iggy-wop comes to mind," I replied.

As Manhattanites hurried around us, we ducked into art galleries. In Central Park, the trails led us through volleyball courts, baseball diamonds, a carousel, rolling acres of grass, a zoo and gigantic rocks for sitting and reading. Stopping to buy hot nuts from a vendor, we also discovered the delights of honey roasted fresh coconut chunks. We admired squirrels in the trees and each other with equal fascination.

"Earth Angel, you know we can't be together on New Year's Eve, so why do you want to know my plans with my wife? Why do you even ask?" Mickey said as we lay on the bed of our Plaza Suite.

"I guess I'm a masochist. I guess I want to imagine where you'll be and of course I wonder what you're doing." I said absently, pulling the top of his hair into neat, little haystacks.

"She planned something. I will show up. Enough said, Angel. But, I promise you I will call you and we can have a great private conversation close to midnight." As he kissed my neck I squirmed around facing the other direction.

"Hmmm, that feels so…" I inhaled deeply as he upped the stakes by nibbling around my ear and kissing the back of my neck slowly.

"Use that sparingly… I am so turned on…." I murmured. Mickey had recently discovered my weakness and when conversations turned awkward, he resorted to the place that blurred all reason. A sudden tide of passion washed over us, and we yielded to the moment, a quiet rapture left us both happy and exhausted. As we silently held each other, amid tussled sheets, my smile at the ceiling faded as his cell phone beckoned.

Remember being a kid, and unexpectedly hearing the song of the ice cream truck? Oh, the joy of possibilities that sound signaled. It's kind of like that, only Mickey's cell phone blasts hideous and jarring notes, causing the opposite effect of the ice cream truck's happy tune. Grabbing the sweet off my lips, it leaves a layer of sawdust in its place. As a kid you never know when you'll hear that happy sound, but a few tinny notes and you're scrambling for change as visions of fudgesicles dance in your head.

The ice cream song can't come at a bad time. It is never that you just ate, or are already doing something. The ice cream truck satisfies a hot summer day as easily as a chilly afternoon.

Then comes the manic and panicky tune signaling Helen Owens. Her beckon comes as a tinny arrangement of *Pop Goes The Weasel*, from his cell phone. Mickey takes the call every time. Once he didn't pick up, and he told me, "I'll say I went down the hall to get a Diet Coke." How pathetic to have to explain your whereabouts every moment of the day. The hourly check-in's never bring in a good message, like she wants to dedicate her life to the Dali Lama and go to Tibet, or join a research expedition in Antarctica. Her life is devoted to the Church of Conspicuous Consumption; their mantra is *gimme, gimme, gimme*.

"Sorry, baby, I gotta take this." Mickey got up, and walked into the other room. As the afternoon sun light faded and the room darkened into night I sat up in bed admiring the bare trees of Central Park for the last time. The city was twinkling with life as my emotional life prepared for hibernation. The days played across my mind like a montage.

I'd hoped to see more of the city, but since we had to leave the hotel at different times, in plotting where to meet, we'd get lazy and not bother to leave the suite at all. Playing inside we entertained ourselves with yoga, dancing, movies, room service, philosophical ponderings and shadow puppet shows. We laughed and cried and loved each other completely. Satiated by the luxurious and romantic vacation, it was a sad contrast to hear the exit music playing; a manic and tinny version of *Pop Goes the Weasel* from Mickey's cell phone. Like a kid at the Make a Wish Foundation, when his pony ride was over, it was time to go back to the hospital, so I dressed.

"Does she suspect anything?" I asked, when my lover emerged from the ten-minute conversation.

"No. She is all caught up in Christmas. She wants a $15,000 watch and to redecorate the den."

"Kinda touching how she got *in the spirit* of Baby Jesus' birth, in October," I said dryly; caught at the crossroads of despising her materialism and envying her ability to spend.

I suspect Mickey has his own little, hellish rooms he peers into from time to time. It came out in a frank conversation yesterday, that at home I have sex a couple times a week, which is more than he is getting. Both of us resent what the other's spouse gets. We are so caught up in this love affair, the border of where he ends and where I begin is blurred. In our possessiveness, we resent that our lover may give away what is rightfully ours.

I turned around to face him, putting the dark thoughts back in their box. "Anyway, as you were saying. It will be good to find each other for a phone call on New Year's Eve. It isn't important where you are going and what you are doing. I'll look forward to the call."

We stood at the window, holding each other in a tight embrace, watching the city prepare for night. Neither of us spoke for several minutes, then he said, "I love you so much.

"Thank you. I know. It's iggy-wop, Squidley."

Chapter 15

THE REIGN OF TERROR

The ax forgets, the tree remembers

Anonymous

Devin's air punches made me a nervous wreck. "I won't hit you!" he screamed as his fist sailed within a millimeter of my nose. The air passing by so rapidly, I flinched and reeled back, losing my balance.

"Yeah, you don't know what hell is, you fuckin bitch! Makin' me get up at 9:30? You don't know what I'm going through!" he added cryptically.

"Giving me all these rules? All of a sudden? I can't do this bitch!"

His shouts were loud and it was exhausting to process the wild threats and curses through the ears of my sedate neighbors, as well as my own.

"What are you trying to do?" Devin roared. Without waiting for an answer, he grabbed at the.phone I was holding. I had just disconnected it from the cord in his room. Clutching it with two hands, I ran down the hall and up the stairs to my room.

"I overheard you talking to Kyle! You're dealing drugs and now the phone is OFF LIMITS!" After slamming his door, and the hall door, knocking over a dining room chair that was in his path, I had the lead outrunning him up the stairs.

"Gimme that, you can't do that!" he shouted behind me, leaping up the stairs three at a time. I rolled onto my bed and laid on my back kicking wildly with the phone cradled at my solar plexus. I'm going down for this one.

"Maybe I spoiled you for seventeen years, but right now you can't deal drugs in my house! I've got the phone and I'm keeping it!"

"Hey, look at the shirt you are wearing? Who do you think made you that shirt, bitch?" he snarled at me, panting like a wolf. I could smell him closing in.

"A sweet boy at camp who didn't call me a fuckin bitch ten times before noon, made this tied dyed shirt – a long time ago!"

Rolling onto the floor, I ducked, narrowly escaping another swipe in the air, by a hand that had "no intention" of hitting me, or so he said. Scrambling on my hands and knees for six feet, I made it into the bathroom door and locked it. Almost deafened by the pounding sound coming from inside my head, I heard him curse one last time and leave my room. I sighed with relief as I slumped to the floor leaning against the tub.

This was day three of enforcing the "up by 9:30 and dressed by 10:30 a.m. rule." Adding to this recipe for disaster, the situation escalated when I picked up the kitchen phone and heard a conversation confirming my suspicions. He was selling drugs. This morning was unveiling like an episode of COPS. Looking at my watch, it was hard to believe it was only 9:45 and I was sweaty and nauseous.

As if the bell for Round Three clanged, I felt some-what victorious on the floor cradling the phone with the cold tub propping up my back. Winning that fight in three rounds meant grabbing the phone-round one. Running up the stairs ahead of him and kicking him away, round two. Escaping to the bathroom, locking the door behind me –still clutching the phone meant I won today's first battle. My insides contract as my body slumps into a fetal position, against the cold tub. Prickly sensation on my back makes me feel like I've de-evolved into a porcupine. The tiny hairs on my back have turned to quills and my skin tingles as if throwing off quills at an enemy.

As normal breathing replaces the pant, I spot an aspirin bottle, shake three out and wash them down with my mouth at the faucet. Settling back on the cold, tile floor, I reflect on the last couple months. There was definitely a soap-opera element to my home life. Because my husband and son *actually look like* soap opera hunks, it all seems more dramatic and manipulative. They are playing handsome villains in my house. Raymond or Devin, just by sitting on a couch, actually enhance the esthetic value of the room. Raymond could turn a shed into a movie set. As most women know, strong jaw lines, great hair and bewitching smiles almost guarantee short forgiveness cycle too. I'm forever turning a Rubik's cube of love and hate, looking for solutions.

After being kicked out of public school, Devin was now a home school student. Home school is an option for kids to graduate from high school at their own pace, at home with mailed assignments. Over achievers could graduate early with this correspondence school option. Devin was working on high school graduation through the program offered by the University of Nebraska Independent Studies. If it could only be in Nebraska, instead of my dining room table. It was a relentless 24-hour nagathon getting him to do the assignments and mail them in. My mantra was, those teachers in public school don't get paid enough. Well, that was one of my mantras. A more popular mantra was, "when are you going to open a book?" quickly followed by, "well, try *and FIND* the book."

I resented every step of the process, to the point of begrudging my dog, which would escape through the pet door when things got loud.

Since Devin's assignments were always returned late and he wasn't in any hurry to graduate, I told my son it was time for a part time job. I started noticing the polite grocery bagging teenagers at Vons Market and sent him there to apply. He didn't even pretend to try. Like pages blowing off a calendar in an old movie, Devin was blowing off months without working or studying. The polite teens bagging my groceries now seemed to taunt me with their courtesy. Why did they have to rub it in that they were raised better? One by one, my resentments, like blocks stacked into a huge pyramid of anger, and I was teetering on the top.

Whenever the subject of job came up, we would have this spirited conversation. Devin would piously inform me he "wasn't gonna be somebody's bitch and get no minimum wage job and be a chump like you, Mom." The brother from the burbs explained further, "I'm gonna make the real cheddar (money) producing my crew of rappers-makin' the beats cuz I know this guy who got a five million dollar recording contract and I'm gonna wait till I get some oh that."

"But, I saw they were hiring at ----"

"I'm not gonna be no loser like you Mom," he hissed with scorn. "You? Ha! You got no job, just Dad bossing you around all day."

"I work for Dad and help him with his bookings and contracts. I'm booking all day, what do you *think* I'm doing on the phone?" At this point, my whine would become a pleading bleat of self-pity, morphing into a roar of melodramatic defiance -- nose to nose with my son. In our own bubble of anger and rush to get the last word in, we were loud enough to be heard by low flying aircraft.

"I'm here for you and Dad all day to help you, to cook your meals and run this household. How do you think the peanut butter gets in the cupboard? *That's* my job!" I would explain, thudding my chest repeatedly with my index finger.

"You don't need to help ME!" Devin would retort with scorn. Then, taking a quick breath to fortify the intensity of his point, (this part was so predictable, the dog knew the cue to scurry out the pet door) he would bellow, "I am 17! I don't need NOTHIN' from you!"

Next the cycle of violence would accelerate with an object thrown, a lanky arm swiping the air, a chair tipped over and more shouts of indignation. The duet of insults is exchanged at full volume, regardless of houseguests present. Onlookers be damned, *I will* have the last word.

Although I started today's altercation, usually the tantrums appeared like a comet headed for Earth, with no warning. It must be the drugs inciting his erratic behavior, I decide. My friends tell me to throw him out. Every last person, who cares about me, gives me the same advice. Aside from the emotional toll of throwing out my only son, he is a minor. So, this course of action would involve family court, lawyers and more emotional and financial expense. Who has the time? Oh, and the practical aspect of throwing him out is a joke. Getting in our house without a key is like breaking into a slice of Swiss cheese. Most of the windows don't have screens, simply sliding the window to one side, puts you inside in less time than it takes to find keys in a purse.

Naturally, I never needed to find my keys, since Devin and Raymond never lock the door. Devin is just careless and since my husband's valuable equipment is locked in his garage/studio, he reckons there is nothing of value worth locking up in the house, like his wife in bed asleep. Once our home became a teen flophouse, it was always unnerving coming into a dark house at night, with all the doors left open. Home? I've lowered the bar so many times I'm *livin'* the Limbo.

Devin is simply a spoiled brat who cannot cope with life's realities, like work and responsibility. I guess I am woefully to blame for spoiling him. Raymond can't even take the blame since he was never around. He has the noble excuse of working outside the home or practicing in the soundproof garage/studio. I guess it is a legitimate excuse, but would things have been different if he helped me raise our kid and face the music at home?

Apparently I dozed off with the comfort of my towel pillow, because the next sound I heard was Raymond pounding on the bathroom door.

"Where is the kitchen phone? Veronica, are you in there?"

"Yes," I replied.

"Devin left a big mess in the kitchen and now he's gone. Hey, open the door!" I reached up from the floor and twisted the handle, with a click the lock released. Glancing at me he snapped, "I wish I had all day to hang out in the bathroom, while the rest of the house goes to hell."

"Oh, here's the phone," I said, handing it to him.

"What the hell --? Oh, never mind. I don't even want to know why the phone is in here." Then, turning to leave he said over his shoulder, "Is everything okay? You better answer your business line. It's ringing."

"Everything is regular," I said emerging from my porcelain sanctuary. I sat down at my desk and picked up the receiver. "Entertainment"

"Veronica? This is Simon Bestep, and I'm having second thoughts. There's a strong probability that I won't be emotionally attached to Gwendolyn, ah -- in the brief period of time our date allows."

"Uh huh," I said lamely.

"It will be such a short amount of time spent together and I wonder if I will *bond with her*. I needed to call and tell you right away, of... my reservations."

"Could you hold for just one moment, sir?" I pressed the hold button on the phone, took a couple deep breaths, cleared my throat and came back on the line.

"Simon, Gwendolyn will be sending you personal emails starting tomorrow, since she wants to get on a closer basis before December. It seems, she...shares your concern. May I pass your email address on to Gwendolyn? She is most anxious to write you."

"Correspondence? via email? Well, oh my, that would be dandy. I say, that would be dandy!"

We hung up the phone and I laid my head on the desk and cried.

&&&&&&&

Chapter 16

DREAMS & COUNSELING

Love is the triumph of imagination over intelligence.

H.L. Mencken

Although Devin would eventually find his way upstairs to use my office phone, for now his homies couldn't call him back. He didn't know my business line number to give friends and Raymond hid our home phone. Talk about inmates taking over the asylum. What a morning.

With Devin gone, and Raymond heading back to his studio, with the home phone tucked under his arm, I decided to unplug my business line, lock the door and go back to bed. I select my two favorite eyelid movies and try to program a sweet dream. The first is a picture of Devin, detoxed from drugs, and smiling sweetly as he returns from a slow moving fishing boat from Alaska, where boys turn into men by working hard in fish canneries. Or, at the very least, fall overboard during rough seas. The other daydream was of Mickey and me in Zihuatanejo, Mexico. You, the reader, may want to practice saying it a couple times, and consider it for your own travel destination. Closing my eyes, I take a deep breath and set my daydream in motion.

Zihuatanejo is a fishing village about a three-hour drive north of Acapulco. The main street is on wooden slats up from the dirt, like Dodge City. There is a post office with a wooden awning. A sign points down the road, with an arrow that reads "Modern Beaches." I love that.

Mickey gave me an envelope of cash, which I turned over to the travel agent and the rest was easy. Well, my part was easy; Mickey had to escape the spouse. This stolen weekend would be a perfect combination of sunning, swimming, tacos, and making love; not in that order.

Few tourists find their way to this remote outpost populated with fishermen and students: two groups of people who know how to squeeze a peso. My sentimental journey recalls the port I knew in my college days. Or, perhaps daze is more accurate. At that time, accommodations were various casitas down a dirt road, hugging the shore. Wide banana tree leaves and palm trees often hid the doors of the modest homes. There were welcoming smiles for strangers, and Mexican children would always be waving you into their patios. The locals rented rooms to student/tourists. The "budget plan" was paying a few pesos a night to sleep in a hammock, strung up in somebody's yard. A guest's backpack was always safe, stashed behind a potted plant on the red brick patio. There was an outdoor shower; with cold water, and a nail driven into a post for your one towel. I mean *your towel*, as no towels were provided. My friends and I traveled second-class. We often took the families' beds, relocating Mom, Dad and the kids to the patio hammocks, swatting mosquitoes. There was one luxury hotel in town. I'd also stayed there.

It's a great little harbor with a tropical jungle just a few feet from the white sand! The public beach is separated by more jungle, about a mile thick with a cove to the north. The public beach closer to town is a harbor where boats are moored, then a bluff, with the one luxury hotel on top of the hill. The "Modern Beach" sign refers to what: young *sand?* It points toward the big hotel where Mickey and I stayed.

A two-mile lush jungle passage separated the two coves, filled with tropical flowers, huge butterflies and a fresh water spring – ready-made for a thirsty traveler. The public beach had palm leaf umbrellas, known as *Palapas,* for shade. Beautiful, dark-skinned matrons walked the beach with mangos and coconut chunks, or the more daring might eat an illegal raw turtle egg, seasoned on the spot with chilies and lemon. Men would crack the top of the shell and suck the turtle egg straight down, some perceived ritual of masculinity, no doubt. No raw-turtle-egg-breath kisses for me.

Mickey and I set out on the long, garden trail heading inland and north of the public beach to the more private *Playa Conejo Cove*. The walk through the jungle was a riot of color; the butterflies had wingspans the size of your outstretched hand. After the long, humid trek, it is a delicious reward to drink the cool water from the natural spring spouting out of the ground. We drank gratefully, splashing our necks and chests and faces. Heading inland toward the soft jungle underbrush, a tunnel of green ferns was an inviting hiding place as we lay down.

Finally, I'm able to relax. Surrounded by nature's bounty, the fear of being lost in this dense jungle had begun to overpower me. Our directions were given in garbled Spanish slang, but with the sound of the waves in the distance, I knew we'd stayed on the right path

Mickey's guidance led us to safety, fresh water and the beach. Relieved and cooled by the spring water, I melted into his arms and slid around on his body, as we became hot, sticky and tropical plants ourselves. We adapted to our jungle surroundings like vines in a fever of growth. Tenderly at first Mickey played his tongue against my top lip and after the playful kisses, deep thrusts followed. With my head on the towel, I looked up to see my lover's face, framed by lush green branches hiding the sky. Mickey whispered, *mine* and held my wrists in place, as an animal trapping his prey, on the leafy, tropical floor.

We eventually made our way back from *Conejo Cove* after a wonderful day of swimming. As we walked back to our hotel through the village, we noticed a local newspaper. There was a picture of teenagers in the harbor, and an article about a fishing boat that had left Zihuatanejo the day before. Apparently, an Alaskan fishing boat headed south to Acapulco had recruited some Californian young men to work tuna canneries in Alaska. *En route*, they stopped in Zihuatanejo for three days, then shipped out yesterday. There was a picture of the young men performing a rap concert in the *zocalo/plaza* of the town.

There was my son Devin in the photo, entertaining the locals, with the small sound system he brought on the fishing boat. He was free-style rapping on top of his own, recorded beats and music. The newspaper reported it was a big success with the local teens in the fishing village, who experienced urban music live, for the first time. The college students were shown in the photo cheering to the impromptu concert as well. The article stated that, after Acapulco, the crew were going to return to the cannery in Alaska.

As I awoke with a yawning stretch, my eyes opened to see my ugly brown dresser drawers with clothes spilling over the top. I was back in my room, my office, and my life.

There was a small sense of satisfaction that my unconscious was able to weave my two favorite fantasies together in one Technicolor dream. Suddenly feeling close to Mickey, I needed to make contact with him. It was risky to call, since his wife was often lurking about, but I took the chance.

"Can you talk, Mickey?" I began, in my just-woke–up sexy voice.

"Just for a moment, I'm heading over the canyon. I picked up some prescriptions at the pharmacy and, is the phone cutting out?"

"Are you sick?" I asked.

"No, no, just picking up Plavix, for my heart, it's just a blood thinner like an aspirin. How are you, baby-baby?"

"I'm great. I just had the coolest dream of you and me in Mexico," I said, with my voice rising over the static. "Can you talk? Where you going now?"

"I'm meeting her at two, for couples counseling on Ventura Boulevard."

"Couples counseling?" I squeaked, "You and your wife …are going to *couples* counseling?" The tight air passage in my throat could barely say the words "I'm going to lose you!"

"No, no, it won't make any difference," Mickey said dismissively. Even on the phone, I could see him batting the air.

"Nothing is going to happen, she's just trying to re-solve her anger issues," he added quickly.

"What does that mean?"

"Anger that, well, frankly that my career has stalled. She keeps harping on renting a villa in Tuscany for a summer, I, don't know, basically, she wants more stuff," Mickey said matter of factly.

"*Stuff?*" I gasped into the phone. Considering all the years of therapy Woody Allen invested, perhaps counseling won't matter in this case either.

"I hate this. What a horrible fate to sit and lie to peo-ple for an hour a week pretending you're not married to a self-absorbed, malcontent-and, discuss *your need for improvement.* What prompted this, tell me!" I insisted as tears formed in the corners of my eyes.

"She's obsessed with the A List. Last week she thought we didn't get the best table at Valentino's Restaurant and that started an avalanche of her insecurities, which led to tears into the Gazpacho, and verbally attacking me on the ride home…blah, blah," Mickey said uneasily, regretting the slip.

"I'm getting into Laurel Canyon, I'll call you lat…" The phone died and I was a ball of angry confusion.

Couples counseling, huh? This concept is like going to the Star Trek Convention, where you pretend to believe in someone's fantasy world. In this case, it is his wife's Victim-land, and Mickey has to play along. "I'm here for self improvement in a world without gravity or laws of decency." Naturally, the therapist has a high stake in finding fault with the husband and exaggerating his wife's complaints, thus fueling the charade, to perpetuate more income. The shrink won't tell her, "Grow up and get a life, you friggin' satellite. And quit whining."

The sign on the therapist's door probably says, "Welcome to Victimland. Our motto is: spoiled women are rewarded for insecurity, and happy people are supposed to be guilty. Please pay in advance."

How many battered husbands are sitting in well-decorated offices sincerely concerned about the cause of their wives' malaise? This hothouse orchid breed of women probably don't feel validated because they have few talents or skills *to validate them*. Sure, the husbands get all the attention, but often wives don't consider *why the hand* that feeds them receives attention. Rather, just throw money at the problem and hope for the sympathy of a well-attended pity party. God forbid the celebrity wife has a skill other than shopping, and getting Thank You notes out in a week.

If Raymond ever made it on a large scale, I know I'd be different. At the very least I'm a team player and not a status monger, what's this A list crap?

The flies on the walls in the office are probably gagging. "Yes, dear, I see, when you have to wait for me as I talk to photographers and press people, *you feel* left out. You hate it when I travel."

Skilled at ducking the obvious solutions, the therapist rings out, "Let's explore that pain!" Instead of asking, how do you expect to maintain this lifestyle without some sacrifice on your part? Or, when is the last time you made a nickel on one of your skills? No, the therapist needs to fan the fires of victimhood to keep those billable hours of income.

Maybe I need to see the shrink and schedule a partial lobotomy, de-activating the synapse of my brain where jealousy and imagination intersect. Mickey said she can't get to the "source of her every day anger." Oh, gag me, the session probably goes like this: "Well, Doctor, I'm trying to get to the root of all the anger I feel for my husband and the fact that he hasn't had a hit in five years," Mrs. Mickey says intently, leaning forward and narrowing her eyes.

The shrink nods solemnly, encouraging her to vent. "That's good, that's good...hmm, perhaps you could describe your typical day? Let's start with yesterday."

Taking a gulp of air, and trying her best to be a brave little soldier, Mrs. Mickey begins, "I awoke to my husband bringing me coffee in bed, took a shower and went for a walk around the beautiful canyon that surrounds our home. Then, I talked on the phone to three friends, directed the gardener about some planting, scolded the dog-walker for bringing Chivas Regal back seven minutes early last week, then got my feet, hands, horns and tail manicured. The shop was unusually crowded, so I barely had time to cross town, to meet friends at my favorite restaurant. We were meeting the celebrity chef yesterday, and the traffic was horrible on Wilshire."

"Don't think about it, dear, go on." Grabbing a tissue, she continues.

"When I met my friends for lunch they asked about my husband's career, and I'm always *so* embarrassed. You realize it's been more than five years since he's had a song on the charts, don't you?" Mrs. Mickey honks into a tissue at this point.

"No, dear, I wasn't aware," the therapist says with a sudden concern for her own financial future.

"My day yesterday, hmmm, a bit of jewelry shopping on the way home, then my private dance lessons with Raul. My husband joined me for dinner at The Little Door Restaurant, after class. What's your point, Doctor?" Sighing heavily, Helen appears exhausted at the task of reliving the events of yesterday.

"Dancing lesson?" inquires the therapist.

"Yes, I started taking them with my husband, but he couldn't keep up, so now I take four private lessons a week with Raul."

"That must have been disappointing for you, that your husband couldn't be a suitable dance partner, when CLEARLY it's so important to you," the therapist would probably coo.

"Thank you. Now you know what I am going through! Thank you. No one understands me," Helen says, vigorously nodding her head. Then bringing her hands to her forehead, she rubs her temples.

"I can see we have much work ahead of us Mickey. I noticed your body language when Helen was describing her trying day. Mickey, did I see you opening and closing your little pocketknife that hangs on your key chain? Hmmm?"

"Oh that? Well ma'am, I thought the blade should be clean in case she chokes on something and I need to rush over and slit her throat--so as to clear her trachea, so she can breathe."

"What did you say?" asks the therapist slowly.

"I said, Tuesdays are good for me," Mickey says.

Because I discreetly inquire, I assure you that is a typical day for the spoiled Mrs. Owens. In a parallel universe a therapist would have the guts to say, "People like you make me regret ever going to college to try and help the human race! Your sense of entitlement came from what? However, due to the poor economy, I suppose I should be grateful you employ an army of people to maintain your lifestyle." Instead, the therapist schedules a Tuesday appointment.

A horn blasting in the driveway signaled Lindy's arrival. I sat up to look out the window and real life came back into focus. It was already afternoon and my best friend and I had big plans. Devin's foiled drug deal in the morning, romantic Mexican holiday dream at noon, and discovering the love of my life is working on his marriage in the early afternoon, meant quite a day. But tonight promises an even more dangerous adventure.

With regards to Mr. Bestock's New Year party, it was time to get a hooker. The actors I'll deal with later, but what about this mild gentleman's mistress? Lindy offered to help, albeit, seemed too eager to help. We decided to step into Hollywood's underworld. Jeeze, what does one wear for picking out a prostitute? Apparently, a wrinkled blouse and denim skirt, I sigh racing out the door.

"I'm coming, I'm coming!" I called to my friend from the window.

&&&&&&&

Chapter 17

LOVE FOR SALE

The art of being wise is the art of knowing what to overlook.

William James

Our household immediately absorbed Bestep's first deposit, so it was clear what remained of his second deposit had to be spent on the actors, to assure they held the date for New Year's Eve. Specifically, an actress to play Bestep's wife Gwendolyn; a polite and stuffy teen to play his stepson Chad, and a prostitute to be his mistress, who would come to his hotel room at midnight, once his wife was "called away." This had to get rolling. I needed to make some decisions on the cast, before I spent all of the second deposit too.

Hastily throwing some clothes on, I motioned to Lindy to come up. She was early for cruising Santa Monica Boulevard, but who could blame her? Who wouldn't want to interview prostitutes for a job on December 31st between 11:45 p.m. and 12:45 a.m.? I didn't imagine we'd be as lucky as Richard Gere was in *Pretty Woman*, spotting a fresh faced Julia Roberts on Santa Monica Boulevard. Applying my make-up, I tried to emulate Julia's familiar laugh as I tossed my curls. (Adding the trademark smile with the hair toss, brown eyes looking skyward and infectious giggle was multi-taskingly impossible.) My terrier sprang from the room, apparently jarred by the loud, throaty giggle of Julia. Buffy's rapid departure discouraged any potential I may have had as an impressionist.

As Lindy and I drove to West Hollywood to find a hooker, I updated her on Mickey's couple's counseling. As a neighbor she was out of the loop of entertainment people and I felt she could be trusted. It was a relief to bitch and moan. Although not optimistic about the outcome, at least she wasn't judgmental about my affair.

"Wow, Lindy, wouldn't I like to be a fly on the wall? We're only hearing one side of the story, do you think Mrs. Mickey *has some real* reasons she doesn't like him, could he be unbearable?"

"Does Raggedy Ann have cotton tits? Damn right, he could be getting on her nerves," Lindy said.

"What if he always breaks into show tunes every few minutes? *He is* cheerful and *does know* a lot of songs," I wondered aloud.

"That would be annoying," Lindy said as she pulled a margarita can out of her purse, and popped open the triangle tin lid.

In a theatrical voice, I said, "'Is everything Okay at your table, Sir?' He breaks in with, '*Okay? Oklahoma, where the wind comes whistlin' down the plain...*"

"'Would you like a Bloody Mary with your brunch, sir?'" Lindy said in a solemn voice. Then, she sang out, "*Bloody Mary? Bloody Mary is the, boom...boom, girl I love!*'"

Recalling the showstopper from *South Pacific*, we sang a spirited chorus in unison. Exiting the 405 freeway at Santa Monica, we slowed down to observe a gender bending fashion show of cruisers, signaling a sex change in the population.

"Now, why are we down here, Veronica? A hooker hunt?" Lindy smirked, as she leaned out the open window for a closer look.

"Yes, I told you, I need to hire one for a client's New Year's party. What is Mickey's fatal flaw that sends his wife to the shrink? Let's talk about me," I pleaded, unsnapping my seat belt and turning off the key.

Lindy unbuckled her seatbelt, fished another cocktail-in-a-can from her purse, popped the aluminum top, took a swig and continued. "Maybe he's addicted to the Internet? It could be anything. He might buy everything he sees on late night TV? What if he wears her underwear around the house? I've seen straight guys who wear their wives' lingerie around the house. What if..."

"Wait a minute, where have you've seen that?"

"Jerry Springer has shows with hairy truck drivers wearing bras and maybe he shares his Popsicle with his dog, who licks it while holding it with its paws. I knew a guy who..."

"Lindy, this man is dignified. He isn't eating Popsicles." I said with mounting irritation, stepping out of the car. "I know she wouldn't tolerate much, so it must be his personal habits that annoy her. Things I couldn't know in a weekend."

Lindy interrupted me with a flash of inspiration. "Okay, we're doing it! We'll spy on his wife and make a plan to meet her, and try to bond with her at the beauty shop. We'll get the real story. Who knows, maybe we'll all be friends for life and have a good laugh about it later."

"Seriously, Lindy, I couldn't. What if *she is* really a nice person? That means I'm the creep. If I discovered she wasn't a shrew, then what? Gimme me one of those cocktails," I said lunging for Lindy's purse.

"What if she was –" I gulped, "I don't know what I'd do if she was like, one of us?"

"One of us? We aren't spoiled hothouse orchids, complaining and bitching for more stuff in between spa treatments and private dance lessons. She can't even walk her own dog!" Lindy bellowed. "Or were you kidding about the dog walker?" she said, grinning.

"No, it's all true. The orchid can't walk the dog. Only dance, shop and *kvetch*. Mickey's kids are from his first wife, and they're in boarding schools -- so she has no responsibility. She doesn't go to church, or do volunteer work, or paint or read books or help out in the community or train for a marathon, or..."

"Stop, I get it!" Lindy wailed.

"She doesn't even do yard work. All she has to do is attend functions with him and not complain."

"Ugh!" Lindy sputtered, then drained her can as if in protest. "Yeah! Down with the house orchid!"

"Yeah! Down with the HOT house orchid and that entire fragile breed of women," I cried, as we clinked our cans in a metallic toast of solidarity. We hard working women had no tolerance for them. Or was it their lives we envied? Either way, the chilled tequila drinks warmed us with sentimentality.

"Nah, she isn't one of us," Lindy confirmed, "We're more like weeds, popping up anywhere, sturdy and…"

"At least can we be a dandelion? A simple flowerish weed?" I asked.

Lindy picked up the ball, "From the way you describe her, Mickey deserves a break from her. That's probably why they're going to the shrink. She's so damned boring, it's somethin' to do…" Then, reaching into the bottomless purse, "I had six, where's the other one?"

Looking around Santa Monica's red light district as my tipsy friend talked to her purse, I realized we were intruding on an unknown world. The attractive hookers all had narrow hips, great wigs, long legs and well, were guys. The females looked pretty skanky and I didn't trust someone from the street to take a deposit and show up later.

"Look how these guys dress! This is quite the fashion scene," I whispered to Lindy as the parade of androgynous model-types sashayed by.

"Hey, I'm wearing that skirt!" I hissed and ducked back towards the car.

"Veronica, don't be so sensitive, just 'cause your legs aren't as long, and he looks better. Hey, you got a better adam's apple!" Lindy said cackling.

"Shut up, get back here," I said, shoving her toward the car. "There's got to be a better way. I can't trust these women people to show up after I pay them a deposit. I can't keep track of some ho for the next six weeks!"

Lindy shrugged.

"Should I call an escort service out of the phone book, Lindy?" I grabbed her arm and began dragging her back towards the car.

"That would be a higher quality skank, but most of the money would go to the agency and not much to the girl doing the horizontal boogie," Lindy observed.

"I have an idea. Let's go by the casino where I used to book entertainment. My friend Sam is a Pai Gow manager, and he probably has experience finding women for the high rollers. Maybe he could introduce me to a hooker over there, at the casino."

In Los Angeles there are card clubs that call themselves "casinos." Only Indian casinos can have slot machines. However there are zoned areas inside L.A. County where poker rooms are allowed. These casinos were great places for Chinese food in the middle of the night, as well as entertainment, too. As former Entertainment Director, I was hopeful my connections would pay off. Driving west on Santa Monica Boulevard and entering the 405 freeway, I felt we were gaining more direction in this strange pursuit. Twenty minutes later, we found ourselves at the Hollywood Park Casino.

By now, Lindy was on the edge of drunkenness and didn't want to leave the car. "You go, I'll just wait right here," she said, sleepily.

"No, I can't leave you in this parking lot! Come on, Lindy, let's go inside, maybe you'll find your eternal love," I said, teasing her while yanking her arm.

"Did ya forget I'm married? I'll tell you what eternal love is," Lindy slurred, "Ray Charles and Stevie Wonder playing tennis!"

"That's so funny, tell that to Sam when you meet him. Let's go inside and meet some new people." She allowed herself to be hoisted from the car and we trekked across the long parking lot toward the casino doors.

The clamor of metal Pai Gow cups thudding against the felt tables, the din of several languages, and garbled announcements from the P.A. system assaulted our ears once we were inside. Walking toward the coffee shop, we brushed past food trays with steak bones and sandwich crusts abandoned by weary gamblers. Quickly, I found Sam who agreed to meet us in ten minutes at the coffee shop.

Sam Griff had the aura of a man entirely in control. As we settled into the red vinyl booth, he discreetly nodded to his bodyguard to take a break. My eyes followed his nod, and I saw the steely-eyed Samoan take his cue and go outside for a smoke. A seasoned Pit Boss, Sam always had an easy smile on his face, which was a welcome sight in a room with so many glazed-over, vacant eyes. His ability to speak a few phrases in several Asian dialects helped him control the Pai Gow Section of the casino, it was a tinder box of tense action. An expensive suit worn with snakeskin cowboy boots was his stylish uniform. The casino owner once told me Sam made about $900,000 a year with all the juice/tips from the Asian section. One wondered if his inner-child was spoiled with all the vice surrounding him.

After introductions and catch up chatter, I got to the point. "Sam, I need your help. You know I'm an event planner, and, well, there is a certain VIP client who needs to have a date for a New Year's Eve party I booked."

"Event planner? What's that? I thought you hired bands," Sam said.

"Well, yes, I hire bands, book bands, booked entertainment –you know. I just need to find a girl who is available, um, to get friendly, um, with this guy, who –who will be at a party—for which I booked the entertainment," I said, and forced a smile.

"Can you line us up with a reliable hooker?" Lindy barked, interrupting my stumbling ramble.

"Oh I see. What's wrong with Tiffany?" Sam said turning his head toward the bar. Next to the coffee shop was the Back Room Bar, a darkly lit lounge.

"The waitress? Oh, *she* might know someone? Thanks." I said, casting a scornful look at Lindy, although I was grateful we were making progress.

Tiffany was a tall, thin brunette about thirty, with the energy of a ferret on a double espresso. She made great tips cocktailing at the bar, with her style of offering the customer something between the bum's rush and good service. Back and forth to her table many times, she could have been annoying if she weren't so cute. A relaxing mood was the antithesis of drinking in her station, I had noted in the past. Now Tiffany's flirtatious smiles and "gotta-go-hons" took on new meaning.

"You know Tiffany does tricks on the side," Sam said nonchalantly. "Everybody knows she is a working girl. Come on, Veronica, how long did you work here, booking bands, and eating Kung Pow Chicken?"

"Oh, how sad," I gushed.

"She don't look sad to me," Lindy volunteered with a throaty laugh. We leaned sideways in our booth for a better view of the lounge just in time to see Tiffany kissing a customer at the table.

Sam got up from the table, tossed an orange chip next to the bill and kissed us good-bye. "Ladies," he said with a small bow. "It was a pleasure meeting you, Lindy." Giving us a wink and flashing the $900,000 smile, he got up from the table. His beefy bodyguard appeared and fell in step with Sam, following three feet behind as they disappeared into the card room.

Lindy had a strong buzz going and was ready to round up Tiffany to close the deal.

My being the last to know the barmaid was a hooker was not a total surprise. One time I was singing in Reno, at Harrah's, and after two months, I commented that I hadn't seen a hooker yet. Apparently, I don't have an eye for spotting an employee of the oldest profession in the world. Reno could be confusing because the tourists wore plunging necklines. Heck, so did I! Finally, a dealer had pointed out that the hookers always wore the 3-½ inch heels. Tight clothes always accompanied by the high, high heels. Once I trained my eyes to notice footwear, I observed the hookers never made eye contact, well, with women. Normally, women might randomly glance around inside the casino. The average working girl has a deadened gaze, the casino landscape had lost any excitement long ago.

We picked up our margaritas and headed into the dark cocktail lounge, which smelled like rotting dreams, if there were such a scent.

"How embarrassing is this going to be?" I whined to Lindy, as we sat down at a small table. In a sticky sweet voice, I practiced my speech softly.

"Hi, Tiffany, we'd like a couple margaritas, and oh, just one other thing. Could you screw a stranger for me on New Year's Eve?" Lifting my shoulders, I wrinkled my nose and put my hands together in a mock prayer.

"You're startin' to friggin' annoy me," Lindy slurred, draining her glass.

"Tiffany, c'mere. I got somebody I want you to meet," Lindy called out to the only waitress in the lounge.

Tiffany was at our table in a streak. With her glass extended in the air like the Statue of Liberty, Lindy announced, "You probably remember Veronica? Well, she's found you a rich, old guy for a date. Whaddaya doin' New Year's Eve?"

"Nothing but serving these pathetic losers," Tiffany said, shrugging her shoulders. "I'm in. You girls doin'it, too? How many *babes* does this guy want?"

&&&&&&&

Chapter 18

ADD PLAGIARISM

*There's always two sides to a story, but in your case--
it's an octagon.*

Steve Perry

"Veronica? Do you have a moment?" Simon Bestep's voice on the phone sounded anxious. So I bid a hasty good-bye to the chainsaw juggler on the other line and I got back to my client.

I inquired sweetly, "How is your day going, Simon?"

"Veronica, I have to tell you the bi-weekly emails from Gwendolyn have really filled an empty spot in my day. Well, they really make a difference." He spoke with a halting rhythm which made him difficult to gauge over the phone.

"Is that to say you like them?"

"Very much. However, I haven't received a letter from her this week, causing this old fool to check his email at least three times daily." He self-consciously chuckled before clearing his throat and continued. "Can you let her know I want to hear from her more often? I don't reply to her, as you might know. It's only one-sided."

"Sure, I'll tell Gwendolyn to write you today, by three o'clock."

"Thank you, dear. I'm happy to pay for the extra letters, if you wish. Another matter, on the night of our evening together, New Year's Eve, what time will Chad and Gwendolyn be arriving? That is to say, at what time will dinner be served? Shall I meet her at seven or at eight?"

"Why don't we say, uh, 8:30, Simon?"

"Splendid. I haven't forgotten how long it takes ladies to get ready for a night out," Simon said agreeably. "Good-bye Veronica."

As I hung up I told the phone in its cradle, "Mister, you have no idea how long it takes." Looking over my list of things to do, I read:

1. Pick up Raymond's dry cleaning.
2. Fill out Washington Mutual loan application and mail today
3. Sew buttons on two tux shirts & find missing studs for tux shirts.
4. Fed Ex Devin's book report/ late again!
5. Decipher astronomical phone bill, confront Verizon,/beg for a payment plan.
6. Find three singing Santas for Mall gig
7. Call the city and give them my license plate numbers, to check for outstanding parking tickets (that reportedly have been ripped from the offending windshield by a family member)
8. Find a harpist for a memorial service

Taking the pencil off the ledge of my ear I added,

9. Email love letter to Bestep by·3 p.m..

The day was getting away from me. I was rendezvousing with Mickey at five, and still had dirty hair, and clothes in the dryer. All afternoon the phone rang off its hook with party planners in search of Deejays, now that the best bands had already been booked for the holidays.

With a quiet "Mickey, forgive me," I opened up my file cabinet, and took out a manila envelope from the back, which read "Pet Documents." Leafing through my hidden stash of love letters from Mickey, I found and retyped one to send to Simon, changing only the pronouns. Then, I sent it.

Until now, I had written every letter, but my words paled in comparison to my lover's prose. Besides, who has the time?

TO: Simon Bestep

FROM: Gwendolyn

>*Darling, I'm glad my words arouse you...I want to love you with my words, and hold you with their imagined sound in your mind, and wish that you could read them with your eyes closed...the Braille advantage: To read my love poems in darkness...imagining my breath on your neck...the soft first brush of our lips and the deep, deep lusty kisses that follow...that moment when you can feel me drinking from your spirit...consuming you with my need...for you to be deeper and deeper inside me...listening for that breath that tells me you're ready. Simon, you're the shelter I dove into during a storm and magically discovered it to be a hidden door into Ireland, a beach hideaway, and a castle we built in the sky.*

>*Your adoring, Gwendolyn*

There, it was done. Now I could cross "write love letter" off my list replacing it with "find an actress to play Gwendolyn."

Raymond and Devin had gone to a sale at Guitar Center, and afterwards they were off to Raymond's gig in Santa Barbara. This was Devin's first experience as a roadie with his dad. We hired our little slacker to pack/unpack his dad's equipment and set up mics, in exchange for buying him guitar equipment. During the gig Devin could hang out in their hotel room, help break down and load out after the performance, and the guys would be back the next day. The timing of this gig coincided with Mickey's ASCAP board meeting at a posh hotel in north San Diego County. Naturally, I was invited.

Driving into the long driveway of the Four Seasons Aviara, I was ushered into a serene world where I somehow didn't belong. Sheryl Crow was fervently singing, "*You're my Favorite MISTAKE...*", blasting from my car, when the valet opened my door and startled me with the question:

"Are you checking-in, or having dinner with us this evening?"

"I, I, I was looking for self park."

"Oh, sorry madam, it is all valet parking." He efficiently pulled out a tablet of parking slips and asked my name.

"Oh? My name? Oh, of course, you want my name, hmmm."

Gee, they didn't ask my name at other places I valet parked. Hmm. Yet, this seemed like a standard procedure, not friendly chat, coming from young parking attendant who stood his ground with a fixed smile, penetrating eyes, and slightly raised eyebrows.

"Ah, yes--Verronica Bennett. I'm meeting a friend." I announced with meek authority. Then, I realized I could have said I was having dinner since "meeting a friend" wasn't one of the two choices I was offered by the Arian Youth Palace Guard. He opened the door to assist me, and the music of Sheryl Crow spilled out into the parking area, "*miss your laughter...but I can't go on this way...*"

I had to decide whether to scramble in the back seat retrieving just the essential items out of my overnight bag or just take the whole thing inside to "meet the friend." The attendant stood watching as I agonized over the organization of this. The open car door beeped a loud pulse signaling door open-key inside, or was it, door open-POSSIBLE HOOKER inside?

My bag was heavy with clothes, candle, small boom box, chocolates and my purse. Should I have layered my clothes? Wearing today, tonight and tomorrow's clothes like the homeless? I could forgo the snacks and music but the large green scented candle was bought just for tonight. Now that he's watching, do I fish through the overnight bag and grab a candle to meet a friend? Or, just hoist it over my shoulder with a smile and enter the palace? With a burst of bravado, I choose the second option.

As I cross the driveway my face is flushing with embarrassment. I decide next time I'm at valet/check-in, I'll put my things in a Nordstrom's shopping bag so I'll look like a guest returning from shopping. Oh no, now I have to buy something large at Nordstrom's, which again is problematic. That still won't solve the name on the register problem. What if I *were* meeting a friend for dinner, and just brought my shopping bag inside? This incident is embarrassing and the optimism of the drive down has been replaced with a throbbing headache. I won't put myself through that again, I resolve with a shudder.

Once inside the marbled, high-ceilinged shrine, I spot a pianist playing in the lobby. Whoops, it's my friend, Lonnie Jayne, playing the soothing, cocktail piano music. Quickly ducking down a hall, I avoid her. As I drift around the vastness of the spacious hotel lobby, I'm hating life. I can't go back toward the reservation desk or Lonnie might see me. Calling Mickey on a house phone to meet me is out of the question; he would be recognized in the lobby and he'll think me an idiot for not finding his number on a door.

The tranquil and elegant setting the architects designed in this luxurious hotel is not working for me. I feel like a lonely imposter. When doing business at hotels, I'm confident; in fact, all this opulence justifies the talent fees I need to charge. Were I a registered guest, I'd be loving life! However, right now, looking around for a freakin elevator to find Mickey's room, makes me feel a notch below the worker polishing the leaves of the silk plants. At least that guy *is supposed* to be there. *I'm what*? A nomad searching for a friend, a registered guest here on business? Is that okay? It sounds okay, but I'm queasy, knowing the back-story.

Is it my imagination, or are *all the couples* walking past me just back from a cover shoot of *Golf & Leisure Magazine*? The perfectly groomed women all seem to be wearing earth tones, real pearls, and make-up airbrushed on by a make-up artist. Although my hair was recently cut and styled, I'm re-thinking my choice of wardrobe. I don't have nice casual clothes, I fret. Just business suits, salsa skirts, old performing-in-clubs clothes, jeans and a bathing suit. Nothing I own fits the "dash-from-parking-lot-to-swanky-room" category. A business suit would have been better, I realize as I look down with scorn at the lacy peach top over camisole and fitted jeans I'm wearing.

Trying to discern the layout of this hotel, without asking anyone, while avoiding the lobby/pianist is a form of slow torture. The high heeled, strappy sandals are digging into my swollen feet and perspiration has now mixed my powder into a thin paste. Reading *Where's Waldo?* books with my kid hardly prepared me for this challenge. Like a building inspector in heels, I retrace my footsteps up and down the quiet corridors, avoiding eye contact from the enemy, which right now is anyone. Friendly faces seem to mock my homeless predicament. The serious faces are undercover hotel security, my paranoia whispers. Ready to bolt out of this stiff, formal, labyrinth, I'm sentimental about the comfort my car once offered.

By the time I tap on the door of room 1426, I'm in a bad mood. Is Sheryl Crow taunting me as she sings in my head, *"You're My Favorite Mistake..."* There is so much tension that accompanies these contrived slumber parties.

Tapping on the door and waiting the thirty seconds it takes Mickey to answer, I review the myriad of steps it took *to be alone* with him. Would anyone else lie to her family, drive eighty miles, and go through the embarrassment this secrecy dance requires? I certainly can't survey my friends, but I think not. Then, the left side of my brain, which governs logic, recalls his words, "I wouldn't have had someone. I didn't need anyone." My confident nature has been thrashed by this ordeal and I'm a bad sport at the end of a race. The quiet elegance and beauty of the hotel reminds me, I'm an intruder. The embossed wallpaper knows who I truly am. I'm not wearing earth tones, the silk plants observe in disgust. The happy girl who set out for a good time began melting with "Are you a registered guest, or, are you having dinner with us this evening?" Forty-five minutes later, the only thing holding up my inappropriate outfit is a bundle of frayed nerves.

A weak smile painted on my face is all I can muster by the time the door opens.

"Hi, come in," Mickey smiles giving me a warm hug. "Sit down. Look at you! Uh oh, what's wrong, baby?"

"I knew the piano player in the lobby, so I had to avoid her. I couldn't ask directions, as I'm not a registered guest. It was hard to find the right elevator. I'm still lugging this heavy bag. I've seen dolphins at Sea World jump through fewer hoops!"

"Dolphins?" he laughed. "You see! I love that fabulous mind almost as much as that perfect body. That's why I love you!" Then, changing his tone to concern, "I'm so sorry you had trouble, Angel. Thank you so much for coming, here, let me make you a drink. Champagne? Let's see what's in the mini bar."

Gulping my gin and tonic, I was back on a roll. "Maybe I should become a building inspector in my spare time, so I can travel freely from hotel to hotel, checking smoke alarms, making these romps more legitimate. You don't know how close I was to leaving..." My voice held the edge of a weary traveler.

"Had you turned around and gone back, I would've been so disappointed, Veronica. You're the best part of my life. I look forward to these hours, moments together..." his voice trailed off as his eyes were sincere and so sad. The power of his words melted me. Then I shuddered, when I remembered earlier this morning, when I recycled Mickey's love letter, emailing it to Simon Bestep, from the phantom Gwendolyn.

"I love this room!" I said, draining my glass as I crossed to the balcony to better admire the hillside view.

We sat in silence on our balcony which was perched between a meadow and a beautiful pool surrounded by tropical gardens. I became more comfortable with my pride-bending experience: Jumping the seven hoops of entering room 1426 at the Four Seasons Aviara.

Would I be happier to meet a lover in the auto-wrecking yard, where he works as the night watchman and we make it in the back seat of a totalled Ford Pinto? That might be an easier tryst, but, nah.

With a second drink in my hand, I leaned back into the plush rocking chair. "I wouldn't mind stuffing this patio furniture in my suitcase. Who knew an outdoor rocking chair could feel so good," I said, surveying the magnificent sunset as Mickey massaged my calves. Safe behind the heavy, locked door, our world began to take form. Our world was made up of witty repartee, show-biz gossip, songs, Spanish TV and repeating phrases, shared secrets about ourselves and eventually making love.

"I met the most amazing artist at the Hermosa Beach street fair yesterday. Her paintings are whimsical and full of fantasy. She's a Russian girl, only thirteen years old. What a talent! I brought you these samples of her work, to see," I said, handing him a brochure.

"Let's go to her web site and see more pictures," Mickey suggested, walking to his laptop, which cast a blue light from the corner desk of the suite. He typed in Alina's Eydel's web site, www.AlinaFineArt.com, and we marveled at the paintings this delightful prodigy had on display.

Although he couldn't physically go to a gallery with me, he did offer the virtual alternative. "I like this one best," Mickey said, pointing to a painting entitled "Two Lovers." It featured a man and woman embracing on a park bench, beside two cats posed the same way.

"That's my favorite, too."

"You must have it then," Mickey pronounced. Then, as I sat by, he purchased it on-line and arranged to have it sent to my house.

"This won't cause you too many questions at home, will it? if I send this print to you?"

"No, it could be a present from a relative, an early Christmas gift. Anyway, thank you so, so much. I'll figure out something." We kissed, and looked back at the monitor screen admiring the "Two Lovers."

"Thank you."

"It is my pleasure," he answered. With a few key strokes he closed out the World Wide Web. He turned to me slowly, and we began focusing on our intimate World-entangled Web, where we would reside for the next 24 hours.

&&&&&&&

Chapter 19

MEET CANDACE

Hope is a very unruly emotion.

Gloria Steinem

Sitting at my desk, leafing through a folder marked "Client: Simon Bestep/Dec. 31", I review the budget and sadly recall the fleeting second deposit of $5,000, which, by now, has also been absorbed by household bills.

At least I'd made the final payment of for Devin's last rehab. Obsidian Trails was the Cadillac of rehab programs run by kind and caring psychologists/woodsmen and was the last tough-love wilderness program my son attended, two years ago. That January professional escorts jarred him out of a stoned slumber at 5:30 a.m. wrestled him into handcuffs, and flew him to rural Oregon, where he trekked over a prairie with a 55-pound backpack and slept under the stars. It cost $20,000 and he "graduated" in three months.

I never minded going into debt for Devin's rehab efforts–the money bought hope. An unsentimental journey of hope entries filled my check book register. Such as a Ju jitsu Master from Brazil who taught marshal arts specifically to discipline wayward boys. We tried Scientology; they kept us waiting so long in the lobby that after he finished the 90-minute questionnaire, his level of cooperation was exhausted, but heck, Mom couldn't resist buying a course anyway. An allergy doctor thought his cranky behavior was brought on by a demon pollen. Yep, a year of allergy shots later and he was still incorrigible. Browsing for hope, I consulted with psychics, as well as psychologists. Had we lived closer to Africa, I'd have laid down beads for a witch doctor. We went to a sweat lodge in a guy's backyard in Laguna Beach where Devin called the Caucasian tribe, "Indian Wannabes." Dancing Lizard may have held the secret to our family's dysfunction, but not that day.

Various family-counseling efforts through the years proved futile. Attention Deficit Disorder experts tested him and claimed there was a tad of ADD, but that ADD couldn't explain his outbursts of rage. Next, we slapped down $5,000 to get Devin's head examined by the UCLA Psychiatric Department. Collectively, they were some of the world's leading psychiatrists. The possibility of a neural disorder explaining his erratic behavior was what we hoped for, since a solution was possible, albeit pharmaceutical. Oh, wise men in white lab coats, give us a dose of hope in colorful capsules and cure our screaming family. (And, throw in some happy pills for Raymond while you're at it.)

With five bearded doctors, three weeks later, the team of experts produced a Psychiatric Evaluation. The 34-page report diagnosing him with "conduct disorder" concluded that the only thing wrong with him "was his conduct," according to the Sages of the Psych Department. They recommended AA meetings, and someone to manage his money since the testing indicated he was irresponsible in that area. Gee thanks, Sherlock, now, can I have my $5,000 back?

I contend Devin is probably just a pothead, who also uses random drugs. Amazingly, UCLA did not come to that conclusion; his drug tests were fairly benign. "Just go to AA Meetings," they said. How do I make him go? Separating him from his addiction was like separating him from his shadow. His addiction was a dark twin, shading all our lives, even after two rehab programs.

Choosing to Home School him, to keep him away from the drug crowd at Taft High School was an idiotic solution. The home school was a punishment for both of us. My day starts with nagging Devin awake for about two hours.

Then after his 25-minute shower, I point out the wet towel and boxer shorts on the bathroom floor. Devin grumbles an insult in my direction and jams the wet things under the sink, so they can begin to mildew along with the rest of the blue clump. "What's for breakfast?" is not my favorite question at 11:30 a.m. Now, along with booking talent on the phone, I'm thrust into the role of perky, patient and knowledgeable U. S. Government Teacher/short-order cook. Unlike the fortunate minimum-wage cooks in a diner, my customers are not refused service for being rude, and I can't go home sick. I can't even send him to the principal's office for swearing at his teacher.

Although Raymond makes a good living as a musician and I eke out a few bucks booking, we're always broke. It's no great mystery; all our money has been funneled into rehab efforts for Devin and producing guitar albums and buying state-of-the-art equipment for Raymond. There is not a more noble cause than spending money on my family in the name of self-improvement and self-expression, so why do I feel like Jack after he traded a perfectly good cow for a handful of magic beans? Jack was buying hope, too. Like Jack, I wished we had more food on the table and less magic vines in the backyard. Bongs under the bed, and cartons of CDs in the garage were our big vines to the sky, reaching out for a better "now."

I stamped some lucky envelopes, and put the remaining pile of bills away. The folder marked, Client: Simon Bestock/Dec. 31, sent a ripple of anxiety through me, so I jammed it in my desk drawer. Once I find his "wife" I need to start auditioning for the stepson.

It was already three o' clock and the actress I chose to play the part of Simon's "beloved wife Gwendolyn" was to meet me at four. Driving away from the house, I felt the full impact of the discouraging day. The last few weeks I'd eagerly anticipated Bestock's second deposit to pay-off the bills; the joy was as short-lived and satisfying as one Raisinette.

Driving to the Mexican restaurant where the actress, Candace, was waiting, I psyched myself up for the task at hand. It was all too clear I had to pay her as little as possible due to the dwindling budget. Yet, Simon has already parted with $10,000 and expects a fantasy date worthy of his steep financial and emotional investment. On the other hand, Candace wants a big payday to give up her New Year's Eve. She will have to turn down a lavish gala with Hollywood insiders - or so she'll say. With her head overflowing with possibilities, she'll need a lot of dough to give up that phantom party. And, sadly, I need a good actress with an "A-Plus" attitude. "Something's gotta give," I warn the steering wheel, gripping it tightly.

Turning off Melrose into Lucy's El Adobe Restaurant parking lot I was still muttering over the details of the budget. Exiting my car, I resembled a homeless person with a furrowed brow, tapping my fingers on the side of my thigh as I reviewed the cost of the dinner, liquor, flowers, and brunch for two, etc. So far only the hotel suite and extra room were paid for. Candace would need a deposit today. My spoiled actress will probably insist on shopping for a new dress. Preparing for her inevitable whine, I reason Gwendolyn's look is so conservative she won't want a new something in *that* style anyway, so I'll find it myself.

Simon's next deposit needs to cover the actor playing "Chad" (Bestep's stepson), deposit on hooker, then there are expenses of flowers, good champagne, all food on site, as well as a few small Christmas presents for the family. The balance will cover the mortgage for January.

Candace was smoking on the outside patio; seated among the clay pots and plants, she was as still as a statue. She wore tight low cut jeans, high heels and a tiny blue tee shirt rimmed in lace. Her vintage jewelry sparkled on her alabaster skin, and she looked like a mannequin from a Melrose Avenue window. The delicious smells wafting from the Mexican kitchen filled the air and I knew a taco was in my immediate future.

She greeted me warmly with air kisses as a plume of blue smoke billowed from her full frosted lips, "Veronica, how great to see you!" This warm, dragonesque greeting didn't fool me; it's been said, if you want to hear an actor complain, give them a job. After a bit of catch-up, I laid it all out for her.

"So I don't have to do anything, except talk to the boring geezer, right?" Candace said with skepticism. The lanky thirty-something, brunette's best feature was her large round eyes. Her ultra thin frame and pale skin suggested a diet of cigarettes and Starbucks. As she chattered on I wondered if the pale, wafer-thin, gaunt, look was the only quality needed for a MAW career. MAW was a flippant acronym for "Model-Actress-Whatever," and described a growing and glamorous breed of L.A. scenesters. Equipped with even features and perpetually bored expressions, these women seemed to get by.

Her eating habits were to my advantage, I thought cynically, when she announced, "I'm famished; I'll have this entire bowel of chips and salsa." She gestured broadly toward the twelve chips in a petite clay dish. "No cappuccino?" she asked the waiter with disappointment, "Okay, an iced tea is tight."

So who was I to judge? Modeling ads proved there was a higher purpose for emaciated females. Perhaps this was her calling and staying thin seemed to agree with her. In between bites and the typically inflated career update, came the hard questions.

"My dressing room is the hotel room? Who is doing hair and makeup? What about wardrobe? I'm to look dowdy? Like this girl in the picture?" The questions were coming quick, as I watched her shaking out five envelopes of Sweet N Low into her iced tea.

"We have two rooms," I said. "There's a room where you can get ready, do your hair, makeup and wardrobe. You retire there at 11:45 p.m. and then your next, shift, hmm spot, *um appearance* is at the New Year's Day Brunch at 10 a.m. I will bring you an outfit for the morning. Size 6?"

"Size 4," she sniffed. "You're lucky I'm available. That Prince Ahmed from Morocco had a great party last year, and the girls and I were supposed to go again this year, but then everybody got all sketchy about flying to the Middle East ...doo-dah doo-dah..." She trailed off, biting into a chip.

The trickle down effect of the Iraq War jeopardizing Candace's ability to join the jetsetters in a palace left me speechless. I stammered, "Who could have predicted?"

"Tell me!" Candace added with annoyance, "Like, the Prince paid for all five of our air-fares last year to Casablanca, and so totally would have done the same this year! Everybody is all, 'I don't know, now, Candace...' So, I guess I'll do this job Veronica, your job with the geezer."

I winced at her nickname for the client, of whom I'd become quite fond. "This character?" she said, shaking the photo, "my character, Gwendolyn? Looks way boring. But, hey, thanks again for the work. But really, Veronica, $1,000 isn't that much when you consider it is two days of acting." She said, pouting her glossy, salted lips. It seemed the gloss caught all the salt from the chips, giving her mouth a spackled-like texture.

"I chose you because I wanted to put a thousand bucks in the pocket of a terrific, young actress who is on her way up. You actually look like the actress Carol Kane, who looks like Gwendolyn. Just speak softly and be a classy, timid mouse. You're an actress, and did you mean to add five packets of Sweet N Low?"

"What else, Veronica?" She asked stirring the tea vigorously.

"He's been receiving email love letters from you - actually me-- from his dead-wife, call her what you want, and he may refer to those love letters at dinner. Just play along. He gave me a lot of background details on this woman - oh, have I mentioned she sounds wonderful? Anyway, I wrote up a character sketch with some dialogue to throw in. You will personify all that he remembers of his ideal woman. Just improvise this script." I shoved a manila envelope across the table. "Be lavish with praise, get him talking at all times and lead him into reminiscing."

"No physical contact at all, right?" Candace winced, cocking her head to the side. She was starting to get on my last nerve.

"Just dancing. Probably the waltz," I said. It was hard to know if her choking was intentional, or just a spastic reaction the salt and Sweet N Low, but I ignored her sputters and continued.

"Once you sit down to dinner in the formal dining room, the clock is running. You don't have to do anything, except look fascinated and say things like, 'Really? And then what?' 'Really? And then what?' keeps a man talking forever. Men don't recognize the phrase, no matter how often it's used." It was my best dating tip, and I valued it like a sacred love-potion.

"The script? Pretending I'm the dead wife? That's weird." She wrinkled her tiny nose as she flipped through the pages I prepared for her. "It might be funny," she smirked and flashed a wicked wink.

"Candace, this is *serious* improvisation. Dramatic fantasy - no comedy, you hear me? Don't try to be funny. Don't even attempt it. Never break character. This man has spent a lot of …"

"What? How much? Wait, *I'm only* getting…" her voice went up an octave, and other diners looked over.

"Did I say *money?* I meant to say he has spent a lot of…*blood platelets* to keep her alive! Actually, that's why he is so thin. When she got sick he spent all his money on transfusions and blood platelets to keep her alive!" In leaning forward my blouse dipped into the refried beans. "Dammit! Anyway, Candace, now Simon's last few dollars are spent on this, uh, memorial to her memory!"

Candace narrowed her eyes. "Where do you *find* these people?"

"He is a veteran. Do it for our country! Do it for the Lobster Bisque soup and filet mignon you can cut with a spoon, do it for the money! Just do it!" I barked at the thin actress staring at me.

"Veronica, that blouse was so much whiter before you started getting so - so agro."

I leaned over, "What? Are you in? Don't talk about my blouse." Checking my watch I realized Raymond would be leaving for work soon and stoners would slowly be infesting my house. After requesting the check, taking a deep breath, and glancing from side to side, I lost my patience. Dipping my napkin in the water and vigorously scrubbing the cotton blouse, I hissed, "Listen to me. This bit of valuable dating advice *more than pays* for the gig, Candace. Forget the money, this phrase will usher you into a lifetime of dating success. Practice with me. Say, 'Really? And then what!' Say it!"

She gave me a blank stare, and, with her head bobbing horizontally from side to side, for emphasis, she said, "Thanks for the tip, but, I didn't see you at the Prince's party last year. I must have been doing all right."

This was dissolving before my eyes, but I wanted to close the deal today. Ignoring the slight, I charged on.

"Every time he pauses just look at him with love and admiration. Remember the song, '*The Look of Love*'?" She shook her head no. I softly sang the lyrics from the Bachrach/David tune, in a last ditch effort to get her motivated. "*The look of love is in your eyes, the look that time can't disguise*" That is you, girl! Now, I'll find this dress and pearls. We'll make the alterations later. You need to take some time to brush up on opera, here are some library books, memorize a few key phrases, they have to be returned by the 15th."

"Okay," replied the starving actress with a shrug. "It is kind of like, improv... like comedy improv, only serious, right?"

"Candace, THIS is the newest art form, Improvisational Drama for Romantic Fulfillment. It is the rage in Europe. It replaced performance art months ago. Oh, one more thing, you have a kid fourteen - an actor will be playing your son." I tossed this fact in with a cheery smile as I got up from the table.

"I'm not old enough to have a kid that age!" Candace scoffed at the prospect.

"I think she had him at 16, so, that makes you 31," I said, gaily. "You two will get along great."

"I am 28, Veronica," Candace spat. "Who's the kid?"

"We will all meet in my room for an hour. Dinner is at 8:30. We can go over the lines and get into character and wardrobe."

"Who is the kid?" Candace repeated. "A professional actor who works in theatre would be better than one from commercials and TV. Do you have someone who knows improv, I hope?"

"A real pro," I assured her. "Dinner at 8:30, so be in the hotel room at the Ritz-Carlton by 7:00 on New Year's Eve. Solid? Okay, I have the 50% deposit check in my purse, just sign this little agreement."

"Solid," Candace repeated slowly, and shaped her lips into a pout as she signed.

"This New Year's Eve will be the highlight of the year!" I sang out grandly, handing over the bag containing the opera books, and envelope with $500 deposit check. All the table tension was gone and amidst air kisses, we hugged goodbye in the parking lot. Candace hastily lit up a cigarette as she walked toward her car. Driving out of the lot I passed her on foot and called out the window, "No smoking that night, Candace!"

There was a slight sense of relief knowing I had secured the second member of the three-member cast. With the final payment spread out so thin, how much was left to pay the kid actor, "Chad, the Preppy son"? Driving down my street, I spotted Devin standing in front of the house, waving good-bye to a departing car. He looked pleasant in the late afternoon sun. Stepping up to my window he smiled and said,

"Hey Mom, what's for dinner? I'm hungry."

"How are you coming along on those acting classes, Devin? Do you like to act in the theater games? Do you like improv? Are you good at it?"

"Oh yeah, piece of cake," he grinned. "I did this great scene last week; the whole class was laughing--it was the bomb..." As he chattered on happily retelling an account of last week's acting class, I looked at my son with a slow appreciation; the old cliché "hope springs eternal" came to mind. His agent's words also echoed in my head, "We could really use a boy like him around here! Look at all that charisma and energy!" Never mind he's not had one acting job from Agency West. He got his break today. As he talked happily about exploits in his acting class, I smiled slowly, and used the handy phrase, "Oh really? And then what?"

&&&&&&&

Chapter 20

Say Hello To The Cast

"If you want fair, go to Pomona."

Anonymous

On the first of December, I felt it was important to call a meeting of the cast for Simon Bestep's fantasy weekend. There was too much uncertainty on all sides, and by getting together once, I was sure I could answer questions and hopefully bond the little ensemble.

Sliding into the booth next to Candice, I was anxious about it, but put on my best professional demeanor.

"Well, first off I want to thank you all for coming to our 'run-down' for Mr. Besteps's fantasy party." My voice sounded like it had been processed through an artificial chirp machine.

"How long is this going to take? I only put change in the meter for 30 minutes," Tiffany said. Her face appeared weary in the harsh morning sunlight, streaming into Victor's Deli.

"Orange juice? Coffee?" Since I only brought twenty dollars, it was important to supervise the food orders, so I covertly piled the menus into a neat stack beside me on the booth.

"No, this won't take long, Tiffany. Let me introduce all of you, I thought it would be a good idea for us all to meet, some of you have questions. Tiffany plays the part of Simon's lover, Candice plays the part of Simon's wife, 'Gwendolyn the opera singer', and Devin is Simon's step-son, Chad, who is home for the holidays from prep school."

"Mom! Mom! Can I have pancakes?" Devin interrupted, as he eyed a plate going by.

"We aren't going to be here that long, here eat these." I slid a basket of saltine crackers in his direction. "I thought we weren't going to mention *our relationship*," I said smiling with clenched teeth. My face got hot and I felt like a ventriloquist bombing during his act.

"But, now that you have—*chosen to do so,*" I addressed the girls sitting across from me, "Yes—Tiffany, Candice, this is my son, Devin. He's an actor who is with Agency West and studied with…"

"Mom, cut the crap, they don't care about that shit, really. I want a Grand Slam. Do they have that here?" As he looked furtively for a menu, my heart sunk. This was not a strong opening for my "cast meeting." Like every other day in my life, the simplest thing turns into a power struggle with my strong-willed teenager. Simple thing? *What was I thinking*? I have a month to change my uncouth son from Neanderthal to Preppy. Avoiding the eyes of my tablemates, I looked around the deli, hoping to spot a poster advertising Charm School scholarships.

"Hey, Devin, just chill, let your mom talk, here's a Snickers." Tiffany fished a candy bar from her purse and tossed it into the air. "We got to get this thing rollin', I gotta bounce in fifteen minutes." Tiffany gave Devin a broad smile as he caught the chocolate and they high-fived, each saluting the successful pass.

Candice made a clucking sound and stared at the wall next to her. Having great illusions of grandeur about her position in the entertainment industry, I could see how easily her ego enhanced the New Year's Eve acting job. To friends, she simply said, she was hired to do a reality-type show to be filmed at The Ritz-Carlton. She may have hinted that it would play later at the Cannes Film Festival. It was a bit on the down-low, at this point, but she was glad to be working on the exciting project. Yes, last New Year's Eve in Morocco with the Prince was fun, but she now regarded that as her decadent period and drew from the experience, enriching her as an actress.

Today's cast meeting and run-down banished any notion that she was among professionals, adding to the disappointing revelation that there would be no filming of the "reality show".

"What, may I ask, is the purpose of this little charade, if not to film, Veronica?" Candice asked icily; her tone said, don't *even* offer me a candy bar.

Devin and Tiffany seemed to have bonded on some low-life wavelength and were drawing tattoos on Devin's hand with a pen I'd left on the table for notes.

"I never told any of you this improvisation would be filmed. You assumed it, Candice, because the gig, the job— in your in your mind—'the shoot,' was over a two-day period. You just *thought* it was reality TV. This is a live play, with only one in the audience. Here are the scripts/outlines, now settle down and read."

"Whoa, wait a minute, don't be telling me to settle down, I'm not one of your kids!" Candice exclaimed.

"I meant to say... wow, I am sorry to have sounded like that..."

Tiffany and Devin's snorts of stifled laughter, interrupted my back peddling.

Sighing deeply I began again. "I am just asking you all to have—*an open mind*." Regretting the quaver in my voice, I passed out the "Character Descriptions and Timeline For Dec. 31st" envelopes.

"Here is the framework, you can ad lib the conversations. Yes, I will have some tea, thank you." I addressed the waitress standing at the rim of the table.

"How ya doin' today, hon? Where's your friend this morning?" Inquiring minds want to know? *How lovely* I think, while shrinking into the booth with annoyance. Returning her question with a blank stare and feeling guilty for acting cold to the innocent waitress who makes a living on remembering the faces and orders of her regular customers.

"I'm not sure, um, where, ah…" I stammer, fully aware that she is referring to Mickey. Our pattern of rendezvousing at the Sheraton on Saturday mornings (when he had permission to golf) is followed by a chance meeting here at Victor's Deli. This familiar spot was freeway close, so it seemed like a good idea to hold the cast meeting here. Maybe not.

"Eggs Benedict like usual, ma'am?"

Gawd! Would she give it a rest? Sneaking a sidewise glance at the others I see Candice is pouting at the wall, and Tiffany and Devin are detailing an ink dragon up his forearm.

"Mom, yo, listen! Dude you know what you can do? Order hot water, pour ketchup in it, add salt and pepper and crunch up these soda crackers, and…"

"Hobo Soup!" Tiffany and Devin said in unison, beaming with pride at the waitress, as if they'd conjured up an exotic recipe.

"That's tight, Wolfgang Puck," Candice said.

Beaming with confidence, Devin asked the waitress, "Could you bring us some hot water?" Turning to me, he said, "Try it, Mom!"

Stuck at the intersection of chagrin and sentiment, I sighed. He was just a kid meaning well. Often in coffee shops we'd split meals and just order water, so he was being inventive, and it was sweet and sad. Meanwhile the waitress wants to know whether to bring "my usual eggs benedict" or, simply hot water for poor man's tomato soup.

Turning to the waitress, I found myself in a rare speechless moment. I shook my head with a definitive no. No for hot water, no Eggs Benedict, no grand slam breakfast, and mostly no friggin' way could this ensemble impress a man who's paying $30,000 for a fantasy date.

"Don't talk to me about hot water, Devin. Read this." The self-important posture of a show producer had melted down to the slumping resignation of a haggard mom. I struggled to regain some semblance of professionalism (for Candice' sake if not my own), and it was impossible. Now she was brooding. Perhaps after cavorting with a prince last year she felt entitled to be pampered, like a great princess/actress. Well, maybe I felt entitled to order breakfast off the menu—but, that didn't happen either.

Observing Tiffany and Devin turned my stomach into knots. They were getting along well and that was good, but they were such *weak* supporting actors. The whole evening depended on Candice' class and her excellent acting skills. Knowing I cannot lose her and she might quit, I'm in a quandary about what to do. She's either furious, or getting into character for some new role as building inspector, concentrating on the cracks in the wall.

"Candice, did you bring back those books about opera?"

"Oh yes, I'm the world's leading expert." She retorted sarcastically. Then, looking at Tiffany with raised eyebrows, she asked, "Have you brushed up on your knowledge of arpeggios, Tiffany?"

"Hey Miss 'Tude, I'm an expert on what I need to know, and that's all that matters," Tiffany shot back, not missing a beat. In an attempt to distract the dueling divas, I turned to my son. "Devin, I think that 'Chad' will have a sore throat at dinner, and mostly just –look at the person who is talking, nod, and sit as still as possible. Do you think you can do that?"

"Hey, that's whack! I'm an actor, too! Now I can't act? What? This is gonna be too boring if I can't do lines," Devin's voice seemed too loud for the normal din of the room.

"Chad would not interrupt. Or draw a snake on the back of his hand. Or catch a candy bar in the air. Chad sits listening quietly, with an intelligent expression," I hissed.

"Hey, don't get all 'Dr. Phil' with me! I can do the lines you wrote here, Hey the candy? I just caught it. Mom, you're such a hater! Why do you have to make such a big deal about everything?" Devin started heating up. "I'm doing these lines right here. That's that!"

"Gotta bounce, hun" Tiffany got up and kissed Devin and me, then extended her hand to Candice, only to take it away as Candice reluctantly raised her hand to shake.

"See ya at room 1267 at the Ritz-Carton," she said, reading from her info sheet.

"Tiffany, remember to dress very conservatively. Bring your date clothes in an overnight bag. Call my cell phone from the lobby." Then remembering I'd have to make sure I had the cell phone that night, and not Raymond, I said, "Just come up to the room. I'll be in the room. Could you please come early, about seven?"

"Hey, yeah, she's dope," Devin said. "Come early and kick it with us in the hotel, Tiffany. Mom said they have seriously, sweet video games like Duke Nukem."

Tiffany smiled as if he had dropped the name of a trusted family friend, "The Dukester! Yeah, Ok, I'll come early and kick your ass on Duke Nukem," she said with spirit.

Candice excused herself and bolted. I looked at the bill on the table, only $7.46. So, my son ordered fries and a malt, I ordered a draft beer, and we sat at the table in silence. And so went the meeting. Next time we would all be together would be at the Ritz-Carlton. What a grim reality

"Mom, why is that guy getting two wives? If I'm eating dinner with Candice, 'my fake mom' and him, then why is Tiffany coming, too?"

Putting down the breakfast beer, I said, "Well honey, I guess this is the time I tell you there is no Santa Claus." Smiling at my joke, I explained. "This gentleman is trying to re-live a perfect time in his life. I will try and recreate a memory of someone he loved. Actually the two people he loved the most, are his step-son, Chad, and deceased wife, Gwendolyn."

"What does dizzyeed mean?"

"Dead, deceased wife, means dead person. And, as you know her son Chad went to his real dad after she died, and he never saw his step-son…"

"Where does Tiffany come in? Why does he have two ladies?" Devin interrupted, sucking up the last remains of the malt with a loud sucking sound.

"I'm trying to tell you, it would be a natural thing for a man to desire to make love with his wife, but I can't expect an actress to, well that's not appropriate for an actress to go all the way. In movies, they show kissing on the screen, but …no sex."

"'cept in porn." My son finished the sentence. "So Tiffany is the coochy mama who's gonna roll with him?"

"Yeah, I guess it's something like that," I sighed.

"Sweet. That's mad crunk. Does Dad know?"

"Dad has a gig in our same hotel in a banquet room. Actually he'll be there, but not where we are. He knows about the client, but doesn't know all that much. He said he didn't want to know anything, that it sounded like one of my crazy schemes."

Then, erupting with laughter Devin said, "I could just hear him. Yo, remember the time you bought all those peep holes, and tried to install them going door to door? That was so funny!"

"It was a good idea. Shut up. The Peephole only cost like 59 cents, then to drill a hole in a door, screw it in, 'install it' and charge $20 bucks, was a good idea."

"Yeah, like someone's gonna *let you* drill a hole in their door!" Laughing again, he added, "You looked more like a fuckin' Avon lady with a drill."

"Yes, we've all been over that failure, Devin. As we are reminded every time we open the junk drawer and see 99 Peephole packages. It is one of your dad's favorite examples of my entrepreneurial skills."

"Oh Mom, don't be all sensitive. It's hilarious!" Putting a thin arm around me he hugged me, "Mom's tryin' to keep it real," Devin said, swinging his head from side to side. He was enjoying himself, the chocolate malt, his first cast meeting for an acting job, and talking to an actual "Coochy Mama" added up to a big morning.

"So seriously Mom, I'm getting like $100 bucks right?" Devin said as we got up to leave.

"Two hundred if you get a good report," I told my son.

"That's off the hook!" he said cackling with glee.

As we emerged from the deli, a harsh winter sun momentarily blinded me. The beer for breakfast wasn't something I would try again. However, Devin's lanky limb around my shoulders was a comfort as we crossed the parking lot. "Don't worry Mom. You worry too much."

"There are so many details, I want it to go perfectly, Devin. I'm worried you'll say the F word and things like that."

"Mom, Mom, he won't notice *everything*. It's just like the Dr. Pepper can."

"Huh?"

"Yeah, think how many times you drink Dr. Pepper, and no one ever notices there isn't a little period at the end of Doctor. It just says D and R."

"No, I never noticed that, Devin."

"See? We're going to be all right. You're just trippin'. People *don't notice* stuff."

"Thanks honey, I feel a little better."

"I love you, Mom"

"I love you too Devin."

With that we drove the familiar route home. I hoped he was right, that people don't notice stuff.

&&&&&&&

Chapter 21

ONCE UPON A ZEN

Suddenly my world's gone and changed its face, but I still know where I'm going

I have had my mind, spun out in space, and yet--I've watched it growing.

And if you're listening God, please don't make it hard to know- If we should believe the things that we see?

Tell us, should we run away? Should we try and stay?

Or, would it be better just to let things be?

Living here in this brand new world-might be a fantasy, But, it's taught me to love, so it's real to me.

Charley Smalls
(Lyrics to *Home* from *The Wiz*)

The sound of the slap on his face stunned us both. My hand was stinging, as a handprint darkened Mickey's pale cheek. Our eyes locked, and we froze. Then, as if this altered state had run its course, time snapped us back into reality. We began recovering from the shock of my violent outburst. Like all good adults, we picked up the "ego-ball" and ran down the field, passing it between us.

"Well, so—that's the way *it is,* OKAY!" I blustered. "I guess this was –just a social experiment. It was something we—found out about each other. It just took several months…" Trying to resurrect my composure, I frantically tossed things about the room searching for my purse. Not finding my keys was definitely slowing down a dramatic exit.

"That's right, I'm not comfortable going out. You know that, Veronica!" He looked away, paused and then met my eyes saying in an even tone, "Sorry, it's who I am. It's just the way it is."

"Come on," I hissed. "This is a little town; we can't even go to a foreign film that starts at 10:00 p.m.? Who's going to see you walk from your car? I told you I'd walk in first!"

"I'm not going out. I can't risk being seen. It's not worth it," Mickey repeated.

"Aghhh!" I made a guttural sound, as I clenched my car keys and slammed the door. As I marched across the parking lot and jammed the key into the slot, I was too angry to cry. Seeing the lavish hotel disappear behind me in the rearview mirror gave me some satisfaction as I cooled off. The steering wheel felt good in my tight grip; finally, I was in control of something.

My best friend from high school lived about five miles from the La Costa Resort, and I had shamelessly used her as my excuse for the weekend getaway. I told Raymond that Jenny and her husband were having serious marital problems and she needed me. I explained it would be rude to call me at their house under the circumstances. Jenny or Ross might answer the phone and be embarrassed to speak to Raymond, so we agreed that I would call him. That was the plan. Now it was time to drop in unannounced. It was some consolation knowing my alibi would be rock-solid, if I called my husband tonight and prompted Jenny to shout out a "hi" while I was on the phone.

As I slowly drove toward her neighborhood I reflected on how quickly this evening went south. Our first argument had sneaked up on us. While we had both enjoyed the La Costa Resort last night, staying in again tonight was too much. Accustomed to the fast pace of my home life, after we were rested, fed and sexually fulfilled, *excuse me* for being restless.

Mickey returned early from a songwriting session and I was at first glad we still had a long evening ahead. As the Entertainment Director of a casino years ago, I wore my

148

title with pride; it was easy for me to find fun things to do. Whether it was a promotional party for a poker tournament or a birthday party for my son, I prided myself on knowing creative entertainment options. This afternoon, I mocked up several great ideas ranging from a foreign movie at the local art house, to throwing back tequila shots in Tijuana while Salsa dancing. Approaching the subject cautiously, I began with some low-key ideas like strolling along the coast and drifting in and out of art galleries in La Jolla (naturally, sporting dark glasses and hats). My vote would be Tijuana. The Mexican border was an hour drive south and its fun-potential soared in my mind to the point I could almost smell the delicious scent of street tacos. But, being a realist (this is the first time I've ever used that sentence), I thought it best to start slow as I coaxed him out of the room. It was so frustrating; he wouldn't give in to me and yet didn't get riled.

"Hey, I'm not asking you to take me to The Ivy on a Saturday night; I've just got to get out of these friggin walls!"

"Maybe you're too young for me," he stated matter-of-factly, like a sociologist pointing at a pie chart in front of the class.

"Well, you'll have a hard time finding someone of ANY age to go along with this program. Never going out? Come on, Mickey! Who's going to be happy, stashed in a hotel room for days at a time?"

"I wouldn't have had someone. I wasn't looking for anyone," he returned my glare head-on. That's when I slapped his face. He didn't move, so I slapped it again. I was mad at his seeming indifference; this had been building for months. My assumption that we would rarely go out was replaced by the *knowledge*—we would *never* go out. It was like reading a bulletin that had been sitting in my mailbox for months. With the exception of the gloriously anonymous sidewalks of New York, it's lunch at Victor's Deli—take it or leave it.

Pulling up to Jenny's perfect house, neighborhood and family, gave me an unfamiliar tinge of guilt. Unfaithfulness is so complicated, I mused as I waited on the porch, nervously shifting from foot to foot.

"Veronica! Wow, hey, what a surprise, come in, how great to see you!" Jenny gushed all at once. "What are you doing down this way?" she asked through a hug.

Noticing her leotard, I jumped at the first distraction of many to follow. "Where *are you* going—to the gym?"

"My yoga class. It's such a bummer, because my teacher is moving—this is her last night here in La Costa and I *absolutely love* this teacher," she swooned, closing her eyes. "So, I'm all ready to go and my babysitter cancelled! Ross is working late, and I didn't know whether to keep calling sitters, and now—you are here..." she trailed off.

"Listen Jenny, go to yoga. I'm not going back to L.A. until eleven or so. I was down here checking on an act playing nearby...so, anyway, I'll watch Carrie. I know how important it is to say good bye--" then looking away I added, "to someone who means a lot."

"Great! Thanks. Carrie just took a bath and she's in her room. I hope you don't mind reading? It's almost bedtime and we are part way through *Beauty and the Beast*."

"I love the story," I said.

"Good, she's expecting it."

"Easy, sure, now get going! We'll catch up when you get back." We hugged again and after disappearing down the hall to say good-bye to her ten-year-old daughter, Jenny left.

Pleased with how well this was working out, I made myself a cup of tea. Whew, I've got a place to land and sort my thoughts and do a good deed. So glad I don't have to answer any questions about my arrival or struggle through normal talk. "*Gee, pardon me if I seem a tad distracted. I just smacked my lover, Grammy-winning composer Mickey Owens, in the face. Yeah, he took it like a champ, so I had to slap him twice —just to make sure he felt it. I left him in the hotel suite. So, what'd ya make for dinner tonight?*"

Perhaps by 10:30 when she returned, I'd know the answer to the only question that mattered: Was I going to stay in this affair with Mickey? Or, return to L.A. tonight and forfeit the clothes I left in our hotel room. It would make quite a statement—not even returning for my belongings. As I sipped Earl Grey Tea, inhaling the familiar spicy scent, I calculated my losses. A black, cloth Lancôme bag was my modest luggage. Hmm, that was no big deal, perfume, cosmetics bag, underwear, two magazines, a candle, cute jeans, belt and top, bathing suit and semi-sheer nightgown. My purse was with me. Uh, oh. My boom box and CDs were on the floor beside the bed. That would be hard to replace.

Imagining Mickey at check-out time was kind of sad. So respectful of people and their belongings, it would be impossible for him to throw my things in the trash or leave them in the room. He couldn't drop them off at my house or take them home either. He didn't know my mailing address and his sports car didn't have a trunk to hide them. Just picturing his dilemma of what to do with the "practical remains of Veronica," gave me some satisfaction. I was sick of his Zen calmness about our relationship. It was time he felt my frustration and confusion, beyond just a stinging cheek. Fuck his poise.

He would have to deal with the emotional remains of me too. Perhaps he was smelling my scent on his pillow right now, since I always sprayed the hotel pillowcase lightly with *Tuscany*. Checking the clock every few minutes, waiting for my return, would disturb his passion for mystery novels tonight. Wondering if I was okay might conjure up some fantasies of me out Salsa dancing with swarthy, handsome Latin men at Papas and Beer in Tijuana. Maybe I would drive back to L.A., never saying good-bye. He knew I was, at the very least, capable of that.

It would be dumb to just go back and grab my boom box and start packing. I wouldn't be able to hold my resolve once inside the door. This caused a dilemma, since the boom box would be costly to replace, and it also had sentimental value. Listening to audio books from the library, I carried it with me all over the house. It was my literate companion, telling me stories while I folded the clothes, mopped the kitchen floor and picked weeds in the backyard.

"Hi Ronica!" Carrie's sweet voice reeled me into the soft world of little girls, pajamas and storybooks.

"Come here, sweetheart. How good to see you! Your hair is still a little bit wet, so let's go and dry it in the bathroom. Then I'll read you a story. You are getting so big!" I hugged the chubby, damp little girl and we walked hand and hand to the bathroom.

"Where are we in the story, Carrie?" I shouted over the buzz of the hair dryer.

"You gave me this book, remember?" Carrie yelled back. Looking up with big brown eyes, she explained, "Well, Beauty is at the Beast's castle and it's really neat. And, she doesn't want to be there, but the Beast is really nice."

We trotted down the hall to the pink bedroom, climbed on the bed and I began to read:

Beauty soon resolved not to make her unhappy situation worse by useless sorrow; she took a view of the palace, and was much delighted with its beauty.

But what was her surprise, on coming to a large and splendid suite of rooms, to find written over the door, "Beauty's Apartments."

She opened it hastily, and was dazzled at the splendor of everything it contained; but what excited her wonder more than all was a large library filled with books and pieces of music.

She opened the library and saw a book on which was written, in letters of gold: "Beauteous lady, dry your tears; Here's no cause for sighs or fears;

Command as freely as you may, Compliance still shall mark your sway."

Beauty began to think that the Beast was very kind to her, and he said, 'Be sure you do not want for anything, for all you see is yours.'

Beauty lived three months in this place very contentedly. The Beast visited her every evening, and she, instead of dreading the time of his coming, was continually looking at her watch, to see it if was time for him to come."

The childhood fairytale transported me into a world of monsters, fairies and spells. How I had loved this story as a child, and since I always gave this book to children, I was quite familiar with Beauty's plight. Beauty was just a simple country girl who, through unusual circumstances, was sent to live with the Beast in a luxurious castle.

The story appealed to me because the Beast exposed Beauty to culture and books. Instead of the usual soup and bread for dinner, at the farmhouse where she was utterly taken for granted, Beauty was now served delicious cuisine on platters of silver. At the end of the evening meal, the Beast would appear in the salon for conversation. He was a polite, kind and gentle Beast who was extremely intelligent and cultured. *Beauty and the Beast* was written over a hundred years ago, when country women didn't have access to wonderful libraries, nor were they encouraged to read and discuss books.

When Carrie left for the bathroom, I returned to my own thoughts. I remembered our lovely suite, and the sound of my banging the heavy door shut. Just last night, Mickey had ordered my dinner and the very formal, room service waiter wheeled in a cart of delicious offerings. The entrees and desserts were on a table with a white linen tablecloth and even a small vase with fresh flowers. After choosing an in-room movie, we dined wearing soft, plush white robes. There was a fire blazing in our fireplace and the balcony curtains danced lazily in the breeze coming up off the golf course.

Even tonight I noticed I was wearing an outfit my lover had bought for me. A low-cut, white, angora sweater, black fitted pants and black and white woven jacket with large black buttons, pulled the ensemble together beautifully. There was never a need to hide any new clothes, since Raymond never noticed what I wore, and if he did comment I told him it was a hand-me-down from my sister, who truly has a shopping disorder. Being the same size, I'm grateful this shopaholic doesn't participate in a Twelve Step program; I've been the stylish recipient of her excesses for years.

Beauty was so happy in the castle, with the opulence inside its gilded walls. However, our heroine spent many quiet, lonely hours alone waiting for the Beast to return in the evenings. I'm not sure what the Beast's day job was, but he only appeared at night, as the clock struck nine. Because she could never leave the grounds, Beauty was a prisoner inside her exquisite cage.

Carrie returned and curled up next to me. As the child slept beside me, I reached and shut off the light. Mentally, I still drifted in and out of the story

Seeing myself as Beauty the hotel captive, imprisoned in artfully decorated suites, I realized I, like Beauty, was always waiting. The charm of the stunning artwork and décor of the suites wore off after a few hours. The rest of the time was spent longing for my enchanting and cultured companion's return. When he did finally burst through the door, I'd feel so happy to see him and, of course, the exuberance of...*at last, someone to talk to.*

"*The Beast loved her exceedingly.*" The Beast was kind, never used curse words and never discussed money. He told Beauty she could have facials and massages in the hotel, to order anything she desired from room service and to enjoy the movies until he returned. He told her she was beautiful, the love of his life, his own special angel. She believed him and loved him *exceedingly* too.

Beauty was gregarious. She needed to be around people, and she wanted to share the Beast with the people of her village, yet he could never go out with her. He couldn't leave his palace.

The clock said 10 p.m. Jenny would be coming in the door soon. As I waited, I wondered, would I spend the night here, go back to L.A., or, return to my Zen Beast?

&&&&&&&

Chapter 22

SCALES ARE FOR FISHES

When we walk to the edge of all the light we have, and take the step into darkness of the unknown, we must believe that one of two things will happen. There will be something solid for us to stand on or we will be taught to fly.

Patrick Overton

With Carrie sleeping beside me, the phone's loud ring jolted me upright. Jenny's voice sounded excited.

"Would you mind awfully, if I stayed later tonight? Because it's our teacher's last night, there's a little party here. Ross should be home around 11, what do you—"

"Jenny, have fun. Carrie's asleep and I'm just reading," I assured her. The truth was I was fake-resting with my head a half-inch off the pillow, and eyes fixed on the unfamiliar shadows of the ceiling. My rigid rest included holding perfectly still, so as to not wake Carrie.

"There are Eskimo Pies in the freezer, magazines on my side of the bed, and oh, go ahead and check your email, if you want to. The computer is on—thank you so much, Veronica!"

Ice cream was a time-honored mood enhancer, so I went there first. I appreciated having more alone-time in the quiet house.

I went to the computer next. Checking my email, I was surprised to see a message that Mickey had sent me an hour ago. It simply said, "want my Earth Angel back...I love you." I could almost hear him say the words softly through the monitor. He must have assumed I went home, and would read the letter there. Without responding to the message, I closed down the computer and went back into Carrie's room to get the book we'd been reading.

In the story, the Beast permitted Beauty to go home to visit to see her ailing father, after a solemn promise to return in ten days. Beauty stayed at the family's farmhouse longer. Slipping back into her old life, she forgot all about the Beast. On the fifteenth day, she remembered the Beast and her promise. He had given her a magic mirror to take home, and she'd forgotten to use it. Missing him and with a terrible sense of guilt, she now ran to the mirror, sensing something was wrong. Saying the spell he'd taught her into the ornate, golden frame, the mirror revealed the Beast at that moment. The book showed Beauty peering inside the glass. To Beauty's horror, the kind and gentle Beast lay outstretched beneath the white rose bush, dying.

Imagining the beige computer monitor to be my modern magic mirror, I too had seen another place, not so far away. Alerted by the electronic chime, supplied by America Online, Mickey's email has caught me off-guard. He assumed I wasn't returning to him. He couldn't have known I would read his email while still in town. Mickey's simple plea, "*I want you back*," was a quiet whisper in the night. My Zen Beast would never beg, or be manipulative. He knew there was a chance of my leaving and, by a certain hour- apparently 9:37 p.m.- Mickey had accepted his fate.

Being the Drama Queen, and center of all worlds, real and enchanted, I imagined Mickey dead on the balcony of our beautiful suite, outstretched, lying face down. A white rose bush in an ornate pot stood in the corner of the spacious patio, and I could even picture the full moon illuminating Mickey's dying frame.

Is this the reality I want? Do I want to break his heart? Of course, he wasn't going to die, but a part of him would: the part that harbored the belief that someone loved him for who he was, a*t this moment* in his life. The one who loved him was not the perennial showgirl he dated while he headlined in Vegas, sharing toots in the dressing room. Nor was she the ubiquitous blonde in the Green Room at the "Tonight Show," who accompanied him on limo booze cruises to nightclubs after the show.

I'm the woman who meets him for walks, and breakfasts in coffee shops. Considering the many peaks and valleys of an artist's career, Mickey had seen better days and I knew I was one of his truest friends. I would be missed. All of the precious hours spent laughing, discussing the rancid music business, books, and our careers flashed by me in a heart-melting montage. Sometimes I would cry, witnessed by food servers shuttling our plates to the table, but mostly these times with Mickey were the highlights of my week. Whatever annoyances I'd be feeling en route to meet him, had always evaporated by the ride home. More accurately, I would depart our meetings with a surge of positive energy and optimism. Like sunshine, his love warms me. He seeks out my virtues, studies them, then invariably describes my idiosyncrasies, finding me fascinating, funny and original. He's tickled that I have *a library card*. He notices my good-hair days. He says the sound of my laughter could start a heart. He listens patiently as I brainstorm on ways to build up my booking business. His attention sustains me.

With a profound admiration for the sum of Mickey's parts, a lump grows in my throat, almost choking me. I recalled how much of himself he gave when mentoring young songwriters. He had a terrible childhood and, although his career was notable, booze and drugs had fed his inner demons. At the time we met, he had already given up drugs, cigarettes, white flour, sugar and even chocolate. Now, he has to give me up too.

Do I really want to inflict more pain on him by taking my love away? What if he gets sick? Or, fell into a deep depression? What if *anything ever* happens to him? Since we have no mutual acquaintances, I would never hear about him, other than news in the papers. They don't report on acute depression and treatment for hen-pecking wounds on *Entertainment Tonight*. Perhaps, by just loving him on his terms and within his timetable, I could keep him alive longer.

Love can enhance one's life and I'm sure our affair would add years to his life. With grandiosity I realized I'd do anything I could to add *even minutes* to his life.

Through his eyes, I'm fresh, and my irreverence matches his own. We drop the happy horse-shit of self-promotion and get real. Our sense of humor is in sync, and if we ever catch ourselves being too self important, we slide into a dialog of elaborate story-topping. By out-doing each other to the point of absurdity, we dissolve into hysterics.

In the book, Beauty returned to her Beast and saved him with a kiss. Maybe through the magic of a fairy tale, the Universe is telling me to save *my* Zen Beast. He would be devastated if I didn't return to the castle. I'm his Earth Angel, and he has told me over and over that I'm the best part of his life. Am I ready to pull the plug on all we have?

We can never be seen together, my busy-head re-minds me. How about women who fall in love with the prisoners? Now, there's a breed of love-struck women, right there. Like me, they can't date their man or bring him home. They settle for love letters scrawled on note pads, purchased at the prison commissary. As for holidays, the most we can hope for is a furtive phone call with quick sentiments squeezed into the phone receivers. The prison-visiting gals can do it. Can I? Is true love the illusive prize that ennobles us? In the end, are we measured by our ability to love another person more than ourselves? The daily sacrifice we mothers make for our children is less easily dispensed to a lover. Is there a love-scale in the sky? Perhaps some grand equation or formula by which we know how *much* we can give away, before we cut into our selves? Is Mickey's feeling safer, more important than my being entertained?

I closed the book, and sat waiting with my purse in my lap. At 10:45 Jenny walked through the door. She thanked me and we hugged goodbye, I was grateful she accepted my choice to get on the road, forgoing our visit.

Driving back slowly, I scanned the sky in search of a constellation resembling a love scale. Not even *my* imagination could conjure that up using the vast canopy of stars overhead. As I got out of the car and headed toward the suite, I said to no one in particular, "Yes, the Luckiest Man in the World, just got luckier." My returning to him will keep us both happy, at least for a while longer.

&&&&&&&

.

Chapter 23

FRACTURED HOLIDAYS

Every argument between two people is likely to sink or rise to the level of a dogfight.

A.A. Milne

The crash of the glass shattering didn't startle me. Perhaps a primal instinct protecting my eyeballs stopped me from turning my head to see the bottle of nail polish sail inches past my head, shattering the large window behind the couch. The delicate glass shards tinkled like chimes in a random tune as they fell to the window sill.

"Okay, are you happy *now*?" Devin's voice boomed. "You see what you made me do? Why do you have to be so stupid? All you had to do was give me the number of your credit card, so I can get back online! Now, give it to me!"

"I'm not giving you my credit card number. I'll talk to AOL and find out why you got kicked off. Foul language is the reason probably; at least it was the last couple times. I don't know how many of these 'citations' we can get before *we're all* kicked off!"

"Citations? My ass, I was just messin' around. Come on! You gotta— "

"I don't *gotta* do anything," I said.

"Gimme the car keys then, I gotta pick up Nicole,"

"Tomorrow is Christmas Eve—so, I guess it will be hard getting someone out here to fix this window. It's going to be cold." I said, stating the obvious in a flat tone.

Enraged, Devin looked again to the coffee table for the next item to pitch. He snatched the remote control and

160

hurled it across the living room; like a missile it detonated into the wall shattering into bits. I remained still. During these outbreaks, I always held very still and willed myself invisible, like a small rabbit near a predator. It was fright over flight—running wasn't an option. Forgetting to breathe, I was just trying to swallow. To accomplish this nearly impossible feat, my saliva must thread its way through the tight eye of a needle that was my throat.

When Devin stormed out of the house, I remained frozen, and it triggered a memory of a childhood game "Statue Maker." A playmate would spin you around by one arm and let you go, flung on to the grass. You had to freeze, holding the pose of how you landed. One kid was The Statue Maker and his job was to assign each kid's occupation based on the frozen pose. I loved that game until I was condemned to play incessantly with my deranged teenager. Without warning, he spins me around, and unexpectedly I fall to the ground. So, like the game, I hold perfectly still, while Devin, the-Statue Maker, calls the shots, telling me what I am and what to do.

Raymond was gone for the night, and it slowly dawned on me, this would be a good time to leave. I grabbed my keys and drove down the street, but where to go? Dressed in pajama bottoms a sweatshirt, I realized my options were limited. I pulled into Lindy's driveway. I knocked on the door while turning the handle.

Thankfully, Lindy was home and quickly made me a cup of tea, as I sat at the kitchen table processing the afternoon's events.

"Where I went wrong," I said wearily, "as a parent was—well, maybe I stressed all the wrong things to my kid by pointing out all the bad things that happened to bad people—instead of talking about people's achievements. My fascination with the underworld made those negative people examples of, oh, I don't know…"

"Wait a minute, girlfriend. He hurls a bottle through your living room window, and you think it's *your* fault? That's crazy talk."

"It wasn't a big bottle. It was just a little nail polish bottle," I said meekly. "Stuff like, I'd point out a bum, pushing a shopping cart alongside the road, and I'd say 'Look, there's a guy who didn't want to make his bed.' Now that I think about it, he probably identified with the bum. Who wants to make his bed and have his mom telling him what to do? The bum didn't."

"One time I was at your house and you were telling a story about some girl who got drunk, and fell from her second story balcony," Lindy said, refilling my teacup. "I guess she passed out and landed on an ant hill. She was taken to the hospital when somebody finally found her but she was almost eaten alive by red ants. Hey, wait a minute! Was that for *my* benefit? Was that one of your little morality tales for me?"

"Actually Lindy, it's no secret you drink too much. Yes, it's a true story about Linda, some chick my sister knows. Was Devin there when I told it? Oh, it doesn't matter. I should've just found positive anecdotes—instead of implying the probable outcome of sipping a cocktail on a balcony was death by red ant bites."

"Or, that not making your bed turns you into a guy with a long, lint-filled beard pushing a shopping cart." Lindy added.

"How does anybody raise a normal kid? Why didn't I tell stories of Thomas Jefferson's life, for example," I moaned.

"You probably didn't remember any, if you're like me," Lindy said.

"When is your husband getting home, so I can stop wallowing in self-pity, in time to get out," I said through my tears.

"He'll be back in a couple hours, go ahead and cry, Veronica," she said, handing me a box of tissues and then, just to get a smile, a roll of paper towels.

"Devin's life is pretty normal, accept for an inattentive dad who has rage problems, but that isn't enough to be as disrespectful as he is. Why is he such a rebel without a cause? Have I just spoiled him? It was me, spoiling him!" I sobbed.

"Veronica, it isn't about your choice of bed time stories. He's on drugs."

"Yeah, I guess." I said.

"You don't want to look at it, and can't see it till a window breaks next to your head. That isn't how normal teenagers deal with frustration. It's over the top. Stop blaming yourself."

"It's just that Raymond won't spend the money to put in a security system so we can lock the doors at a certain time and insist on a curfew or punishment...and I can't go along with calling the cops on him, so... so...so, he goes to jail for having pot or selling pot, and a restraining order costs—" with my head over my folded arms I began reciting the same old conundrum to the table top.

"Stop crying and come out to the backyard. Let's look at the sunset," my friend urged, pulling my arm.

"You don't know what it's like living with him...snatching away any dot of tranquility I find. No matter how I start the day—meditating, or reading something positive, like *Guideposts Magazine*, as soon as he gets in those moods, I'm a nervous wreck. Weekends are the worst..." My voice trailed off as I took my whining inward.

Now, emotionally defeated, I'm merely sleepwalking through my house. The living things that I once cared for are insignificant. Now I stare at my dog as she dances around her empty dog dish. I miss the cue. My newly potted plants threaten to die of neglect. In my haze I've abandoned the life that exists around me, the flora and fauna are on their own.

"It's okay to talk about it," Lindy said softly as she tossed me a blanket. The sun had gone down and now in the semi darkness, life was bleaker.

"I'll just sit here for a few minutes. You can go inside. Thanks for the blanket," I told my friend.

All these years I had unfairly judged those who had no personality. Now I had joined the flat-line zombies. The human desire to laugh or care has been replaced by nothingness behind empty, tired and red eyes. Like an amputee experiencing phantom pain from the lost limb, I faintly recalled the bubbly personality I had before it was cut off by the tourniquet of Devin's abusive behavior. From now on, I bond with all the sad, dull people who, in the past, I would have arrogantly scorned. Give me your bland, your boring, your mono-toned, depressed foot shufflers, for these are *my people.*

****

Dear Diary,

It's Christmas Eve,

No sleigh bells ring, instead sad hearts creak like old floor boards of a house, remembering a better day.

The ghost of Christmas present is a haunting sad mist hovering above.

Peace? Such a humble prayer; yet so difficult to attain as an individual, as a family, as a world.

Our wringing hands must instead form a fleshy steeple, and believe our prayers will make it true. That we must first be living examples of peace and romantic love. One person at a time, we dare to cast a twinkling light, suggesting love's power. Then, perhaps, a tiny spark of hope may shine through our eyes and lighten someone else's heavy heart.

****

Christmas was uneventful and drafty. We awoke at the crack of noon and had our traditional Christmas morning breakfast: the top layer of a Sees Candy box.

Devin gave me a letter of apology, in poem form, and a box of incense. Raymond gave me a couple of CDs, still in the plastic bag from the Wherehouse Record Store. We gave Devin clothes and gift certificates to the AMC Movie Theater and Baskin Robbins Ice Cream Store.

Raymond was gifted with renewals to *Acoustic Guitar Magazine, Fret Magazine, Guitar Player Magazine and Jazz Guitar Quarterly Magazine.* If the gifts seemed uninspired it's because money was tight. Renewing the subscriptions was meant to be a gesture of thoughtfulness, rather than inevitability. Quite like my husband's gifts to me. He would have bought those CDs for himself. Tossing in a Salsa CD was *his* gesture of thoughtfulness. Wrapping it up would have been too sentimental, I suppose.

We spent a pleasant afternoon at my sister Dana's house. I disappeared behind an apron in the kitchen, Devin disappeared into the garage with his cousins and Raymond made all of us disappear behind closed eyelids. With the exception of the time it took him to crawl up from the floor onto a chair to eat, he laid on the floor sleeping. After the last bite of pie was swallowed, he returned to the floor, like a giant walrus sliding off a rock.

"Why do you let him sleep through every holiday, Veronica?" my sister inquired, as we carried dishes into the kitchen.

"Oh, I don't know. Since he has to be social in his job, I guess he feels like it's a commodity he's giving away for free, if he talks to us on his day off," I said, defending the 160 pound lump on the carpet.

"Well, I wouldn't allow it," Dana said, closing her eyes and shaking her head, as if that would somehow diminish the buzz of snoring. "Don't be fooled. Right now he doesn't want to see people are helping, *we are cleaning up*. When he got here, he didn't want to answer questions about his son, album sales, or why your house was so cold yesterday. Did you get your heat turned off?"

"You don't want to know," I said. She really didn't.

"He tunes us out. It's as simple as that," Dana said, pressing the dishwasher's start button with finality.

Hmmm, the prospect of answering those well-meaning questions *did* sound worse than being rude by sleeping. But knowing how she felt, it was too late for me to curl up on the floor.

"You're a good sport, Veronica."

Raymond tunes out most of family life, it's true. He escapes to that place where musical notes just hang in the air, waiting to be selected, put into exquisite order, then admired. In fairness, his manner of tuning out is more productive than the crutches Devin and I use.

&&&&&&&

Chapter 24

GUTTER BLUES

Sitting on the curb in front of my house, I looked down. My feet were rather pretty. Even though it was winter, my pink toenails denoted cheery, happy, little feet. Unfortunately, they led me to a cement seat next to the gutter at 11:08 a.m. on December 28th.

Candace's voice on the phone machine was clipped and distant. Like a guy at the Radio Shack saying, "We can't fix your camera, lady. Sorry, it's not what we do." Candace's message was, "Hey, Veronica, you know, I just can't be a part of your little acting job at the Ritz on the 31st. Sorry, I know it's only a few days away, but you know a lot of people—that could maybe do it, huh?" A pause, then a short gasp of restrained excitement was evident. "I'm invited to Monte Carlo for a party, a few of us girls are going. Let's see...hmmm, you don't need to call me back. I'm sending you a new check for the deposit I already cashed. Oh, and the lost library books..." That was the point at which I slammed the phone down. Apparently *her* invitation came in late.

After running away from my phone and desk, I went outside and plunked down at the curb like a bag of rubbish waiting for pick-up. In the middle of the day the street was quiet and I had a few moments of outdoor privacy for soft wails of defeat amid small hiccups of self-righteousness.

Devin was asleep and Raymond was at a voice lesson, so my impending doom could play itself out without distraction. This latest disappointment was too big for my bedroom office; I had to take my pounding heart and heaving chest outside. Through the flood of tears, I imagined myself melting a tear at a time into the gutter's stream.

Did I deserve to be shot down? Was I *too greedy?* I had only tried to save my house from foreclosure. Was this a karmic response to my adultery? Would I be sued for trying to make a stranger's fantasy come true? Simon's fantasy? Where could I find the money to pay back his deposit? *I hate Candace,* I seethed. Simon's fantasy was important, but what about my fantasy of becoming financially solvent for a few months? It was all falling apart, now that the disloyal bitch was going to Monte Carlo.

How did a cute, clever girl like me wind up financially bankrupt? A clever girl could make enough money to live. A pretty girl could surely marry a man capable of supporting a family of three without resenting it to the point of fostering rage. Why was I the only attractive, thin blond shopping every week at the *Nothing Over 99 Cents Store?* When did shopping at the mall become a pipe dream?

While other girls dined at fine restaurants on a date, my experience was entering through the kitchen and setting up my microphone stand at the piano. However, as a musician, spying on loving couples was definitely a perk— not to mention free salad. "Yes I know that song I'd be happy to play *The First Time Ever I Saw Your Face.*" My singing and piano accompaniment were a valued accessory to many romantic evenings. From the stage I admired those anonymous customers; the girls toasting, giggling and swooning at their very own lobster tail. Rationalizing that these men were probably boring, the table chat consisted of discussions on annuities and phosphorus, I wasn't bitter. *I have the soul of the artist.* The gypsy in me waited for an artist to marry me. My soul-mate would be a talented man who, like me, didn't buy into the corporate world of commerce. Who wants financial security? When you marry at 25, life is defined by love and music.

Admittedly, putting all my eggs into the love of art basket was idealistic, but the main problem was now the person *holding* the basket. My basket was filled with only the hope of artistic expression, support and love. Oh, P.S. Veronica—*Raymond flew solo.* Eventually, I gave up singing and playing piano to help manage Raymond's career, in a matter of weeks I became his valet.

Sure, the life of an artist usually consists of struggle, but to feel *unloved after seventeen years* of marriage was harsh. Raymond contributed a thimble of love, and Mickey risked the wrath of Mrs. Owens about once a month. I did the math. Hmm, these two halves don't make a whole. The quality of love I received was shortchanged by my husband and the quantity was short-changed by my lover. What now? Introduce a third entity into my bed, because Raymond's silver thimble can't stretch any easier than Mickey's metal leash tethered to the tree? Where does love leave off and slutdom begin? If either one of these men could take care of me, I would cut the other loose. Beyond being faithful, I'd be damn grateful to have a husband *be there for me* emotionally. Financially would be an added bonus. Isn't that what all women want, and most women have? After believing in art and not selling-out for an average Joe with a good job, it seemed I backed the wrong horse, and I was headed back from the track completely busted. Raymond put me in this fix, I decided in a flash. He was constantly taking lessons, buying expensive equipment, fifteen hand-crafted guitars and self-producing four albums, then building a recording studio in the garage. He wasn't a partner; he was a baby I had to protect from the financial facts of life. Now I was out on a limb with this stupid stunt. I hated Raymond and Candace.

Raymond was too lazy to woo me. Would it kill him to steal some obscure lyric, scrawl it onto the back of an envelope, *and pretend* it was for me? Could he toss me a bone? Come on! A simple lazy, insincere, five minute gesture would've made me incredibly happy.

Love is over there, for someone else. The happy, Korean fisherman putting squid on his fishhook and casting-off the Redondo Pier, for example. He has his rotund, and contented wife sitting next to him in the cold, drinking coffee from a thermos at midnight. They are together. They share the secret of true love. Me? I'm just an agent who's waiting for the phone to ring so I can send entertainment to liven up someone else's party. The only party I'm going to is my own pity party. Oh, and I've yet to see any "Mother of the Year Awards" hanging on the fractured walls of my house either.

"Veronica, are you all right? Of course you're not all right."

"Oh? Uh, hi Janna. I was just, ummm, I don't know."

"Would you like a cookie? I baked too many for Christmas boxes and we've been eating them all day," she handed me a soft cookie tree sprinkled with green sugar.

"Thanks." I lowered my head again and watched as the crumbs drifted past in the gutter's now familiar current.

"The kids were watching a video and I was doing dishes at the window and I watched you for the longest time, just sitting here. I thought maybe you needed a cookie and someone to talk to." Janna smiled her beautifully innocent smile, implying she had all the time in the world to listen. She was a mother of five. It was hard to imagine she would have the emotional energy to invest in a wayward neighbor. Hey, if my five kids were occupied, it would take an explosion to get me out of a bubble bath. But, here she was.

"Thanks Janna, but I don't think you'd understand."

"Start at the beginning," she encouraged me, as she pulled another cookie from her apron pocket. "Sometimes another person can see things differently and help with a solution. Is it Devin?"

When I didn't answer, she assumed the neighborhood's bad boy was responsible for the tears. "Veronica, think back when you were pregnant and remember how you were happy in the first few months, yet in your ninth month your feet were swollen and you got so big you couldn't sleep and you were so uncomfortable?"

"Uh huh," I said lamely. Part of me wondered where this was going and the other part of me wanted to be left alone.

"Well," Janna continued, "that's what's going on here. Your baby's getting ready to leave the nest. To start an independent life and that process is painful. Where we used to want our babies safe inside us, by the ninth month we want them out—and we count the days! That's what's happening to you. It's much like the painful process of childbirth. You have to go through it again—to get him out on his own, so the child can begin a new life without you. The teenager is preparing you by acting awful, so you won't mind the separation. It's God's plan."

"That sounds pretty good, Janna. Actually, Devin and I did have a blow out last week, but he wrote me a poem saying he's sorry, and he's been a pretty good guy since. But that isn't the thing that has me sitting out here today."

"Go on," she said.

"I just found out that an actress I had hired to pretend to be this gentleman's deceased wife, just cancelled out. I got nobody, and this poor man is going to be so disappointed." Crying again, I couldn't help myself; once the words were spoken, it solidified the predicament. Trying to make it a short story, I filled her in, leaving out details like the evaporated $15,000 advances, paying off Devin's rehab, late mortgage payments, the impossibility of paying Simon back, a probable lawsuit and the frisky hooker on stand-by.

"Is this an uncle, did you say?" she asked softly. By now we were both seated on the curb with our legs outstretched on the street.

"Yes, my uncle. I just want him to...oh, forget it," I sighed.

"I think I understand more than you know," Janna shook her head. "We had a situation like that in our family. It sounds like the same thing. Uncle Morris stayed with us, one time, at Easter. He was down from Provo, Utah, and we were looking forward to his visit. It had been a while since we spent much time with him and when we picked him up from the airport, it wasn't long before we realized he was a bit senile. Oh, he talked a heap about his wife, forgetting she had passed away. He was always asking us if we had seen Aunt Barbara and got upset when we reminded him of the truth, that she had passed away last February. Finally, we humored Uncle Morris. Since he was staying two weeks, we had to do something!"

Recalling the memory made her laugh and she threw both her hands into the air and clapped them together. As she went on with the anecdotes, I noticed what a pleasant voice she had, as well as a country maiden's natural beauty. I always admired her statuesque height and shiny brown hair. Or maybe it was her dancing eyes, wide smile and beautiful white teeth that made her so appealing.

"Veronica, you are such a loving person. You are so kind to care about your uncle. What is his name?"

"Simon, uh, Uncle Simon," I said, clearing my throat.

"Look how blessed we both are, with our health and having our husbands alive. My Uncle Morris and your Uncle Simon are adjusting to a terrible loss. You are so kind to try to make him happy by finding an actress to pretend. Why don't you get someone else to play-act his wife?"

"Oh, it isn't that easy. To start calling actresses..." my voice trailed off.

"Why don't you ask a friend to be his pretend wife? Did the actress who quit look just like her? Is that the problem?"

"Well, not *just like her*. She was about 38, tall, thin, with brown hair and eyes," I said.

"Since he's senile, why would he remember they were supposed to get together? Maybe he'll just forget about that, like he forgets where he left his keys."

"Janna, it's not that simple."

"Why is that?"

"Well, I humored him by saying Aunt Gwendolyn would have a big evening of dancing and dinner at their favorite spot on New Year's Eve." As I floated tiny blades of grass in the slow moving gutter, I kept my eyes averted from my well-meaning neighbor.

"Uncle Simon kept talking about his deceased wife; asking me about her, and wondering why she didn't come home from some trip. Finally, it was easier to just finally say, she was coming back. I took it too far; in a moment of weakness I promised him she'd be back. He assumed it was for their traditional New Year's dinner. He remembered talking about it, *hung on to it*—in fact, he now fully expects it." I started feeling better, sharing my burden with another person. I started believing my own bullshit about the lonely, elderly uncle.

"Let's put our heads together and think of someone who could meet him. It sounds like it means so much," Janna said.

"It's very serious," I said.

"When you think about it, all they have to do is show up, eat a great dinner and play along, huh, Janna?" Maybe it was Janna's benevolent presence or just a sugar cookie high, but I started feeling better. Janna wasn't shocked at all, and took my predicament in stride like a scraped knee. She started sailing her own dried leaf boats, which followed my blades of grass as we sat on the curb with our heads down watching the microcosm of vessels floating past in the murky water.

"How much do you know about opera, Janna?"

"Quite a bit. Why?"

&&&&&&&&

December 31st

Brioche, Quail Egg and Caviar

*

Terrine of Fois Gras and Apple, Onion Marmalade

*

Scallop and Black Truffle Carpaccio, Micro Green Salad

*

**Pheasant with Cabbage in Pastry,
Celery Root and Sauce Salmis**

*

**Warm Liquid Center Hazelnut Cake,
Vanilla Bean Ice Cream**

*

Migardises and Coffee

*

**Pierre LaTorre
Chef De Cuisine**

&&&&&&&

As Devin would say, we were "kicking it" in Tiffany's room, which was a floor down from Simon's suite.

Tiffany raised her cocktail and called out, "Happy New Year, everyone!" She was wearing a t-shirt that said 'Stud Muffin Magnet' and a cardboard, feathered tiara. Her carefree *joie de vivre* was a welcome change of pace for me since I was feeling the stress typical of a producer on opening night. Problem being, the main attraction of my show would be the equivalent of "Tonight, Standing in for Meryl Streep, in the starring role, is Edith, from accounts payable."

Attempting distraction, I busied myself at the bar in our room. Pouring from a bottle I had stashed in my purse, I turned to my son. "I guess since *it is* New Year's and you are 17, it's okay to have a cocktail with Tiffany and me," I chirped, handing Devin a fizzing green, icy drink.

"Hugs, hugs, everybody!" Tiffany cried. Devin and I responded in kind and we exchanged a round of good-natured embraces. The big night was ahead, and now, at 7:45, we all tried to loosen up and relax with a cocktail. Devin seemed to have mellowed out with the Nyquil and Perrier beverage I made for him.

"Whoa, this is mad strong," he murmured to himself as he gulped the bright green potion. Dinner was at eight, and I wanted Devin to be on his best behavior and that included sedation. Now, before you judge me, consider all the kids with colds getting shots of Nyquil on this very evening. It could be said it was "preventive medicine," preventing me from strangling my hyperactive, preppy-from -hell.

I thought of Simon. It was enjoyable turning the already lavish suite into a banquet for the senses. A well placed candelabra and pale peach candles would assure mood lighting for later, and the air was scented with several dozen white roses. I placed See's Candy Bridge Mix in crystal dishes and a basket of fruit, with gourmet pates, crackers, sausages, and a champagne bucket. A sexy feather fan concealed a boom box loaded with music by Michael Feinstein, Charlotte Church, Diana Krall and Luther Vandros. The suite was, indeed, a promising setting for sensual delights to come.

In these last moments alone, I imagine Simon in his suite resting. Perhaps he's smelling the roses and tasting the chocolate as he listened to the pristine voice of opera singer, Charlotte Church. He may even run his fingertips across the soft pastel feathers, imagining the sensation of it grazing across smooth, young skin.

In 15 minutes, the evening would begin to unfold. Simon's appetite was whetted through the e-mail correspondence with Gwendolyn; the prosaic letters sustained and supported the fantasy of his dream lover. They also supported my household with the extra income from additional letters he requested. Gratefully, Mickey had more time on his hands than I did; his love missives were recycled as quickly as they came in. As I sipped at a White Russian, I reclined in my chair and enjoyed the idea that the curtain was about to rise on my biggest production, the gig that hopefully pays me $30,000.

The symphony I'm conducting is a discreet fantasy; fine-tuned to satisfy a man's appetite for sentimentality and lust. The passionate plea of the mistress at midnight is designed to thrill. Tiffany knows her lines, requesting permission to visit his room after his wife is unexpectedly called away. The next morning, playing the role of successful, upstanding family man, he enjoys the brunch even more, with his attractive and adoring wife at his side. By my sewing romantic and erotic patches on his tattered self-image, my client, Simon Bestep, jump-starts the New Year.

Then there is the dreaded chat with Simon's friggin' attorney. No time to dwell on that, I told myself. As my drink took a calming effect, Devin and Tiffany chatted in the bathroom. Seeing myself as the puppeteer with strings which pulled at all the complicated emotions of a wealthy and powerful man, I was jolted from my delusions of grandeur. Sounds of violent vomiting and groans came from the bathroom. Devin was spewing green liquid in the bathtub. In a macho move, he had drunk down his "Nyquil Fizz" too quickly and was paying the price.

"Bro, you're the bomb in that suit," Tiffany said, punctuating her remark with a hearty laugh. "Don't be getting any of that nasty stuff on yourself!"

Devin was wearing a suit combining the *huate de* thrift store and Raymond's clothes. Hanging over the tub and toggling back to the toilet, he managed to keep the navy blue blazer and gray flannel slacks clean. The white shirt was going to need a spot clean.

"Oooh, yuck," Devin groaned. As he looked up from the toilet, it occurred to me that he looked like a preppy at a frat party, turning vivid shades of green as he prayed to the porcelain god.

Tiffany grabbed a washcloth and started dabbing it on his shirt. I needed to meet with Simon. Looking at my watch, I said to my son, "Chad, be prompt. At 8:25 the Maitre d' takes you to Mr. Bestep's table. Remember how to find the restaurant from here?"

"Mom, you're heartless. Yeah, I can find it. I feel horrible! Did you see me hurl?"

"Gwendolyn will make her entrance at 8:15; you'll come in at 8:25, like the script says. Honey, I'm sorry you drank your drink too fast. Just smile and keep your mouth shut. Here is your toothbrush," I handed him a brush already pasted. "This evening will be over before you know it. Remember to ask *Father* what he suggests you order for dinner and choose that."

"Mom, come on! This sucks! I feel horrible!"

"No Coke at the table. No caffeine, and don't try to fool your Mother, Janna-Gwendolyn."

"Mom, you're cold! Listen, for reals, I feel sick!" he continued in-between spits, "How long is this gonna take?"

"Two hundred for a good job, Devin. That's what we need to think about. How long will it take? We can't be exactly sure; I'm sure the service is good. You should be finished eating and say your good bye lines at 9:45. Or, how about when the couple take their first dance? That can be your cue to thank Mother and Father for the delicious dinner and remind them you are taking the train back to school in the morning. Whichever comes first: their dance or 9:45. You have your watch on? So you'll know when to say good-bye?"

"Do I say the bit about playing the cello in the school band? And water polo?" Devin croaked.

"Yes. Remember? That was before the salad. Look at the notes again. You have a couple lines between each course, and keep your answers short. Be a good actor. You never know, a casting agent might be at the next table."

"Yeah, right, Mom." I wasn't sure if he was being sarcastic, but no matter.

"Memorize those lines again, *Chad.* Tiffany, work with him."

"Has Gwendolyn called from the beauty shop? Her hair and make-up should be done by now."

****

Simon looked snappy in his tuxedo. He stood up as I entered the library; I smiled and sat down. There were a few awkward moments before the brandy spun its warm magic. Simon leaned forward and reminded me that Edgar Freis would be joining us after brunch in the morning.

"Frankly, Simon, I wish you wouldn't be so mysterious about why you want me to meet him." Ignoring the question, he stood up and took my arm as we walked toward the formal dining room.

"Veronica, I know I'm an old fool. I lost Gwendolyn when she was just 44 years old. She was the light of my life...now, to imagine that I could see her again...." He

178

cleared his throat and said in a whisper, "If she only had a twin, heck a clone…just to look at her again." He shook his head, and his voice trailed off.

We arrived at the entrance of the restaurant, and the Maitre d' led us to his table. In front of the Maitre d', I casually drew Simon's attention to the two, slightly different, silver champagne stands. Since Gwendolyn only drank special, imported champagne, *any* other champagne would produce hives, due to her sensitivity to certain grapes, I explained. The waiters were briefed on this arrangement, and instructed to only present the lady champagne from the bottle covered with a fake label, containing sparkling apple cider. This was an important detail, since, as a Mormon, Janna couldn't drink alcohol. Simon seemed content with the grape allergy explanation.

The band played a couple of instrumental numbers and then the leader invited me to join them on stage for a song. Simon raised his eyebrows in surprise, then rose from his seat as I slid past him making my way toward the bandstand.

The nine-piece orchestra opened the music for the song I had prepared.

"Thank you," I said, nodding to the audience, acknowledging the applause. "I want to wish you a very Happy New Year and take this opportunity to sing one of my favorite songs. This goes out to a special friend. Kenny Asher wrote the music and Paul Williams wrote the words; it's from the movie, *A Star Is Born.*

> *With one more look at you, I could learn to*
> *tame the clouds and let the sun shine through,*
>
> *Leave a troubled past and I might start anew,*
>
> *I'll solve the mysteries, if you're the prize,*
> *refresh these tired eyes…*

With one more look at you, I might overcome
the anger that I've learned to know,

Find a peace of mind I lost so long ago, your
gentle touch has made me strong again, and I
belong again!

As the band played the verses instrumentally, I glanced around the room to see Janna enter, right on cue. Her chestnut brown hair swung to her shoulders simple and elegant. The rented pearl and diamond necklace sparkled beautifully on her white neck. The dark blue velvet dress fit her size 6 frame perfectly. Professional make-up completed the look inspired by the photo we had been given of Gwendolyn. Remarkably, Janna looked the part; more than that, she looked radiant. Her ruddy cheeks from time spent outdoors made her look sporty and her full lips made her look sensuous. She moved toward the table with a comfort and grace rivaling any society matron.

Janna is the holiest person I know. Tonight was the ultimate test of my instincts to see if her aura of godliness and beauty would translate to a stranger. On my street, at least, she had the power to warm a lonely soul with a smile.

Simon Bestep stood up and I read Gwendolyn's lips say, "Happy New Year, Darling!" As she planted a kiss on the cheek of her table companion, I took the microphone in my hand and continued singing,

For, when you look at me, I'm everything and
more that I had dreamed I'd be,

My spirit feels a promise, I won't be alone,

We'll love and live more, love and live
forever more!

With one more look at you, I'd learn to
change the stars and change our fortunes too!

*I'd have the constellations paint your portrait
too. So all the world might share this won-
drous sight,*

*The world could end each night, with one
more look at you, one more look at you...I
want... one more look at you!*

&&&&&&&

DECMBER 31ˢᵗ, 9:30 p.m.

As I reached for the tiny jewelry box my heart
pounded. Inside a diamond ring sparkled, and tiny emeralds
shimmered. "Oh, my!" I gasped, admiring the exquisite
stones and setting.

"You know what this means, don't you?" Mickey
said softly.

"I get to keep it?" I blurted out.

"It's an engagement ring. I just don't know when or
how, but *someday*...that's my promise." Then, snuggling up
beside me, he whispered, "I belong to you too."

"I, uh, don't know what to say, I'm so happy! That
book I gave you for Christmas?" I said looking around the
room, "I was just kidding--I want you to have this, uh,
lamp," I reached for the lamp on the nightstand. We both
laughed, replacing the tension with much welcomed comic
relief.

"Really, this lamp is *your* gift, um—I just plugged it
in to —to show you!"

"Hush up," Mickey urged as he gently covered my
mouth in slow, little kisses.

181

"You are my favorite bigamist! I love the ring, what a surprise! Thank you, Mickey-man," I said, sliding the ring on my right hand. It fit perfectly.

"I love the commitment," Mickey told my neck.

"Me too," I whispered, barely able to speak with his lips on mine. As we leaned back for a moment, our eyes locked and he smiled, "Happy New Year, Darling. I love you so much." Mickey paused and took a deep breath, "Eventually, we will be married. You reminded me I once said I was the 'luckiest man in the world', now with your promise to marry me –sometime in the future—you've made me *the happiest man* in the world!" While kissing, I nibbled the top of his bare shoulders as he rolled me over, I landed on top of him.

Wearing the engagement ring on the ring finger of my right hand, I admired its brilliance, as I gently stroked his face. With our hands clasped together, it decorated our ten fingers intertwined, and I framed the picture in my mind. He was as excited as I was with this bold step, and the sheer energy heated up our private party even more. As he kissed the side of my neck and shoulders, a sensual chain-reaction rippled through me.

"Ma'am? Are you all right?"

I screamed to see a large man in a uniform looming over me.

"Ma'am, you fell asleep. Don't worry! I'm not here to hurt you. I'm Henderson—hotel security." The guard stepped back as I sat up.

Blinking my eyes, I realized it was cold outside in the pool chair and I shivered.

"What? Who?" Looking around I regained my bearings when I saw the moonlight reflecting in the still water of the swimming pool. Then it came back to me. After I sang, I left the dining room and came outside for some air. Stretching out on the chaise lounge, I'd found a private spot for star gazing. Then, there were the dreams.

"I must have drifted off," I offered. "Sorry." Suddenly hot with embarrassment and yet chilled by the night air, I rubbed my arms.

"Lady, you can't stay out here. This here area is closed."

"I was just dreaming," I said defensively, scrambling for my purse and shoes under the chair.

"Well, ma'am, you can't be dreaming out here. This is off limits to hotel guests until 7:00 a.m."

"You're right. I can't be dreaming out here. That was a dumb thing to do." Gathering my wounded pride, the click of my heels on the deck seemed deafening in the quiet night. Quickly reentering the hotel, I stood in the hallway as the door closed silently behind me.

****

Stumbling into the ladies room, I caught my reflection in the mirror. A sleepy dreamer peered back at me with confusion. How embarrassing to be busted sleeping outside like a frilly vagrant. Rinsing my face with water helped erase the tears and as I staggered back to reality. Bitterly, I realized dreams belonged in sleep.

With whimpering hiccups I slid onto the plush, gold love seat, ashamed at what I had dared to dream.

The dream was so vivid! Inspired by moonlight, pure exhaustion and drinking two White Russians, I had been lulled into a fantasyland. But the security guard's eviction from Engagement Island whiplashed me into the dark possibility that I was just some guy's mistress. Mickey was a professional writer who made a good living as a romantic lyricist. One only had to listen to his music to hear the skillful, romantic prose. Had he silver-tongued me into bed? Had my hungry heart colorized the black and white reality?

Through the dream my subconscious had actually offered a romantic and do-able solution to our plight. A long, long engagement would be wonderful, as we gradually pruned the vines that were strangling us. Why not? Or is a ring just a bourgeois fairy-tale ending for women dating married men? Is there a bigamist chat room on the Internet? What exactly is engagement protocol when both parties are already married? While I was applying my lipstick, Janna entered the ladies room.

"Oh, Janna!" Catching sight of my face in the mirror, I reminded myself of the cartoon character Charley Brown; my smile looked like a sideways "S", as I tried to draw lipstick on.

As we looked at each other in the warm glow of the plush powder room, we exchanged compliments on our out-of-the-neighborhood transformation, giggling like sorority sisters at a dance.

"You look *so* glamorous, Veronica! When I first entered the room and heard you singing, I was very impressed. Your voice is beautiful. Are you going to sing again?"

"Thank you, Janna, I mean Gwendolyn," I winked. "No, I just did that one song for Uncle Simon. How's it going?" I looked at my watch. "Gee, it's already 10:00."

"Simon is not as senile as my uncle was," Janna said, nodding earnestly. "Singing in the church choir for, heck, 15 years? I guess it's been that long; anyway, has helped me follow the music and opera parts of the conversation."

"How did Chad do?" I asked, stiffening.

"Oh, he is so adorable. I think he was having fun with it, although he didn't eat much and seemed, well, sleepy," she said with a motherly concern. "I needed to correct his manners more than once, but Simon joined in, too. He left at 9:45, just like you said he would."

My biggest concern was the way my son hunched over the plate. Devin had developed an eating style I had seen in Japan. Specifically, businessmen hovering over their steaming hot bowls, furiously whisking food into their mouths with chopsticks, and never looking up. For the last two weeks I had strapped a bungee cord across Devin's chest to attach his back to the chair while he ate. He hated it, but I felt it prepared him for life outside the Orient.

As Janna happily chatted about the unrecognizable food served, I observed her. Earlier in the evening I watched the women from the stage, trying to gauge how Janna fit in with the high-brow clientele. Clearly many of the women came directly from tanning booths; Janna's sun-kissed cheeks had an apricot hue from planting daisies in her yard. Her flawless skin glowed like a twenty-year-old's, not a woman of thirty-eight years. Without cosmetic surgery, facials or expensive skin care products, Janna possessed the natural beauty women pay dearly for. Janna's friendly nature came from the confidence and satisfaction of caring for a large family. She could teach algebra, sew, sing in the choir and living like a Spartan, when given lemons in life, she didn't make lemonade; she made lemon meringue pie. Janna's loving brown eyes emitted a beauty and tranquil peace that blessed the object of her gaze. Without a personal trainer to stay in shape, her strong legs and trim frame were the result of walking her children to school and daily trips to the store. Their family only had one car: a van which her husband, Rusty, used for work. Rusty was a hard working wallpaper hanger who did his best to keep saltines on the table, supporting their family of seven on a modest salary.

"I'm delighted you're enjoying the evening so much. You really are helping Uncle Simon relive the memories of Aunt Gwendolyn," I told her, as I adjusted the necklace on her swan-like neck. "You are honoring Gwendolyn too, by being the lady she was—just for this evening, I mean. Thank you again."

"And you have given my children the best New Year's ever, to send Santa *and* Mrs. Claus and an elf to baby sit!" Janna exclaimed with appreciation.

"Well, actually, after the 25th, the Claus family *is* pretty available," I answered modestly.

"You should have seen their faces when the three of them came to the door tonight! I got back from the beauty shop, oh, I guess about 7:00, and when they came to the door carrying all those platters of food and new board games, it was like Christmas all over again! Now tonight Rusty can just read his sports magazines and let the kids entertain themselves. Thank you so much, Veronica. I don't think anyone even noticed I left!" she said, laughing.

"It was a pleasure to do that for your family, believe me Janna. Devin should be waiting in the lobby at 11:45. Thanks for driving him home."

"Don't worry about a thing! Jeepers, I better get back!" Janna said grabbing her purse as she held the powder room door open for us to leave.

"You tried on the dress and shoes I sent over for the brunch, right?" I asked, suddenly remembering tomorrow's brunch. "Does everything fit?"

"They not only fit, but I can wear them to church, too. Are you sure it's okay to keep them? I can pay you something, maybe..." as we moved toward the lobby.

"Think of it as a gift from Buffy, she enjoys the bones all year! Enjoy the dress. Tomorrow, Simon will be expecting you at the penthouse suite at 10:30 a.m. Together you will go to the patio for brunch. At some point, I'll stop by the table and say hello. Mr. and Mrs. Claus are scheduled to be back at your house at 9:30 in the morning with a ham and deli tray.

"Just remember to stay in character, no matter how comfortable you feel with Uncle Simon. We don't want to jar him, I mean, if it ain't broke, don't fix it." I said cautiously, noting there was a cliché to fit any occasion. Even this one.

As Janna entered the narrow, wood paneled hallway leading to the dining room, she turned to me, "Veronica, what an exciting life you lead! Singing in a fancy place like this *and* being on a first name basis with Santa!"

"Sometime I'll tell you about the water-skiing squirrel," I replied. Bidding Janna goodbye, I checked my watch. Raymond and I had planned to meet at the lobby bar for a quick drink at 10:15. Checking my cell phone, I saw there was a message that he had canceled. Apparently, security was tight for the private party on the 11th floor, and now that he was already inside and set-up, it wasn't easy to exit and return. There was some nonsense about showing a metal coin, issued only to the guests for security access. That was okay with me, since I didn't want Raymond to spot Devin cruising around the hotel tonight, if father and son crossed paths. Busy with his own world, Raymond didn't think to ask about Devin's plans for the night.

It was too early for my cell phone appointment with Mickey at 11:30. I couldn't bear the thought of hanging out with Devin and Tiffany in the room and I was 86'd from the pool area, so, I headed back to the ladies lounge. Mickey had better make that call and escape the acrylic-nailed clutches of the ball and chain, I thought snidely, as I sank into the plush chair of the restroom. What had seemed like fun — welcoming in the New Year together by phone—now seemed stupid and juvenile.

My second concern was becoming more bothersome with each tick of the clock: the meeting with Simon Bestep's attorney, Mr. Edgar Freis. The original reference to the casual meeting had graduated from a *suggestion* to meet, to, "I am counting on you to be there," to, "he is most interested in discussing a serious matter with you." Every night I fretted over the implications. While Raymond lay next to me counting eighth notes and Devin counted stoned sheep, I counted the egregious crimes I may have committed.

Is impersonating a dead person for fun and profit legal in California? Is there an old law on record protecting decent women from adulterous neighbors who trick them into lying, dancing and eating rich foods? How about that little prostitute upstairs? Heidi Fleiss did time. Simon wouldn't bring that up, *would he*? I don't have a business license to run a talent agency, but who does? Everybody knows all you need is a pencil and a phone to be an agent. If I don't get the balance check tomorrow, I'll be in business with only a pencil.

I combed my hair again, touched up my makeup, sank back into the plush chair, and went back to brooding. What if Janna got too comfortable with Simon? She said he didn't seem senile. What if he got wise that she was *not* a highly paid actress, schooled in opera? What if she admitted I said he was demented, and that she played along out of sympathy, for a Honey Baked Ham and some Parker Brothers Games? He would have a right to be angry.

How was Devin's portrayal of the preppy, Chad? What if Simon saw through the facade and recognized Chad's physical resemblance to me, which would raise pointed questions for Janna? Where did his $30,000 actually go? He had a right to ask. My agency promised discreet, professional actors for this private play; he got a juvenile delinquent family member and a sympathetic neighbor who thinks he's nuts. At least Tiffany was a pro. Me? I'm a pro, too. I set the stage months ago and furnished it with heartfelt, enticing, love letters. My only crime was an inability to pay a professional cast due to bill collectors, broken windows and mortgage payments. What else could I do? Give a pint of blood?

Seeing the lawyer friend was probably a veiled threat. Maybe Bestep felt he had to do it to make sure the services met his $30,000 expectations. Regardless, 1:00 p.m. tomorrow was about fourteen hours of worrying away from now. One could only hope the cardboard, paper moon sets would hold up, and that the millionaire's imagination and nostalgia would gloss over the amateur cast.

As I slid back into self-pity, a few tears fell with the realization that my happiest dream of Mickey and me came from sleep. Lindy was right: he was never leaving his wife. The cage was too comfortable with all its toys. There I sat, cursing myself for being too greedy: expecting a husband to love me, financial security, and a kid that wasn't selling drugs.

&&&&&&&

Alice followed the rabbit to the hole, the rabbit dived into the ground and Alice tried to follow. I must chase the rabbit...

Lewis Carroll
Through The Looking Glass

Devin exited the formal dining room with a confident swagger. He felt his first professional acting job had gone well. After a season of auditions resulting in only two callbacks, perhaps his luck had turned. The eternal dreamer, Devin was undaunted by the fact that his first paid acting gig had come from his mother. His role as the preppy son to Mr. Bestep, and the convincing, albeit abbreviated conversation during dinner, seemed to go well. Something told him this was going to be his year.

Walking through the exquisitely decorated, formal hallway that led to the main lobby, Devin wondered how many of these cake jobs were out there. He had made a hundred bucks and eaten a weird dinner, all in a mere hour and a half. He could get used to this, he thought to himself, as he stopped at a table to inhale the scent of orchids springing from a huge floral bouquet.

"Hello," a pretty girl in a uniform called out as she rushed past Devin.

"Oh, hi, where ya off to?" Devin asked the young redhead.

"I'm a relief bartender in the Moonlight Sonata Room tonight," she smiled over her shoulder and disappeared into the dimly lit bar, a few feet ahead.

After dinner, Devin was instructed to go back to the room and wait with Tiffany until 11:30. Then, since his mom was staying late, he was to meet Janna in the lobby and go home. Considering the friendliness of a pretty girl and some unsupervised time ahead, Devin saw the red ponytail as a waving flag, and followed it into the lounge. The effects of the Nyquil had worn off during dinner. Pledging never to drink anything bright green and fizzy again, he ordered a 7 Up and took a seat at the bar.

"That will be $4.00, sir," the burly bartender announced with a smile.

"Wait. No, dude, for soda?" Devin exclaimed, suddenly sounding 13 years old, despite the blazer and flannel pants. Then, disarmed by the young girl who walked up from the other end of the bar, Devin said, "Oh, yeah. Here. Here's a five, keep it. I mean, you know, it's a tip."

The male bartender went toward the sink; the girl grabbed a cloth and started wiping the marble near Devin.

"What are you doing here tonight?" the flirty bartender asked. "Here's two cherries for your 7 Up." She dropped them in his glass with a plunk. Leaning over she said softly, "Here with your folks?"

"Wow, I can't believe you said that. I'm an actor. I was doing a job here tonight." Devin leaned back, holding his hand over his heart. "Hey, you really know how to hurt a guy!"

"Sorry," she answered with a giggle. "My name is Terri. Are you with Mr. Goldman and his group?"

"No, I am with Agency West. I'm Devin." Extending his hand, he asked, "Who's this Goldman guy?"

Her head swung toward the table past Devin. He turned and spotted the nattily dressed man, sitting alone, furiously working a cell phone.

"I thought you might be with that songwriter guy's party upstairs. It starts about ten, and some of the guests have been in here tonight."

"Whose bash is upstairs?" Devin asked eagerly, leaning across the bar toward the friendly informant.

"Oh, I guess it's okay to tell you since you're in the business and everything," she volunteered. "Sitting right there is Mr. Goldman, Mickey Owens's agent. It's Mr. Owens's party upstairs. I usually do banquets, but the composer guy's wife said, 'No female wait staff.' So, they moved me down here for tonight."

"For reals?" Devin gasped.

"For real. I guess she's jealous or something."

"Who is Mitzy Owens?"

"Oh, you know, some old guy who wrote songs, a singer I think. Anyway, he's like our parents' age. You have pretty eyes."

"Thanks, you too," Devin answered, moving in closer.

"What would you normally be doing tonight if you weren't acting?" Terri asked, searching for a clue about this cute, street-smart guy who was dressed like a preppy.

"Tonight? Wow, I'd probably torch up a blunt, and get a major freak on." Cackling at his candor, Devin reeled back on the bar stool and they both laughed. Suddenly, customers started tapping their glasses on the marble surface at the other end of the bar. New Year's Eve brought out the unruly behavior in thirsty patrons who were unaccustomed to poor service.

"There better be a dead bug under that glass," Terri said good-naturedly, heading off toward the clamor.

Turning his stool sideways, Devin was able to observe the important agent at the neighboring table. He recalled his mother remarking earlier that there may be agents in the hotel tonight. Devin made his decision to approach the man just like every other decision he ever made: on sudden impulse. He drained his glass, left it on the bar and approached Mark Goldman. After all, he was fresh off an acting job himself, and he knew this was going to be his year.

"Excuse me, sir, I don't want to take up too much of your time, but I wanted to…" At this point Devin's smooth introduction got lost as he noticed the huge diamond pinky ring and monogrammed cuff of Mark Goldman's salmon colored shirt.

Lifting his fourth martini into the air, Mark's tired eyes met Devin's Windex blue eyes, and in a voice flat with boredom he said, "Happy New Year, my friend."

"Friend?" Devin looked behind him to make sure the salutation was meant for him, oblivious to the agent's tone.

"Oh, yeah, ah, me. Happy New Year, sir, and might I say, what a cool monogram on the cuff of your sleeve there." Nodding vigorously, buying time, Devin added awkwardly, "I've never seen that…like that."

"Well, how are you going to 'not take up too much of my time?' I'm surprised they let minors in here. This is a bar."

"Hey, I know the bartender, and besides, they serve food here," Devin said with a furrowed brow, as though impersonating someone serious, rather than *being* someone serious. "Sir, I am an actor, a rap artist, musician, and I would like to know if I could have your card. I'm also a big fan of Mitzy Otis."

"So am I. But I make money for my client, Mickey Owens, and that keeps us both happy."

"Oh…yeah, uh did I say 'Mitzy?' I meant 'Mickey,'" Shielding his laughter with his hand, he stepped back, and Devin regained his composure. "I'm an actor, my name is…I'm Devin." With a broad and endearing smile he saved for special occasions, Devin extended his hand, bowing slightly.

Having waited for his companion in the lobby bar since eight o'clock, the cranky agent was annoyed with the prospect of attending his client's party alone. Mark's boyfriend, Kevin, had returned that day from Hawaii, where he had been gainfully employed as a Haines underwear model. None of Mark's frequent calls had been returned and it was time to go upstairs. Setting down his glass, he sized up the handsome kid for an instant appraisal.

"Devin? Devin," Mark said, as if trying the name on for size. "Devin, let me tell you something that Hunter Thompson once said. *The music business is a long shallow money trench overrun with pimps and thieves, where good men die like dogs,*" he recited with impeccable accuracy.

"Whoa, that's harsh, sir," Devin said. "I still want to be a rap producer though, sir, well and… an actor."

"Would you like to go to a party?" Mark asked.

"When? Really, sir?"

"Stop calling me 'sir' It makes me feel like we're in the military. The party is happening even as we speak. It's upstairs actually."

"I'm down for that, sir…uh dude," Devin beamed, clapping his hands together in one large swing. Yep, this night was shaping up, indeed, he thought to himself.

Mark exploded in a barking laugh at being addressed as dude.

As the unlikely duo headed for the elevator, Mark's martini-laced logic reasoned that an appearance with a young actor was not such a bad thing. This actually might perk up the evening. What was Mickey thinking with this Renewal of the Marriage Vows' party, anyway? Mark was convinced it was a publicity ploy set in motion by Mickey's wife, Helen, as an attempt to get herself a feature story in *Redbook Magazine*. It was bad enough dealing with the egos of his clients, he thought to himself, but the spouses' egos were often worse. Who could understand love anyway?

Moments before they reached the elevator, Mark excused himself and stepped next to the wall for some privacy. Hitting the redial button on his phone, he hissed, "Kevin, you can kiss my ass. Aloha, you prick," and hung up.

When they reached the elevator, Mark fished into his pocket, found the brass VIP disc for his guest, and put it in Devin's hand. Flipping his own disk, he asked, "Heads or tails, Devin?"

"Heads, sir," Devin responded.

As the elevator door opened to take them to the eleventh floor, Mark read the coin. "Well, there is no head or tail on this brass disk, so I guess that means we both win."

"That's tight," agreed Devin as he stepped into the elevator. Turning to the other guests already inside, he called, "Happy New Year, everybody!" This salutation was met with friendly cheers of agreement by the partygoers, already primed for a big evening. As the doors closed, and the metal rectangle zoomed to the eleventh floor, the happy chatter subsided.

&&&&&&&

DECEMBER 31ˢᵗ 10:50 p.m.

Sitting on the plush loveseat of the ladies room interior, I had time to ruminate on my damned mortgage payment. If I neglected two payments, foreclosure would begin; I had missed two, paid one with Simon's last deposit and in a few days would be back to being behind again, if I didn't leave with Bestep's check tomorrow.

Why did Raymond get to be the *artiste in residence* his whole life, without the worry of bills? The answer was easy: early on he had told me to handle the money, readily admitting he didn't want to be burdened with details. At first, I liked the arrangement. No husband looking over my shoulder to see what I spent seemed good on paper. Then, when push came to knock out, I couldn't tell the maestro we weren't making it on his salary.

He played so well, and practiced so long, it seemed unfair for the universe not to reward him. Assuming the universe was only tardy in making him the next *Big Thang*— I maxed credit cards, took out a second mortgage and dodged bill collectors. Meanwhile, he spent thousands of dollars producing CDs while our garage became a warehouse of Raymond's original music.

He felt he was slumming even *coming home*, so I never told him home was on the edge. Number one on my list of "Stuff To Do" everyday was, "Get Raymond signed to a major record label." That had been on my list for fourteen years. I simply did not have contacts in that area of the

194

business. How our family got by was not my husband's concern. His concern was how to augment a D minor 13 chord with a flat 5th. Today was December 31st and the piper must be paid. GMAC Mortgage Company was the piper who would allow me exactly 45 days to bring my account current, including the outrageous penalties.

Could I be more frugal? Currently the closest thing to an affordable luxury was an olive next to my tuna sandwich. Now, the olive has to go.

Muffled sobs in the powder room led to my whining, "Too bad there isn't a cardboard, feathered tiara that reads, 'Unhappy New Year.'" I told my blotchy reflection in the mirror. "Oh great! Red, puffy eyes are a good look this season." These mutterings were cut short by the sound of the exterior door opening. Animated voices got louder as two ladies entered the lounge, and sent me scurrying for a stall.

"Well, I think the dining room would be the right size for the luncheon. The burning question is, will sixteen-year-old girls regard it as too stuffy for a Sweet Sixteen Party?"

A nasal voice mused, "She is so spoiled, and that is a consideration, ungrateful as she is."

"It would be divine of you to host it here, Darling," her friend exclaimed in a la-de-dah voice. "She should be thrilled a stepmother would even go to the trouble. After all, you're paying her way to come all the way across the country for the weekend, too! Now, you need to get back to your own party upstairs. What a wonderful evening is ahead!"

"Thanks for coming downstairs to inspect the dining room with me, Sylvia. You are such a dearie-dear! How does my hair look?" the nasal voice asked, and then, "I suppose it doesn't matter since I'll be wearing a veil, remember?"

"Of course. You still have your original veil? How sentimental of you to wear it to your renewal ceremony," said the deeper voice.

"Absolutely, I'm wearing *the same veil* I wore on the day Mickey married me, eight years ago. God knows, it's the only thing that still fits me!" Laughter ensued as the ladies exited the restroom.

Perched on the toilet lid inside my stall, I felt my scalp tighten and tingle. Mickey is an unusual name. Mickey had been married eight years. Raymond was playing at "some wedding-type deal" on the eleventh floor for a big shot. Mickey's wife was the stepmother of a sixteen-year-old girl.

Bolting out of the powder room, I stood in the hall looking in both directions for the departed women. Rushing up to the elevator, I spotted them chatting. The doors opened, they stepped inside. I followed.

"Which floor madam?" the elevator operator directed his question to me.

"Uh, eleven?" I suggested weakly.

"Fine, madam. That is a private event this evening; may I see your VIP coin?"

The two ladies swished past me as they got inside. They seemed to smile approvingly at the man as they presented their brass discs, but his eyes fixed on me.

Fishing through my velvet clutch purse I uncovered a half-eaten roll of Tums, matchbooks, and various entertainers' business cards—clearly remnants from other events.

"Eleventh floor, ladies. Sorry ma'am, I need to see your VIP coin before I can permit you to enter the eleventh floor." His voice was officious, as the women peered at me from the corner of the elevator.

"Oh, here it is. Here's my card. I'm entertaining at this party. I am, um, Madam Tanya, The Psychic." Handing him the card, I added, "I'll be doing readings at tonight's event."

The elevator operator looked at the card first, and then at me with suspicion.

"Well, *I think* my event is on the eleventh floor," I added hastily, "It is a big party. I was hired by one the guests to…liven up…the evening with psychic readings." I smiled.

"Well, if you were a psychic, it seems you would *know where* the party is," the redhead remarked in a snarky voice as the elevator door closed and we rose skyward together. Glancing at her friend for support, she cleared her throat and said, "Dear, this is a Marriage Vow Renewal Ceremony and party. I doubt *very* much that a psychic's presence would be required here."

With that, the shorthaired woman with copper hair narrowed her eyes, and stepped off the elevator. Her friend, the brunette, joined her side as the elevator doors closed behind us. Both seemed intent on solving this mystery before rejoining the party.

Stepping further into the room and away from the elevator, I addressed the women.

"Actually, I was hired as a surprise...a gift—to the couple, from one of their guests. The gentleman who hired me thought it would be entertaining for the party, you know, it being New Year's Eve and all. I was told to circulate during the band breaks." I smiled weakly, and handed her the (somewhat worn out) card that read, "Psychic Readings by Madam Tanya."

The elevator doors closed and zoomed away. Standing before the two ladies, who challenged my right to attend this shindig, was bringing on an anxiety volcano. Could this be *Mickey's wife?* Was she the brunette or the redhead?

"Whom do we get to thank for this, ah, unusual gift?" asked the redhead, whose eyebrows seemed to rise off her forehead, punctuating the question.

Would she really call security? I considered mentioning Raymond's name, but I didn't want to get him involved; musicians aren't allowed to have guests at private affairs. Now, having identified myself as Madam Tanya, Helen Owens and her friend were staring at me with skepticism, enjoying their power. I felt like a butterfly in a biology class; with one woman holding tweezers and the other a magnifying glass. With the elevator gone and them blocking the entrance to the party, I had to think fast.

&&&&&&&

Standing still, I tried to act casual as the redhead squinted at my card that read, *"Madam Tanya Psychic— Celestial Readings, Private Parties and By Appointment"*.

"Well, Madam Tanya," she said as she nudged the brunette next to her, "whom do we have to thank for this *Celestial* party gift?"

My face was getting hot, wishing I could freeze this moment and absorb everything in slow motion, but I couldn't. With sensory overload, I was face to face with Mickey's wife and her friend, Sylvia. Matching the voices I figured the redhead was Helen Owens. The appalling circumstance for this party was a future horror to sink in later. Closing my eyes for a moment, I took a chance. "I'm getting something about..." I began haltingly.

"You better not say 'a party about a couple in love,'" Helen challenged. "I want specifics."

"I sense that there is a very beloved, old dog, and you are having trouble releasing him to the afterlife. His name is," I paused for effect, "Chivas Regal?"

"Oh my, Helen, that's your dog's name!" Sylvia exclaimed with astonishment.

"She *is* good!" remarked Helen.

"That's extraordinary, my dear," said Sylvia.

Helen noticed the elevator door open. "Oh my word, look who's finally arriving! That damn Mark, and he looks three sheets to the wind." Mark Goldman and Devin stepped off the elevator.

"Who is the young thing with him? A good-looking boy! Where is the usual hunk..." then, suddenly aware they were speaking in front of me, Helen became quiet.

Adding another layer of artificiality to an already affected speech pattern, she turned to Mark, who had managed to stagger our way. "So nice of you to make it dear, the ceremony is in half an hour." She glanced at her friend, and then leaned into Mickey's agent, frosting her words, "The bar is over there; however, I see you are adept at finding bars on your own."

"Am I late? So sorry, Helen. I know how sentimental you are and how much this day means to you. Has the *Redbook* photographer arrived yet?" With that he grabbed Devin's arm and headed to the bar.

Devin's eyes were large. They pleaded with me to play along as he looked over his shoulder. He was as big a fraud as I was! I had no intention of giving away my true identity any more than he wanted his mom to bust him for not waiting in the hotel room.

"Oh, he is *so intolerable*," gasped Helen through clenched teeth.

"Who do you suppose that young man is?" asked her friend.

"He's a young actor. Your friend met him tonight in the hotel. The actor is new in the business..." I said cryptically using my newly found psychic powers.

"Hmmm, interesting," said Helen. "Well Tanya, go ahead and circulate, don't give anyone bad news." Then, gazing off toward the dance floor, she claimed to no one in particular, "This is going to be my year."

"You *must* do a reading for me!" Sylvia gushed with a new respect and enthusiasm. Then, feeling Helen's tug on her arm, she added, "I mean, after the ceremony."

As the two ladies entered the sea of people, I took in every inch of Mickey's wife. She must have a lot on her mind, to not be amazed when a perfect stranger knew her dog's name and that it was dying. Perhaps she assumed I was briefed on their background.

Helen Owens was poised and immaculately groomed, I'll give her that. She seemed to move around the room smoothly and at the same time stiff. Like an upright piano on casters. She looked so conservative; it wasn't her age that made her a lady instead of a chick, it was her style. One could imagine her walk-in closet being full of beige and white. She was attractive, it could be said, but looked more like a banker's wife, than that of an artist. Whereas Mickey was funny, casual and spontaneous, she was measured and controlled. She spoke in an exacting, calculated way. Arrogantly, she was moving through the room like a giant, puffy poodle at a dog show. She was rude to me and had tried to throw me out of the party! Fortunately, the psychic trick bought me time to spy on them. Oh, if she only knew, I thought shaking my head. In the back of my mind, I knew I should be looking for Mickey to kill him, but I couldn't take my eyes off of his wife, following her at a safe distance.

As I snatched a champagne flute off the tray of a passing waiter, I heard my cell phone ring from inside my purse. Glancing at the number, I saw it was Mickey.

&&&&&&&

DECEMBER 31st, 11:15 p.m.

After guzzling cocktails like a farmhand downs lemonade, Devin was feeling pretty heady. This being his first adult party, he had succumbed to the lure of the open bar. Combined with the rich dinner and desserts he had eaten, his stomach was cued to purge. He darted into the men's room and entered a stall whimpering, "Oh no, I gotta hurl," for the second time of the evening. This time it wasn't the bright green hue of Nyquil, it was a Vodka Seven, conspiring with quail egg and caviar. He was sitting on the lid of the toilet seat, in the last stall of the restroom, wiping his mouth, when he heard the voice of a man entering the men's room.

"I love you, Angel, you just have to trust me on this. *It's for her*—her publicist scheduled it. Baby, baby, baby, don't *say that*. I love you, Earth Angel. You're my Christmas. This vow nonsense doesn't mean *anything*. It's nothing!"

Devin stumbled out of the stall and exchanged glances with the man clutching the cell phone in the corner. Obviously surprised that he wasn't alone, Mickey met Devin's eyes head on, then he turned into the phone and added, "I can't talk here, call me back in five minutes." Mickey sped out of the restroom quickly and Devin was back in his own spinning world. Confused and moaning, he staggered to the sink to wash up.

Re-entering the party, Devin tried to get his bearings when, again, he tasted the rush of stale booze rising up. Darting into a service kitchen door and hearing the noisy preparation inside, he turned right and ran down a narrow hall, entering a door that had been left slightly open. The linen supply room had aisles of shelves. His relief at finding a hiding place was surpassed by the curious sound of a woman crying on the other side of the large shelf of linens. Holding still to listen a moment, he heard the voice say, "You show me no respect! How could you go along with this? This...sham! It is so disrespectful to me. *That's* your excuse? I am *so* hurt. *How could you do this?*"

****

Bolting around the shelves, Devin found me leaning into a corner of the small room, my face to the wall. Seized with emotion, Devin approached my trembling shoulders and spun me around, "Mom?"

I immediately hung up the phone and dropped my arm, awash with sorrow and new guilt. Devin hugged my shaking frame with a bony embrace.

"Mom! Mom, don't be sad. Don't cry. Who was...?" Suddenly, pushing me aside, he stepped forward and threw up on the freshly laundered pink tablecloths stacked on the table. Grabbing a folded napkin, I wiped his face, feeling grateful his suit had survived yet another putrid geyser.

201

Looking around at the foul smelling mess dripping off the linens, Devin croaked out, "I'm sorry, Mom. I had to do that."

"Hey, I don't care if you puke *all over* this place. Let's just get out of here without being seen."

Peeking out of the linen supply room, I saw the narrow hall was empty. I grabbed my son's hand and led the escape down the hall, through the service kitchen and back out to the fringes of the party in session. Once we were safely against a wall, we stopped and looked at each other.

"Wow. Devin, go in the bathroom and wash your mouth and face and I'll do the same thing—oh, and I guess I should find you some soda water." We were standing in the back of the room away from the party, and I was trying to scout out a bar.

"First, I've gotta do this, Mom." Devin grabbed my cell phone and pushed the redial button.

"Veronica, listen to me!" a voice answered on the first ring.

"No dude, you *listen to me*! I don't know who you are, I only know you made my mom cry, and nobody can do that—well, no one but me. Well, I mean…she's a really good person and she don't deserve any more grief *from you,* asshole! I don't know who you are, but you watch out, there's gonna be trouble now—with me, dude!" After screaming his message, he clicked the phone shut and handed it to me, smiling.

Just then the lights flickered off and on. A man in a tuxedo walked past us playing chimes to signal the event was about to take place. An announcer requested that the guests take their seats.

Raymond's resonant classical guitar filled the air with Beethoven's *Ode to Joy.*

The marriage vow renewal ceremony had begun.

&&&&&&&

The Ceremony

Devin took an aisle seat on the back row of chairs facing the flowered canopy. After draining a glass of water, he was starting to feel better. With mild interest he noticed his dad for the first time. Raymond was playing guitar with his quartet to the left side of the wedding pulpit at the front of the room.

Raymond began playing the traditional prelude music, and soon switched over to the specific music charts furnished by Helen Owens. Up until this point, this had been like any other job for Raymond. Since his natural curiosity did not extend to things beyond himself, it wasn't surprising he didn't scan the room for faces, perhaps spotting his son or wife in the gathering of 200 guests. In all fairness, both his family members *had* spent the bulk of the evening in the bathrooms and linen closet. Raymond was one part bored, and two parts resentful upon realizing the host of the evening's party was a celebrated singer /songwriter.

This Owens guy must be doing well to rent out this banquet room and floor of suites for one night, Raymond thought to himself as he plucked the strings of his Stradivarius. It was particularly irksome to the classical guitarist to not be able to choose the material. He was hired to play a lengthy medley of Mickey's pop hits. Helen Owens had given the charts of her husband's compositions to the banquet manager handling the event, who passed it on to the band leader hired by the hotel.

Helen's musical surprise was unbeknownst to Mickey. As he stood waiting uncomfortably at the front of the room, Mickey viewed the medley of songs as an unending tribute of shameless self-promotion. His embarrassment turned to anger as he feigned a calm exterior. With his face getting hotter he found it difficult to find a place to rest his anxious gaze, with everyone watching him. Faces from his professional life and people he hadn't seen in years were attentive and still. The party atmosphere had vanished and was replaced by a solemn respect for the songs Mickey Owens had penned over a lifetime. The rows of chairs represented an elite community, assembled now to witness Helen's slow journey up the aisle.

The musicians played well, but just when the discomfort of one song ended, another one began. The notes formed a daisy chain of memories through the years. His whole musical life was now brilliantly strung together in this interminably long musical tribute. Each song represented a different era. The first hit songs were written and recorded when he was a young man married to Debbie; when they had their two children. Monetary success led to years of drug abuse and excess. The songs from that period were included, too, and those rock solid hits sounded watered down now with tonight's semi-classical arrangements, causing Mickey to wince.

Next were songs written for movies. These musical reminders earmarked the last eight years with Helen. It was clear now, how "right" it seemed to have found a secure nest on which to rest after all the high flying. Hidden in the soft nest was a rusty, metal trap thwarting any creative freedom, and keeping him immobile. Where did the safe sanctuary end and the prison of Helen's control begin? Her constant hovering over him was suffocating. He felt the walls were closing in on him. At what point had he lost control? He reached under his coat to feel his heart pounding. He thought this was just going to be a New Year's party with friends. A few hours ago Helen announced the evening included a marriage vow renewal, as a surprise. This was probably the idiotic suggestion of their couples' therapist, he thought, as he spotted her face beaming in the crowd. He pulled a handkerchief from his pocket to wipe away the perspiration beading on his forehead. How long an entrance does his goddamned wife need, he wondered to himself as he felt all eyes upon him.

The phone call to Veronica was a catastrophic disaster. He even had a cute poem memorized for their New Year's Eve toast, but never got to it. What about that kid— *yelling at him?* Where did that come from? What on earth were the chances of her showing up? No, things had not gone well at all and her son was a wild card. This was not dignified and now he just wanted the night to end with no more surprises. Helen's instructing the musician to play all these songs made his stomach queasy. He felt himself shrinking every time another hit segued into the medley.

Why was Helen always in control of his life? Why was she constantly promoting him? Why was their life one long press release, whenever she was involved? What was her obsession with the A List? This party was just an excuse to invite famous people whom he hadn't seen in years. Who was she kidding? She knew he wouldn't go along with this, and that's why the vows renewal was a surprise. What was he doing up here? Did regret for the choices he'd made during the drug years leave him too crippled to trust decision-making now? Should he stand up to Helen and say "no" to this charade, he wondered. Could he? Or, was it his fate to always doubt his own judgment? Was he the monkey or the organ grinder in this cheap sideshow for *Redbook Magazine?* Mickey felt his chest tighten.

****

"No shit! Is *that* the dude getting married up there?" Devin asked Mark in a stage whisper, after sliding into the seat next to him.

"Yes, that's my client, Mickey Owens," Mark said wearily.

"That's cold if he's getting married. Is he?" Devin asked incredulously.

"Yes. To his same wife, actually."

"Wow. That's whack. Cuz he's playin' some chick called Earth Angel and they were beefing on the phone a few minutes ago!" Devin said in a voice loud enough to draw the attention of the row in front of him.

"What do you mean?" Mark asked.

Pointing at Mickey, Devin said, "Yo, dude, really, I heard *that* guy talking in the bathroom. He was telling somebody named, uh, Angel, that he loved her and all this mushy crap, for real, about 10 minutes ago."

"The person was in the bathroom *with him*?" Mark asked.

"Shhh, please, they're ready to begin," reproached a woman from the row ahead of them.

"Do they do that deal, like in the movies, where if someone says it's bunk, they don't go through with this janky marriage?" Devin asked Mark undeterred by the heads turning. "Like someone calls out to stop it?"

"Well, I guess we'll just have to see," Mark remarked, still lost in the translation of the last few exchanges.

He was in the business long enough to know that any scandal involving clients wasn't always a bad thing. If the kid was onto something, there could well be a scandal surrounding Mickey's marriage. He didn't care. He regarded Helen as a self-righteous priss anyway, and felt no loyalty either way. He idly wondered what effect having been gay played in his lack of reverence for the occasion. He remembered Kevin with a twinge. At least he showed up Kevin by finding a younger date at the last minute. This Devin kid was hard to keep track of all night, but now, Mark wondered, had he heard something interesting?

As Helen paraded slowly down the aisle, she acted more the monarch at a coronation ceremony than a bride. She turned her stately head toward the flashing bulb of the photographer walking backward up the aisle in front of her.

A woman swooped in beside Mark, and with a sweet smile, informed him that he was in her seat. Before he could respond, she pulled his arm into the next empty chair, and plunked herself between him and Devin.

"Hi, I'm Pam. I couldn't help overhearing. You overheard Mickey Owens ten minutes ago? Saying?"

"Oh wow. Are you Angel? Sorry to dime you out... that was harsh, ma'am. I heard him saying he loved you on the phone, and all that."

"Oh, it's not me sweetheart, thank you. But where *was* Angel? You just heard him talking?" cooed the reporter from *Redbook,* leaning in closer. "What did you hear, *exactly?*"

&&&&&&&

DECEMBER 31ST 11:50 p.m.

After Gwendolyn's hasty exit, Simon Bestep looked at his watch; it was 11:50 p.m. Due to a "mix up with Chad's transportation back to school" she was called away to make new arrangements. Regretfully, she explained she would see Simon in the morning, and kissed his cheek good night.

Setting down the crystal glass flute, he rose from the empty table and walked toward the exit, satisfied that the dinner and dancing had made for a grand evening. Gwendolyn was not as articulate as her emails had indicated, but holding her delicate figure in a waltz was certainly a beautiful new entry into what had been a closed file on his deceased wife.

Leaving the lively music and atmosphere of the dining room to return to his suite, Simon felt trepidation about the next phase of tonight's entertainment. This anxiety was heightened as two burly paramedics rushed past him in the hall, heading toward the elevator. They almost knocked him down, carrying the heavy equipment. Personalizing the unnerving rudeness, Simon wondered what was ahead of him this evening, and felt a twinge of comfort knowing there were medical experts in close proximity.

When the elevator returned to the lobby, he stepped inside and pressed the button for the penthouse. As the metal cube rose, he caught his reflection in the brass panels. He looked good in his tuxedo, he reckoned, and tonight he had enjoyed the pleasure of a beautiful woman for the first time in years. Straightening his tie, he mentally prepared for another beautiful surprise. Simon whistled his favorite tune, *"Young at Heart."*

Slipping the plastic card key inside the lock, he heard the phone ringing.

"Yes, hello, Simon here."

"Simon? *Oh, Simon,"* gushed the voice on the line. "This is Tiffany. Oh honey, I have to apologize…Simon."

"Oh and how is that?"

"Well, I know how much we used to like this hotel," she giggled, "and I know we haven't seen each other in a long time, but I was feeling all, well, missing you…so I took a chance coming here tonight. I'm in the hotel right now—actually. Simon, I hoped you'd be alone and want to see me, too. We were such good lovers together—do you think I could come up? One last time for old times sake—Oh shit! That's hot! Goddammit!!"

There was a loud crash, as Tiffany's foot accidentally kicked over a lamp. By lying on her back she was able to command a deeper more sultry voice, but absent-mindedly batting her right foot on the fringe of the hotel lamp shade proved disastrous. Her toe brushed the hot bulb, causing her foot to jerk and accidentally kick it over.

"Now young lady, there is no cause to use that language! What was that crashing sound?"

Tiffany regained her composure quickly, saying softly, "I told you I've been a *bad girl*. Now, can I come up?" She grabbed a towel and bit down hard to quell the pain.

"I don't like profanity. There will be none of that. What was that loud sound I just heard?" Simon asked sternly.

"The lamp broke. I guess you better put me over your knee and spank my bare ass! My toe was playing with the fringe, oh, I was just lying on my back thinkin' about you, honey, when my foot hit the lamp shade, then that darn hot bulb. Anyway, why are we talking about that? I'm close by and hot to see you again. Oh, *where's that ice bucket?*" she said, waving her foot in painful agitation.

"I have an ice bucket filled," Simon said.

"I'm so sorry I cursed, Simon. I won't do that again—it's just that now I have an owie–zowie. If you only saw that lamp go over! Whew! Well, what should we do?

"I'm in the penthouse," he said following a pause.

****

At 1:15 a.m. there was a tap on the penthouse door.

"Room service, sir," the night waiter announced.

The door opened and the waiter scanned the place for a spot to park the room service cart that was piled with dishes of ice cream and cakes resting on doilies. He wheeled it to the side of the bed next to a girl playing a TV video game with one foot in an ice bucket.

"Nice room, sir." Referring to the scented candles and romantic accessories, the waiter smiled broadly, then caught himself for being too familiar and looked down at the cart. "Is right here okay, sir?"

"Yes, that will do."

"Thank God there's more ice," the girl said, barely looking up. "C'mon Simon, it's your turn."

"Duke Nukem calls," Simon said gaily to the screen, and then turning to the waiter, "My son Chad used to be pretty good at these video games, but it wasn't until tonight that I tried them myself."

"Yeah, Chad was damn good. Oops." Tiffany's poor choice of words was not heard, because the waiter blurted out, "I'm the Duke Nuke champ in my apartment building, sir." Suddenly mindful of interrupting a guest, the waiter slipped into exaggerated stiffness. Simon handed him a $20 tip before he exited the room.

"Hey Simon, thanks for the desserts, doll," Tiffany said, removing her foot from the bucket, dabbing it on a towel on the floor and hobbling the few steps toward the cart of sweets.

"Well Tiffany, this has been quite a night. Why not top it off with ice cream and cappuccino cheesecake? And, of course you, my lovely." Pausing a moment, "Who am I leaving out?"

"Duke!" they said in unison, and laughed. Simon picked up his controller and was quickly absorbed in the video game.

"You know what I think?" Tiffany offered, "I think our lovemaking was so good, *the neighbors* had a cigarette."

"We weren't that loud, were we?" Simon whispered, a smile taking shape. "Well, if we were, then to heck with them!" They giggled as he dropped the controller on the floor in reckless abandon and grabbed her.

"You wanted a little sugar, *did you*?" Simon said playfully.

"Yes, why not? It's a new year and time for more sweets and video games and I might be licking you, if you're in front of that cart I'm headed for," she said, delicately lifting his hands off her waist and brushing past him. Seeing Simon's thin body wrapped up in a plush hotel robe, controller in his hand, eyes glued to the screen had lit a spark of affection for this genteel man – he enjoyed the game as much as she did. This was definitely not the usual trick.

Plunging her spoon into the melting ice cream, she said, "This is the strangest, safest, funniest," looking around the room, "most decorated," taking a bite of the ice cream, "sweetest ...most toe-burning-est..."

"*Simonest,*" Simon said.

"*Simonist definitely*, New Year's Eve party I've ever been to. I love it!" She said, spearing a triangle of cheesecake with her fork. "Thanks for having me stay, doll, and teaching me to clean up my language. Simon, you know where heck is? It's where people go who don't believe in gosh."

"Happy New Year, Darling!" Simon said with a hearty laugh, staring at the TV screen and waving the game controller over his head.

&&&&&&&&

DECEMBER 31ˢᵀ

Midnight

When Mickey collapsed the room became silent. Raymond stopped playing, Helen stopped walking, and Devin stopped updating the reporter with whispered details leading up to the ceremony. Mickey's best friend, John, who was presiding over the ceremony, asked in an anxious voice, "Is there a doctor? Someone? *A nurse, a medic* in the house?"

"I'm a doctor!" I said as I rushed from the back of the room and confidently began CPR on the still body stretched out on the flowered carpet. I put my hand inside his wrist to feel his pulse and then my head on his chest to listen. I tilted his lifeless head back and without hesitation, I pinched his nose and breathed into his mouth a slow, measured breath of life—lasting seven seconds. Then, I pressed on his chest methodically, counting five thrusts, and gently leaning over him again, with my lips on his, I began the second series of life-saving measures.

John, although relieved that this emergency seemed to be handled for the moment, felt the need to be in charge again, prompting him to say, "Thank God... someone has called 911." Turning to me, he said gently, "Thanks for all you're doing, but uh, *who are you*? You're a doctor? I didn't get your name."

Ignoring the question I continued fighting for his life. Those close to the scene observed tears falling on Mickey's face and tuxedo.

The guests began to whisper among themselves and move in closer. John spoke louder this time, "I repeat, where is it that you practice, Doctor? Pardon me, I didn't catch your name?"

Peeking out from Sylvia's shoulder, Helen shrieked, "Wait! That's Madam Tanya, *the—psychic!"*

"No—it's Veronica Bennett, the talent booker!" Raymond's voice boomed sternly.

"Mom?" Devin yelled from the back row.

Unconcerned with the identity collision around me, I kept pressing and breathing life into my lover. Too worried to pause, I just kept repeating the pattern of CPR I had learned years ago as a summer lifeguard. Holding the back of his head, I whispered to him and pleaded, "Mickey, Mickey, *you can do it! Breathe baby*, I'm right here." In a tiny voice I squeaked, "No Mickey, don't die! I can't lose you now. Breathe one time, a baby breath, try...come on, Mickey, try!" Oblivious to the stares and whispers, I diligently kept pressing on his chest in a steady rhythm and breathing into his mouth.

"Get AWAY from my husband!" commanded Helen. "What's taking the paramedics so long?"

John was exasperated when he put his arm around her shoulder and said, "Now, Helen, dear, I know how upsetting this must be for you... but this woman seems to know what she's doing, so is it wise to...?"

Helen dropped to her knees, quickly adjusting her dress to cover her legs in the ungainly position, and shrilly barked, "Get off him, I say!"

Helen began yanking at my arm, and John interceded by unfolding her clenched fingers from my arm. When I refused to move, Helen had to save face by shouting out another command to someone clearly on tonight's payroll. Her arm swung up like a jackknife, and pointing at Raymond from her spot on the floor, she ordered, "You! Play something right now!" A ripple of murmurs spread from the inner to the outer circle of guests surrounding Mickey and his *Doctor*.

Not looking up and undaunted by the growing hysteria of Helen Owens, I continued to work tirelessly on the still body.

Raymond, always the professional, complied with the ghastly demand and began playing a stirring rendition of the first thing that popped into his mind, *What's It All About, Alfie?*

"Well, we need music to fill *all* the moments of our lives," Helen said, sniffing. "Don't look at me like that," she added defensively, responding to the wide-eyed stares of Hollywood's elite gathered at her husband's feet.

"Mickey, it's me, Veronica. *You can do it*. Come on! Choose life!" With tears splashing on his pale face I pleaded, "Don't give up, baby, it'll be all right. *We'll be* okay through all this."

It's impossible to know if it was Heaven's Gate or the photographer's flash, but before Mickey's frail spirit traveled toward the light he opened his eyes and seemed to smile as he spoke his last two words, "*My Angel.*"

****

When the paramedics burst onto the scene, they saw a dead man in the arms of two weeping women, and in true Hollywood tradition, music was playing. The sound track to Mickey Owens's death was a breathtaking classical guitar arrangement featuring Raymond's interpretation of *Alfie*. There were wails of sorrow coming from the two women, each holding and kissing one hand, amidst other random whimpers from various corners of the room. The guitar's

213

chordal melodies added a sad and haunting ambience which lay heavily on the guests, stunned into silence

By coincidence, the composers of the song were in attendance. Witnessing their friend's cardiac arrest, Burt Bacharach and Hal David, for reasons they didn't understand, gravitated toward Raymond's band. While Burt sadly sang the words, Hal stood with his arm around him for the first time in memory. The successful songwriting team hadn't done a song together in years, but at this moment the old friendship surfaced once again, as life surrendered to death.

Helen insisted, "Music is to fill *all areas* of our lives," and she was right. Guests felt helpless, caught in the tragedy of a man's life ending before their eyes, several guests joined in singing the ballad with a touching reverence

> *What's it all about, Alfie?*
> *Is it just for the moment we live?*
> *What's it all about when you sort it out, Alfie?*
> *Are we meant to take more, than we give?*
>
> *I believe in love, Alfie,*
> *Without true love we just exist.*
> *Until you've found the love you've missed*
> *you're nothing, Alfie.*
> *When you walk, let your heart lead the way*
> *and you'll find love any day, Alfie."*

None of the guests will ever forget that New Year's Eve and the death of Mickey Owens at midnight.

****

Running out of the ballroom fueled on adrenaline, I grabbed my son's hand. There would be an eternity to grieve my lover's death—but, for the next ten minutes I had to hold it together. *I only have to be normal for ten minutes. I only have to get through the next ten minutes...* was my mantra.

"Devin, let's not talk."

"Sure, Mom," he said. We were late meeting Janna in the lobby for Devin's ride home. She had been sitting primly in the wing-backed chair since 11:45, the appointed time. Devin was still "processing" the first adult cocktail party he had ever attended. It must have been similar to Alice's Adventures in *Through The Looking Glass*. Since we both had so much to explain, I suppose we both could have begun with, "What were *you* doing there? Or, who were you supposed to be?" But with an agreement to *not go there*, we rode down the elevator in silence.

As we walked briskly down the carpeted corridor, past hotel security, paramedics and curious partygoers, Devin finally broke the strained silence.

"Weird, huh?"

"Look honey, when Dad gets home and asks you about tonight, you just tell him you're sleeping and can't talk. Let's see, hmm, he has to break down his equipment and won't be back for at least an hour after you're home. You know how to be rude. If he wakes you up tonight or in the morning with questions—just say you're sleeping. Here's my cell phone. Just take it and leave it on the dining room table. That way he'll see he can't call me. Do that for me."

"Do I get paid for that acting job, too?" he asked with a vexing grin.

"Shut up, Devin," I hissed at his brazen question.

"Hello Janna," I said in a high-pitched voice accented by a weak smile.

"What a fuss! Something's going on; I saw someone carried out on a stretcher! Veronica? You look upset. Are you all right?"

"Yes. Uh, no. Sorry we're late," I said, then with the tight jaws of a ventriloquist I added, "Devin got caught on the wrong floor."

"Well, let's go, Precious. You must be sleepy; it's after twelve." Janna said tussling his hair. Devin rolled his eyes at the notion of midnight being *late*, and said, "Peace out, Mom."

We hugged a long, tight hug and I said, softly, "Devin, honey, thanks for standing up for me, uh a while ago on the phone. I noticed that, even in the craziness." We squeezed each other, let go and then waved good bye.

Janna walked purposefully toward the valet parking podium, with Devin behind her. Looking over his shoulder, Devin's and my eyes locked and we simultaneously made a "*psss*" sound, and shook our heads. Sometimes my family and friends need odd sounds to explain the unexplainable.

When we fled the ballroom Raymond was still on the bandstand, so amidst the chaos, he never got any explanation. I left a message on his voice mail saying I would be home after brunch with the client and then, explain everything. That had been the original plan anyway. Plan? *Original plan?* Bilking a millionaire sounded so childish now, I thought with an aching heart.

****

My room became available at midnight, once Tiffany limped up to Simon's Penthouse. Unlocking the door, I let out a sigh of relief to be alone at last. The makeshift green room for the cast would now be a living tomb for me; a place to bury myself till dawn. With Mickey gone forever, I barely noticed the messy glasses, empty bottles, full ashtrays and clothes strewn all over. Once inside, I stepped over the broken glass on the floor from a lamp overturned. The bathroom light cast a white beam toward my bed.

I sat down and picked up the phone, instructing the desk to hold all calls. Gratefully, Raymond didn't know my room number, and I knew the front desk wouldn't give out a guest's room number at gun-point, if Raymond started making a scene trying to locate me. Kicking off my shoes, I got under the covers still wearing my cocktail dress and sank into a mental abyss that left me numb until daybreak.

The love of my life dying in my arms while my husband played beautiful, classical guitar twenty feet away was an exquisite irony. Beyond the grief and crippling loss, was a small blessing. Coming to his rescue, I was the one in the crowd who showed strength, then tenderness, at one of the most intimate and personal moments two people can share. Our guarded secret was played out for the world to see and in the end, he *was mine*. He had been my hero, saving me from my lonely life, and in the end, I might have been his hero, saving him from death. But I failed. Now, my only comfort is that our eyes had locked in a gaze, a last embrace in his final moment. He looked *at me and said good bye.* I had that.

"*We had no future,*" I cried into the wet pillow. It was 5:07 a.m. and all I could think of was my begging him *to choose life*. Perhaps he chose death. Heart failure? Did life's lessons have to be *so literal*?

&&&&&&&

JANUARY 1ST, 11:00 a.m.

Since I lost the power to pretend, there could ever be a happy ending, that bell is rung out— that song is sung out. He was the life that I led. He was my last chance for happiness, So, God, give me strength.

Elvis Costello
God Give Me Strength

As in a trance, I walked down the long, sunny hallway en route to the gazebo where the champagne brunch was in progress. The distant voices of happy chatter floated over my despair. After crying all night there wasn't a tear left to fall. Taking in a shallow gasp of air and exhaling with a frozen smile, I reminded myself that I only had to get through the next couple hours. Again, my mantra from last night was in use. *I only have to act normal for two hours...I only have to get through two hours...*

It suddenly occurred to me they may be aware of what happened in the hotel last night. Even so, they couldn't possibly connect me with Mickey Owens's passing. Was it in the news? Considering announcements between descriptions of marching bands and floats on the morning broadcast of the Rose Parade, I was getting a new breed of headache.

What possible horror awaited me with Bestep's lawyer and this cryptic meeting? I wondered. Emotionally flat, I felt numb to all of life's *future* disappointments too; the next bomb would drop following brunch, I imagined.

No matter what happened, I'd be home by about 3:00 p.m. then it would be business as usual, except for new fire works. I could anticipate Raymond and Devin's Q & A. session. Yes, the House of Overreaction would be most curious about my claim to be a doctor, and my relation to the patient, I thought, sourly.

Slowing my steps, I deliberately inhaled the tranquility around me. Here in the garden, everything was pastel, sweet and orderly. People spoke in lowered voices, and excused themselves if they passed by too closely, infringing on someone's personal space. I loved that the servers were distant and polite. Might I take some courtesy to go, perhaps a small ration to savor later in my foxhole at home? *Home*— the thought of it jabbed me in the gut. "Just get through these couple hours," I scolded myself, coaxing my tired brain to perform.

As I was shown to my table, I impersonated someone whose life was in order. My life had become a pinball shot out of control by a swinging wedge, only to roll back down and be spun out again in a new direction. Today's pinball game was *Widow With No Place To Grieve*.

"Good morning, Veronica! Oh, join us, join us, your chair is waiting." Simon Bestep's voice sounded energetically charged, which was unusual.

"Good morning! Oh, nice sunglasses, Veronica," Janna chirped.

"Hard night?" Simon chuckled.

You could say that, I thought and caught myself wincing. "Oh, actually, thank you for noticing. These shades are new," I smiled and adjusted them on my nose, "It seems so bright outside."

"Allow me to introduce the eminent Mr. Edgar Freis. This is Veronica Bennett," he said turning to me. "She is an event planner, and talent agent, providing entertainment for many events large and small." We all shook hands and the men sat down.

Edgar Freis didn't look as stern as I imagined. He looked like the actor Gene Hackman, relaxing on the set in between shoots of a police drama.

"You look lovely this morning, Gwendolyn," I observed.

"Thank you. We're just sorry you didn't join us earlier for this fabulous brunch," she said.

I murmured some response about not being a morning person, what an extraordinary ice sculpture, delicious aromas, and then spent a few tedious moments concentrating on steadying my hand as I leaned in to unite my lips with the rim of my coffee cup.

"Do you have pets yourself, Mr. Freis?" Gwendolyn asked, apparently resuming a prior conversation, since it seemed like an odd opening remark.

"Well, no I don't, Gwendolyn, and please call me Edgar."

"Do you find your work is mostly seasonal?" Gwendolyn continued.

"I'm busy all year round with the quarterlies," Edgar said with a nod.

"Well, I think it is just marvelous what you do. The animals I've seen are so life-like," Gwendolyn said agreeably.

"Excuse me dear, what animals? Life-like?" Edgar bobbed his head back, as if trying to put Gwendolyn in focus.

"Well, I appreciate the life-like qualities of the animals I've seen, preserved. You being a taxidermist..." Gwendolyn said slowly.

"What?" Edgar said, "When you asked what I did, I said, 'tax attorney,' *not taxidermy!"*

The table erupted in good-natured laughter, with Simon slapping his attorney's back, and Gwendolyn shyly covering her smile. How pleasant it was to see them all getting along. The unassuming and unsophisticated beauty had these two worldly men rather captivated, it would appear. Janna was advised to stay "in the present" at all times, to comment on the surroundings and avoid anything which may take her out of Gwendolyn's character. Regretfully, she must have strayed from the plan; the next comment alarmed me.

"We've been getting quite an education about the Mormon faith," Simon said, and nodded appreciatively in Gwendolyn's direction.

"Oh. Gee, Mr. Freis, now that we know you aren't a taxidermist, and you are a tax attorney, I hope you have a great year! Tax season is coming up and well, oh...." I didn't know where this sentence was headed, but I had to shift the conversation since Gwendolyn was starting to sound like Janna.

"I would like to propose a toast to start off the New Year!" I recovered. "The past is history, tomorrow a mystery, this moment is a gift and that's why it's called 'the present.'" Raising my glass of water, I stared at Gwendolyn when I said "the present." Gwendolyn raised her glass of orange juice and nodded at me, getting my message to stay on track. The men held their champagne flutes in the air as we clinked in agreement and sipped. Cynically, it occurred to me a more fitting quote would be, "cheap entertainment isn't always inexpensive." But, I kept that to myself.

While the three chatted like old friends, I was able to withdraw again, recalling the debacle last night. How could Mickey go along with that sham? Could our affair have survived *that?* Was this affair one-sided? While I created a paper moon for Simon Bestep's fantasy date, perhaps my own love affair was the *real* illusion. Perhaps Mickey loved his wife, and just wanted extra sex. Yet, the love letters were inspired. Those thoughts couldn't just occur to him—if they weren't true. I'm prettier than his wife and easily more fun. *He is a writer,* my busy head screamed.

"Now it's your turn, Simon. A quote for the New Year, please!" I said suddenly, in an effort to calm the dialogue-taking place in my head.

"All right," after thinking a moment he cleared his throat and began. "Work like you don't need the money, love like you've never been hurt and dance like nobody's watching." With raised glass in hand he seemed pleased with himself, and looked around the table for a consensus of approval. We all nodded vigorously and smiled as we toasted again.

Then, turning to Gwendolyn, Simon said softly, "My dear, we did some great dancing last night, wouldn't you say?"

"Oh yes, you have always been a wonderful dancer," Gwendolyn cooed.

"My dear, you are a deep one. Do share your favorite quote, something to usher us into the New Year with success. Come on, Gwenny. Come on," Simon encouraged.

"Hmm, I would have to say that you three know more about success than I do," she said with a demure smile.

Edgar encouraged her with a waving-to-himself type gesture. "Come on, come on, teach us something, oh modest one."

"I suppose my thoughts about the New Year and success are the same as Ralph Waldo Emerson's. Are you sure you want to hear it? It's a nice definition of success. Oh, I guess I memorized it some years ago.

To laugh often and much; to win the respect of intel-
ligent people, and the affection of children; to earn the
appreciation of honest critics and endure the betrayal of
false friends; to appreciate beauty, to find the best in others;
to leave the world a bit better, whether by a healthy child, a
garden patch or a redeemed social condition; to know even
one life has breathed easier because you have lived...this is
to have succeeded."

Gwendolyn's toast was delivered in a clear, sweet and convincing voice. The words left her mouth effortlessly, as if she were speaking off the top of her head. We three self-proclaimed "successful people" sat at the garden table quietly reflecting.

More pleasantries and then amid a flurry of embraces, Gwendolyn bid us good-bye and the gentlemen guided me up from the table toward the library for our discussion.

&&&&&&&

JANUARY 1ST, 1:00 p.m.

The Library was the hotel's conservative lounge. One imagined it had been the center of robust cigar smoking and expensive brandy consumption in an earlier time. Today, we sat amidst the dark paneled walls surrounded by paintings of freckled hunting dogs. Our aromatic coffee was delivered by a silent waiter, whose uniform was so starched he seemed brittle.

"Now that it's just the three of us," Simon said, as he gently replaced the china cup to its saucer, "we can talk about the business matter I've been alluding to with respect to my attorney, Edgar. This won't take long. We have a game to watch and it's starting soon."

Edgar leaned forward and looked earnestly into my eyes. "I'm a tax attorney, and I'm also partners with my brother in a publishing house called Kendal Street Press. Have you heard of it?"

"No," I answered softly.

"Being an avid reader, the last few years I've become more involved working as literary counsel for that publishing house. I work with agents, and make deals for writers who don't have agents; at any rate, my brother and I secure books to be published by Kendal Street Press. When I see something I like, it gets published. Simon has given me a stack of love-letters that he calls 'Periwinkle Promises.'"

I gasped and felt my face get hot. I looked at Simon; he narrowed one eye, and nodded, holding up a thumb. Edgar continued.

"I love football more than anything so I'm going to get directly to the point. There was a little book out a few years ago, *The Bridges of Madison County*. It seems people like to read love stories, and the prose in that book inspired a few books of contemporary romance poems. That is a genre that we at Kendal want to tap into. I read the letters Simon got from Gwendolyn and frankly, I think we have something here. He and I have been friends for years, and he felt at liberty to share them with me. Simon has informed me you are the author."

I felt myself sink into the overstuffed chair. Gripping the leather arms, I hoped it would hold me.

"I don't know what the circumstances are, but if you grant me permission to go forward with publishing the letters into a book, well, we may all be quite successful with it."

Turning to Simon, he said, "You suggested the name 'Periwinkle Promises,' is that right?"

"Yes, it refers to the seldom-seen color periwinkle. When added to one's 'life palette'—to extend the meta-phor—the landscape of one's life is enhanced by the new shade. It's subtle yet vivid. Simply put, periwinkle is a shade of violet and gray that not everyone has seen," Simon explained.

"A color that didn't exist before but the awareness of it enhances and completes the picture," I said slowly, trying to pluck words from the air.

"Periwinkle? Could it be the color that bees see? The hue of blue that indicates which flowers to pollinate?" Edgar asked.

"I don't know," I said. "It is blue, violet and gray. Maybe it is the bees' color," I said with a shrug.

Looking at his watch with tempered annoyance, Edgar Freis sighed and sat up straight. "How does a book advance of, say, $20,000 sound to you, Ms. Bennett?"

"Okay. Um, very good," I said, feeling suddenly shy.

"I like this girl, Simon. She knows a good deal when she hears one. It appears the letters are all ready, unless you have others to contribute." I nodded and slightly shrugged, like a mute. He continued, "If it's popular and goes into another printing, we'll have this meeting again. Simon has generously paid my commission, so the $20,000 advance is free and clear. Now, I have some ale to drink and some last minute wagering on the Rose Bowl."

Standing up with a slight bow, he continued, "Thank you, Miss Bennett, for your time. Here is my card. I will have the paperwork sent to your office. Do you have legal counsel? "

I shook my head no.

"Have an attorney look it over, if you agree to the terms, sign it, return it to my office and the check will follow within a month," Edgar said, standing up. Simon also stood up and slapped Edgar's back as he beamed a smile in my direction.

"Thank you for the interest in the letters," I said. "The book deal, uh, opportunity, sounds like a dream come true, very generous. Please forgive me if I stay right here and don't walk you out?"

"Fine, fine. Let's talk about success again next year," he said formally. "After all, *I am* a businessman," and, as if his inner-child just peeked out a window, he winked. "Oh, I have a good feeling about this one, Simon!" he added, tossing some bills on the table to cover the tab.

It wasn't clear if "this one" referred to the book or me, but I was in agreement, nodding with wide-eyed amazement.

"Good day." He shook my hand, bowed slightly and turned to leave.

"I'll join you in a moment, Edgar," Simon said.

Edgar made his way across the library, then turned around to face me with a smile and said, "Happy New Year, Ms. Bennett!"

Simon lingered behind to hand me the envelope with the final $15,000 payment.

"Thank you, dear. I now have wonderful new memories to add to my old ones. It was my pleasure to introduce you to Edgar and this fine opportunity; I hoped you wouldn't mind," Simon said, smiling.

"What did you tell him? How did you say you acquired those letters? You didn't mind telling him about the fantasy date?" I asked.

"Him? Oh, I told him the truth. It was my wish to relive even one evening with my deceased wife and stepson. Any man can understand that desire. Also, Tiffany was both fetching and delightful."

I leaned toward Simon and whispered, "I spoke with Tiffany this morning. She called and confided in me that she enjoyed your company," I lied. I had forgotten all about Tiffany, even neglecting to include her on my 4 a.m. what-else-can-go-wrong list."

We embraced stiffly, and with that he walked out of the room. I had felt old and used up when I got out of bed this morning. Now the fog of malaise was lifting and there were possibilities ahead. A new year, new opportunity and money to buy a lobster tail of my very own.

As I headed back to my room to collect my things, I passed the piano player in the lobby. He was playing an old Sammy Cahn song, which, on any another day, I might have regarded as schmaltzy. The tuxedoed musician singing the song may have looked like a tired cliché, but today, I slowed down and listened to the words. He seemed to be singing to me.

Fairy tales can come true, it can happen to you,
If you're young at heart,
And, as rich as you are, it's much better by far, to be young at heart,
You can go to extremes, with impossible schemes
You can laugh when your dreams fall apart at the seams...
And, life gets more exciting with each passing day,
Love is either in your heart or on its way
Don't you know that it's worth, every treasure on Earth...
If, you are among, the very - young - at heart.

In moments I would be in the Honda Accord headed home. My eyes clouded over realizing the computer monitor on my desk was now a boarded up old post office in a ghost town. I willed the tears back and distracted myself by focusing on a bouquet of flowers at a distant table. I sat down at a small table and decided to linger over another cup of coffee.

Perhaps, in this last outpost of serenity, I should contemplate the lessons of this last year, not just grieve over the loss of Mickey. What wisdom could be garnered from this treacherous journey I had taken? What tools, if any, had I now?

****

When I began writing this a year ago, it was a confessional exploration of the hungry heart. Like any diet,

226

becoming more aware of the thing I was deprived of, increased the craving.

Because Mickey was unavailable, I never got enough. Like Skinner's lab rat proved, in well documented experiments, partial-reinforcement increases craving. The dynamics of love are the same as food for the rats: partial reinforcement strengthens desire. Lab rats scurrying? Mickey and I savoring crumbs of time? There must be more than this.

Think, Veronica, what did you learn from this? It's over. Mickey is over. What good came of it? Think. Allow the answers to drift into your consciousness so that the price of loving and cheating and dying leaves a residue of wisdom. If I gained a smidge of personal power or strength, perhaps my tears would dry and I could participate in life again, rather than observe life from this shell .

Picking up a cocktail napkin, I took out my pen and wrote: *Things I am glad for*. The first thought that came to mind was a gladness Mickey wouldn't be with his witchy wife ever again. Then, chiding my unchristian thoughts, I began again, this time directing my consciousness to higher planes. A waitress brought me a cup of coffee; more time passed. I wrote the following: I'm glad I never contacted Mickey's wife, forcing a showdown. If he chose me over Helen, it had to be honestly won. Not by default because he got caught. In the throes of love, I still acted maturely and my hungry heart retained some dignity—I never groveled or presented an ultimatum. Through it all, I was feminine and strong. The arrow in my quiver? Fairness—I played fair in love and war.

While loving Raymond and believing in him, I over-looked his ordering me around; I didn't mind serving him. I enabled him to thrive and develop to his full artistic potential. He was able to study, take advance lessons, practice, record and achieve his artistic goals without the distraction and demands of a family life. Most musicians need to take straight jobs, once they have families or at least help with the children. I'm proud I never asked for more than what he *could* give; not even time. Because I asked so little,

Raymond developed into the musician he always aspired to be. Someday, hopefully, huge commercial success would follow.

When we met, he told me he only loved two things, sex and guitar, and it never got any deeper than that. Raymond's love was the size of a thimble; and although in time, his thimble runneth over for me, I needed a bucket. Aware of his emotional limitations, I didn't chide him. I quietly gave up and spent the last seventeen years supporting his guitar addiction. Today, in Los Angeles, his reputation is: "the guy who plays guitar like a god." He developed into the consummate artist, and my arrow honoring art had hit its mark.

Because the hungry heart haunted me with romantic cravings of my own, I was resourceful enough to use imagination and my entrepreneurial skills to cover my mortgage for a few months. With hot love letters paving the way, I fulfilled a stranger's romantic fantasy. I made a rich, no calorie dream date that satisfied my client, Simon Bestep.

The hungry heart jerked me through this year with passions, surprises, yearnings, cravings, envy and plunked me back down to Earth, with what? I looked at the notes on my napkins and took a sip of my now cold, bitter coffee.

I always knew the Power of Love. Perhaps these trials have equipped me with "arrows" or points of strength in fairness, art, and feminine resourcefulness, to better accept love's elusive nature.

In some future moment when I may falter, perhaps this little warrior will reach back to her quiver of resources and intuit the *fair* thing to do, and be patient in the process.

I will always support art and talent, through my little agency or as a patron. Now that I have some money, maybe *I* can be the artist this time around. Maybe I can write more than a list on a napkin, or a love letter delivered by AOL. At the very least, I deeply appreciate and have been transformed by Raymond's exquisite music and Mickey's profound lyrics and prose.

My friends teased me about having a 50's-style marriage. Whatever. *I knew my feminine power*. I went out ravenous, hunted down what I needed and dragged it back. I brought back whispers of adoration and sensual secrets to relive, over and over. I sought adventure; with Mickey I traveled to cities I would never have seen otherwise. It was a thrilling roller coaster ride of emotional highs and lows.

Like so many of my predecessors, I preserved my feminine dignity—even when verbally abused. Eventually, we sisters do things *our* way. My romantic imagination will someday be unleashed again; there will be a healing. Maybe these tools will serve me; or, perhaps I'm an amoral adulterer, who fancies herself a writer with something to say. Either way, I reached for my purse, shoved the napkin inside, stood up and headed for the door.

&&&&&&&

Epilogue - a year later

VERONICA

    Edgar Freis and Kendal Street Publishing made good on their promise to publish *Periwinkle Promises: Love Letters,* enabling Veronica to leave the house of over-reaction. Mickey's legacy of inspired emails accidentally provided for her future. With the book advance, she legally separated from Raymond, rented a small beach house, and currently is making a modest living writing copy for greeting cards, and is working on a romance novel. The hungry heart and arrows were put in the back of the closet amongst the water skis and tennis rackets: all various endeavors she once enjoyed.

    After Mickey died in her arms, Veronica's flair for the dramatic canonized their love affair in her mind, catapulting Mickey into romantic sainthood. Since leaving his wife would most likely never have taken place, she was spared from the crush of that romantic dream. Their love story was preserved and bound in a book and this gratified Veronica. She appreciated the irony, and with the success of her book, *Periwinkle Promises*, she was in a better position to sell the novel she was writing. She enjoyed appearing at the bookstore promotions, and with her deft social skills, *Periwinkle Promises* was almost flying off the shelves. Her hungry heart believed the love prose and poems inspired young lovers.

RAYMOND

    Raymond rebounded from his wife's swift departure with the consolation of his favorite agent, Suzanne Dubonnet.

Too busy to find a date, he considered placing an ad with an upscale dating service, but once writing down his requirements, it appeared too crass for *even him* to submit. He wasn't alone for long. The wealthy, attractive and keenly ambitious Beverly Hills booking agent, Suzanne, was happy to have him as her escort. She often dated from the stable of classical musicians she hired and, with Raymond's good looks and glib personality, he was the current flavor of the season. Both workaholics, they were only available a few minutes a day. Thus, their needs were met in a shallow and fulfilling connection—most often aboard yacht parties.

DEVIN

Living a bachelor's existence at home with his father, Devin started growing up. His mother's life-saving efforts, witnessed by a room full of people, inspired him to work toward becoming a paramedic. He liked to be in front of a crowd shocking people anyway. To him, the heroic CPR effort seemed like a bigger buzz than rustling up a paying audience every week to watch him and his crew rap. He received his GED from Home School and is taking classes at the community college to become a paramedic. Devin imagined the easy access to amyl nitrate was a perk that came with the job.

HELEN OWENS

The scoop by the reporter from *Redbook*, was never printed since Devin, the only source, had disappeared. Helen was able to spin the tragedy to a hungry press, gladly repeating it as often as possible. She never tired of sputtering through the tale of their delightful marriage and a life filled with Mickey's love and devotion to her. All the sympathy and attention gave her a purpose, and she enjoyed every minute of it. She explained away the mysterious woman's CPR efforts performed on her husband as a valiant effort by a deranged fan from the hotel catering staff. At the service, she had numerous well-wishers. Her therapist, masseuse, dance instructor, chiropractor, manicurist, dog walker, personal trainer, tennis coach, cosmetic surgeon, colorist, meditation coach, florist, interior decorator, all paid their respects. Mrs. Owens was a cottage industry. Her personal maintenance team outnumbered her friends three to one. For exercise and mental health, she engaged in shopping therapy and since her comfort came through chocolate, she was headed for an entire wardrobe of black caftans, size 18.

As was her habit, Helen opened a tin of Almond Rocca at bedtime and started a new book that her hairdresser raved about, called, "Periwinkle Promises: *Love Letters*."

"*My Angel, how did I ever find you? You are my Christmas...the best part of my day....*" With a slight snort, she told the pet Iguana she kept at her bedside, "I don't see what all the fuss is about. No one talks like that."

SIMON BESTEP AND JANNA

For many people the New Year is a time of reflection. At the New Year's Day brunch, Janna revealed the source of her love of opera: it began with singing in the choir at church. Encouraged by Simon's comment, "Oh, really? And then what?" patterned after Janna's conversational style, a brief and heartfelt description of Janna's devotion to the Mormon faith followed. The discussion of her religion was a forgivable departure from the fantasy, since by day two, the couple had exhausted the light banter. Neither were heavy drinkers, and without dancing to divert them, music appreciation led to church appreciation. (Understandably, many of us have had to resort to reality on the last lap of a long date.)

Janna's glowing account of her rich spiritual life was not lost on the searching soul of Simon. Encouraged, she told the story of Joseph Smith and The Book of Mormon; narrating like an Angel, she stirred the soul of the millionaire. He converted six months later and is happily married to a widow from the church, and very involved in raising her three sons.

TIFFANY, THE HOOKER

Veronica helped Tiffany leave the street life by finding funding for Tiffany's invention, the "Chalk Cane." This clever cane, when dragged on pavement, is designed for drunken customers to find their way back to their cars in parking lots. Edgar Freis put up the initial capital and patented this clever device. It was meant to be used in shopping malls to reunite seniors with their automobiles. Wearing a bikini, Tiffany sells Chalk Canes on the Venice Boardwalk. In good weather, she enlists other bikini-clad associates to help; her booth is one of the highlights on the beach.

CANDACE, THE ACTRESS

Returning from Monte Carlo the first week in February, Candace had finally exhausted Prince Akbar's hospitality. To help meet living expenses, she sold the trinkets she brought home. Then, she resigned herself to work as a waitress until pilot season. She is currently dating a Sweet-N-Low sales rep.

&&&&&&&

Happy New Year, Darling! is Veronica Bennett's debut novel. After earning a Bachelors Degree in Psychology from the University of the Americas, in Puebla, Mexico, Veronica worked as a pianist/singer. Her music career took her to such exotic locations as, Casa Blanca, Morocco and Japan, as well as cities throughout the U.S. Her second dream of becoming a writer, is working out better than her first dream, becoming a ballerina. She acknowledges, "Unlike dance, you can practice while lying in bed with a bag of chips." Bennett lives in a So. California beach town with her husband; she has raised a wonderful daughter and son.

To contact author: Write2Veronica@aol.com